MORE THAN BEAUTY

WATCHDOG SECURITY SERIES
BOOK 7

OLIVIA MICHAELS

ONE

Five months ago

Even with the motorcycle helmet on her head, Samantha Collins knew the moment she turned out of her parents' drive she was being watched. Next, she'd be followed.

Who is it this time? she wondered as she revved the stolen Indian motorcycle—*no, not stolen, it should have been mine all this time, not Jake's*—and picked up her pace. She'd left her parents' house in total darkness just to avoid being spotted but that hadn't done any good, dammit. Someone had lain in wait for her again and the possibilities as to who that person was were endless. Her spine prickled.

Her brother Jake could have gotten a buddy from his job at Watchdog Security to keep an eye on her—per Mom's request, she imagined. Bette Collins did not like being kept in the dark and she'd missed her calling as an interrogator, opting to become a Hollywood star instead. *But, Mom hasn't cracked me on this secret.*

Sam smiled to herself, remembering the email she'd read the day before. She could hardly believe it.

Of course, it could just be Jake confirming that yes, she'd stolen —no, *borrowed*—their dad's old bike during his visit, and he planned on taking some sort of revenge. Normally, that would actually be fun—trading pranks and teasing each other—but lately, her easygoing brother had been on edge. Overprotective, even for a bodyguard.

Sam turned down the winding road that would lead out to Santa Monica Boulevard. No one followed behind her, but that didn't mean anything. *I could be up against a team.* One to watch and one to follow. She scanned for anyone pulling out behind her, but so far, nothing.

Or, I could just be turning paranoid in my old age. She smiled again. Twenty-four was hardly old, but she still felt like she had yet to make her mark in a family that tended to make their life decisions early. No—that prickling up and down her spine had never led her astray. It was a finely honed sense that let her know when a stray photographer was about to catch her with her mouth full, or out on a dancefloor, shaking it too close to some starlet's boyfriend-of-the-moment.

Prickle, prickle.

Sam looked around again and saw nothing unusual.

Wait.

She slowed down enough to safely look in the one direction she hadn't considered.

Up.

And there it was, twinkling in the dark. A drone.

At the next intersection, Sam stopped and flipped it off.

The drone hovered off over the treetops and disappeared.

So, maybe it *was* her brother and Watchdog messing with her. Or, it belonged to one of the papps and she'd open social media later to see herself giving the bird to the world.

Great. Whatever. She refused to become obsessed with her online image. That way lay madness.

Sam turned onto Santa Monica and joined the traffic, surprisingly heavy for this early hour. She noted anyone that changed lanes to get behind her—three vehicles back. She'd learned a thing or two growing up in the public eye, including how to spot paparazzi.

Or fans who wanted to take things too far. Sam shivered, trying not to think about that. She was no stranger to stalkers. There were some real sickos out there. Sam's pervs had mostly been online, poking their ugly heads up on websites with names like *Samantha Collins' Coming of Age Countdown Clock* that appeared when she turned fourteen and ticked off the seconds until she'd turned eighteen and therefore legally an adult.

Yeah. Legally fuckable by another so-called adult.

Even years later, people online still speculated on when and if she'd lost her virginity and who she'd lost it to. All sorts of men bemoaned their lost chance to 'tap that first.' They even took *bets* on who she'd slept with first.

Sick.

Stop psyching yourself out.

Except...yup, she was definitely being followed. Another motorcycle shadowed her quick lane changes. The owner of the drone maybe?

Sam turned off, then made three right turns.

The motorcycle kept pace.

Years spent riding had taught Sam to read the movements of vehicles like other people read body language. Motorcycles were even easier to read than cars. Every rider had their own style, and Sam was beginning to suspect who this asshole was behind her.

But just to be sure...

She turned onto a tree-lined street she knew had a particularly sharp, unmarked curve ahead and slowed down. The bike started to catch up but then hung back.

Then she floored it. Predictably, the bike behind her sped up, desperate not to lose her. Sam needed to make sure he was close enough behind her that he wouldn't see what she had planned—if he even realized she knew who he was.

And that she knew his weaknesses on a bike.

Or, she could be wrong about who it was and this would cost her.

Only one way to find out.

The curve was just ahead, and difficult to see with the trees and the low light. Sam slowed again and wobbled, which had the desired effect. Like a predator spotting wounded prey, the bike sped up to catch her. When she knew she had him, she put on speed, then shot around the blind corner.

Sure enough, the guy behind her misjudged and almost laid his bike down.

"Woo-hoo!" Sam shouted as she watched him stop in the rearview. "Serves you right, Anderson."

God, she was sick of that prick hounding her family. Yup, she knew this guy well. Ron Anderson, who had crashed one of Bette's Backyard Bashes over a year ago posing as a waiter with the catering company. He was after photos of a politician's family—specifically their twins who weren't even teenagers yet, so gross. He'd stalked Sam with his camera through her teen years, too. He just loved going after vulnerable targets.

Sam took a circular route even though the prickling had stopped and she was sure she was in the clear. She regretted that she'd be getting to her appointment late, but it was worth keeping her privacy. Especially now.

Sam had checked her email for the billionth time like she had every day for a week, hopeful for a response. She scanned the list of senders until her gaze screeched to a halt on one name.

Quincy Torrent.

Not his newsletter. Not even his personal assistant. Quincy Torrent, the man himself.

Subject line: *Congratulations!*

"Oh, God." Sam covered her mouth as her body started trembling.

This couldn't be happening. There had to be a catch, right?

"Breathe, girl. Slow. No hyperventilating. Be a professional."

Samantha inhaled through her nose to the count of five, held her breath for another count, then breathed out for the same count, a calming technique Jake had taught her from his days as a Navy SEAL. She did that three times before she opened the email.

She did it three more times as she read Quincy's response to her pie-in-the-sky inquiry.

So soon, too. I'll barely have time to train.

As if she hadn't been training non-stop for this already.

She read his words over one more time, just to make sure she wasn't getting ahead of herself.

Nope. She was correct.

Bette was going to kill her when she broke the news.

Kill. Her.

Sam emailed back, requesting an early-morning meeting—he did say he'd see her any time—and hit send. A few minutes that took an eternity later, she had her response. He'd love to see her the next day to finalize the details.

Sam's entire life was about to change.

No, not change—start. Finally.

Her life, not her mother's.

Her life, not the one everyone—strangers and loved ones alike—wanted for her.

Except that she thought the catalyst for that change would be her meeting with Quincy Torrent.

Nope.

For Samantha Collins, it would all come down to an unplanned car ride and the awful, wonderful afternoon she was about to spend with Eric Armstrong, a bodyguard with Watchdog Security—and soon-to-be pain in her ass.

When Samantha got back from her meeting with Quincy she wasn't surprised to see Jake waiting for her in the garage their dad had converted into a motorcycle-restoring man cave. She wondered if Jake realized that he was standing in the exact same position their dad was in on the movie poster hanging behind him. Arms folded, legs spread to shoulder width, chin forward. Only, Grant Collins was in full super-spy costume with a mask over his face, and the name splashed across the poster was not his but the actor Grant doubled for.

So with the mask, you couldn't see whether or not Grant shared Jake's scowl.

Sam rolled to a stop mere inches from her brother's feet and killed the engine. Now she could hear her dad's prehistoric eight-track player painfully churning out Journey's "Still They Ride" and sounding like the band had recorded the track in Atlantis after the lost city sank. The distortion was the soundtrack of their shared childhood whenever they hung out with their dad.

"Hey, big brother. What's shaking?"

"Where'd you take my bike, Sam?"

She swung her leg over and off the Indian, then removed her helmet and tucked it under her arm. "You mean the bike Dad should have given me? I don't ride and tell, do I, baby?" She gave the warm leather seat an affectionate pat.

Jake wasn't budging. If anything, he looked even angrier.

"Why so paranoid? I know how to ride better than you do."

"Do you even remember what's happening today?" he asked in a voice dripping with disdain. So unlike him, but then again, his wife Rachael had been putting in long hours at the recording studio and he got twitchy without her.

"Um..." Her eyes went wide. "Shit. I was thinking that was tomorrow but it's today, isn't it?"

Jake blew a very not-calming breath out his nose. "Even if it was tomorrow, I don't want you out by yourself right now, okay? We are under attack."

"We are *not* under attack—"

A mechanical *bang* startled both of them and they jumped.

Sam snort-laughed. The eight-track player had finished 'Still They Ride' and clunked as it started playing the B-side.

"Okay, maybe we're under attack from Dad's eight-track."

Jake was not amused.

'Escape' started playing, which was exactly what she wished she could do at the moment.

"Fine, we're under imminent attack from the media if they catch wind of Annalie coming over today."

Yeah, probably shouldn't mention Anderson at the moment.

Sam ticked off her fingers as she spoke. "Okay, first, they have no idea who Auntie Annalie is yet. Second, I'm not her. Third, I chose to leave the house early in the morning to deflect any attention." She put her hand on her hip. "See? Responsible."

Jake was anything but convinced. "*First*," he said, mocking her, "Once they know Annalie is the author who created Mom's big break-out character, they'll want quotes and photos and whatever else they can get from Mom." He ticked off his next finger. "Second, if they can't get to Mom, they'll get what they can from us. Third," he dropped his chin, narrowed his eyes, and glared at her, "you took *my* bike."

"I'm a better rider."

"You're a more reckless rider, I'll give you that."

"You're just jealous because I can do all of Dad's old motorcycle stunts and you can't."

Jake's eyes widened comically. "Tell me that's *not* what you were doing this morning."

"That's not what I was doing this morning." Sam turned away and opened up one of the saddlebags to retrieve her bag.

Jake studied her. "Yeah. I believe you because you're too dressed up for it." He squinted. "Wait, are you wearing makeup?"

Shit. Busted. "What, now I can't wear makeup?"

If Jake's eyes had been wide before, now they were the size of headlights—and Sam was caught in them. "Is this actually a walk of *shame*, Sam?"

Sam laughed. "Okay, that's hysterical." She started walking past her brother and clapped him on the shoulder as she passed. "But go ahead and think that; my non-existent love life thanks you."

"So, where *did* you go all made-up this early?" he said to her retreating back.

"MYOB, big brother," Samantha said as she reached the door leading to the house. She paused. "You want to tell me why you've been so cranky lately?"

He paused. "MYOB, little sis."

The living room was tricked out in every wig Bette owned, each one sitting on a mannequin's head, which, to be honest, made Sam giggle. If anyone had been looking through a window and seen the backs of the heads lined up on a table, they would've probably only nodded and thought to themselves *Bette Collins really is a psycho killer just like the one she plays in the movies.*

In addition to the wigs, a rack of clothing stood beside a screen where Annalie could make quick changes. An entire steamer trunk of makeup waited to be plundered in case the rows of lipsticks, makeup brushes, and eyeshadow palettes already spread out on a table weren't enough. Hats and glasses covered another table propping up a full-length mirror. If Annalie still recognized herself by the end of the day, it would be a miracle.

No, it would be a very bad thing. Auntie Annalie was there to learn how to disguise herself in order to hide not just from the papps, but from a stalker.

Sam wasn't supposed to know the details, but of course she'd snooped. Annalie Givens was a worldwide bestselling author of horror and thrillers—under a well-guarded pen name. But now the secret was coming out in a few days, right before she was due to go on her first book tour.

If Annalie was Samantha's adopted aunt, Murray Ackerman, Annalie's agent, was her adopted grandpa. Murray had received a pretty gnarly letter from someone claiming to be the real-life killer from Annalie's first bestseller. No one knew if it was legit, but Murray wasn't taking chances. So now Annalie was stopping by with Murray and a couple of bodyguards from Watchdog.

A beep from the security system told Sam that the front door had opened. They were here.

Voices grew louder as people approached. Sam could pick out Annalie and her mother talking, with an occasional remark thrown in by Murray. A much deeper voice and then another told her both bodyguards were there too. Finally, the clicking of doggie toenails on the wood floor assured her they were indeed from Watchdog.

Annalie was in the lead, walking beside Bette's wheelchair. Murray walked behind her and Sam's heart sank at the serious look on his face. But the second he saw her, his usual smile snapped into place and he winked at her like he always did when she was a little girl, a wink that made her feel like she was in on the joke, that he considered her an equal and not a kid who could be easily fooled.

And she still wasn't fooled. Grandpa Murray was worried sick.

Annalie darted across the room the minute she caught sight of Sam.

"Hey, Auntie," Samantha said as she hugged Annalie. "I'm so sorry this is happening to you."

"Thank you, sweetie. I appreciate you and your mom's help."

"Anything," Sam said. She looked past Annalie to the bodyguards.

Is he even human? The first guy was huge—had to be six-four, six-five, and built like a mountain. Hot, in an older-guy way, but also scary in an *I'm built like a battleship and could kill you with a toothpick* way. His steely, possessive gaze resting on Annalie told

Sam that this stalker guy who was after her didn't stand a chance. He introduced himself as Malcolm McCoy.

The other guy was in charge of the dog, who trotted next to him as he emerged from the hall into the room.

He had that just-right level of stubble lining his jaw and a mole on his cheek that just begged for a kiss. His hair was the color of wet sand and a lock of it fell over his forehead just so. The man's upper arms had to be as big around as Samantha's body and made of pure steel. His extra-broad shoulders tapered down to a trim waist.

Stop. Looking. Below. His. Chin.

Moving back up into the safe zone, Sam focused on his face— his ridiculously perfect face—which she suddenly realized was a big mistake.

One of Sam's favorite things in life was to take her dirt bike into the canyons and find a nice steep-sided ravine to play in. She usually skidded down the sides, using all her skill to keep upright as she navigated the rocks and sand until she got safely to the bottom, and that was great, really. But now and then, she found a ravine that let her play Evel Knievel and jump across that sucker. When she was feeling really brave, that ravine was maybe—just a little bit —too wide for the jump. But Sam would jump it anyway, just to feel that *oh-shit* moment in the middle when she was sure she wasn't going to make it turn into the sublime bliss of *I've got this.* It was damn close to an out-of-body experience and sometimes she swore her soul hung over her body, carrying her across.

Looking at that second bodyguard gave her the very same feeling, but heavy on the *oh-shit.* Goddamn, he was gorgeous. A man like him belonged on the screen. No—better—a man like him belonged in a trailer marked 'stunt double'.

He locked eyes with her and his stern expression softened. It wasn't the awestruck gaze she was used to getting from strangers, the one that turned her from a normal person into something inhuman and unapproachable. It was as if he'd been searching for an old friend and now was thinking *There you are. Finally.* And then she was outside her body watching herself watch him, and the *oh-shit* feeling turned to *I've got this.*

He was on the other side of the jump, the solid ground waiting for her to land.

Bam! She remembered where she was and slammed back into her body. There was absolutely no way in hell she had time for this. And no way in hell he really looked at her like that. It was just her overworked imagination. She glanced away, but when she looked back he was still staring at her.

To distract herself, Sam dropped to her knees to call the dog over, not caring that the German Shepherd was not a pet but on the job.

"Come here, girl." When the dog trotted over, Sam felt Mr. Handsome watch them quietly while Annalie and Bette talked about her situation.

He's just worried that I'll break his dog or something. She peered up through her lashes and he quickly looked away, focusing his attention on Annalie. Sam's stomach was back making that jump over the ravine. She coaxed the dog over to the couch and sat down. She felt more than saw the bodyguard walk over.

"Her name's Blaze." Wow, he had a great voice, too, one that sent shivers right down her spine as she looked up at him.

"Cool name," Sam said, trying to keep her voice even.

"I'm Eric Armstrong."

She almost blurted out that he had a cool name too, that it fit a bodyguard. Flustered, she turned her full attention back to the dog out of sheer self-defense. "It's okay that I pet her?"

"Yeah. For now. Safety level's yellow overall, but it's white right here and now. If that changes, get ready for her to forget you exist."

"If only that were true with some people," she murmured, thinking of the sickos online. Eric surprised her when he suddenly stepped back. She looked up but his attention was off her and back on Annalie, a frown marring his gorgeous face.

Wow. Okay. Conversation over, I guess.

For the next hour, Bette had a field day helping Annalie try on different wigs, outfits, accessories, and use makeup to change her features.

"Remember to change your walk, dear," Bette said. "We all have a unique body language that a skilled eye can pick out."

"As distinctive as a fingerprint," Malcolm added. "Let's see you walk with a little bit of a limp."

"Just what I was going to suggest." Bette gave him an approving smile.

Score one for the walking mountain Sam thought. Actually, Sam was taking notes, too, though she'd never admit it. Her mom would get the wrong idea and it was going to be hard enough to tell her about her meeting with Quincy Torrent without getting her hopes up in the wrong direction.

Bette coached Annalie through moving differently depending on what disguise she was wearing. She picked out a skirt and top, paired it with a long wig, and sent Annalie behind the screen to try everything on. Annalie came out from behind the folding screen looking like she was in her early twenties.

"What do you think?" Annalie asked, turning around to show off her outfit. She did a little shimmy.

Whoa! This is crazy. And, it might just work in her favor. Samantha stood up from the couch where she was still scratching Blaze's head.

"Hang on." She ran over to Annalie and stood right next to her. "With that wig, I could be your double. Look at us." She turned Annalie toward the full-length mirror.

"God, you're right."

"Wait a minute." Samantha grabbed a dark-haired wig off the table that matched Annalie's hair color and dashed behind the screen. She put it on her head and adjusted it in the smaller mirror hanging on the back. When she came out a minute later and checked the mirror, sure enough, they looked alike. *Perfect. Now to drop the suggestion and test the waters.*

She elbowed Annalie. "Hey, maybe I could tag along and be your double—"

Samantha felt the wall of pure 'nope' before she saw him.

"The hell you preach," Jake said as he walked in, cutting her off mid-sentence like their argument in the garage wasn't over. "We already have one woman in danger, we don't need two targets."

Upgrade that to overbearing jackass. "How dare you?" Samantha hurled the words at him like throwing knives. "I know how to handle myself. I'd make a great double."

Dammit. This was not going as planned. It never helped her case to lose her temper, and Jake knew exactly which buttons to push to make her do just that.

Her brother counted off on his fingers like he had in the garage. "One, you are my little sister. Two, you are my little sister. Three, you are totally untrained for a potentially dangerous situation like that. Four, you are my litt—"

She couldn't contain her fury anymore. "Okay, okay, got it." Sam threw her hands up in the air and walked back to the couch where Blaze waited, her head tilted slightly as if she were assessing the threat level.

"Kids," Bette warned, using that condescending voice that made Sam feel like she was five years old. "No fighting."

"Come *on*, Mom. He treats me like I'm made out of spun glass. You all do. I'm better on a motorcycle than him, I could probably punch him into next week—"

"Samantha!"

And there it was.

James Earl Jones had his scary Darth Vader voice, which he'd used on his kids to get them to go to bed when they were little.

This was worse than that.

This was Bette Collins' stage face, the one on countless movie posters depicting her as a stone-cold psychopath. The one that gave grown men nightmares.

It almost—*almost*—still worked on Samantha and her brothers. But she knew it was time to change tactics. Sam schooled her voice into something she thought might pass for reasonable.

"I'm just saying, all of you treat me like I'm a fragile little girl and I'm not. Like, at all."

Her mother wasn't buying it. "Apologize to Annalie."

Annalie shook her head. "Bette, it's okay."

She didn't acknowledge her, never breaking eye contact with Sam. Samantha watched the angry spark in her mother's eyes dance. "My daughter will apologize for acting like a two-year-old while ironically asking to be treated like the adult she's supposed to be. Now."

This couldn't go any worse. She'd have to put off breaking the news about Quincy. "I'm sorry."

God, I sound like a bitch, and to my poor auntie, no less. As her haze of anger dissipated, Samantha felt terrible about that.

"I mean it, Auntie. I'm sorry all of this is happening to you because you don't deserve it. You're one of the nicest people I know, and I just want to help you." She really did. She'd do anything to protect this woman who didn't deserve her snotty temper tantrum.

Sam would just have to punch her brother later, out of sight.

Auntie Annalie pulled her up off the couch and into a hug she didn't deserve. "Thank you."

Sam squeezed her tightly. "Sorry," she whispered into her ear.

"Hey, guys."

Everyone's attention went to Eric, who was looking at his phone. "Bad news." He tapped the screen and turned the phone so everyone could see and hear it.

Shitballs. It was "The Prue and Jaylee Show" and it was streaming live. Samantha hated the show with its twits who couldn't wait to dig up every last bit of dirt—both real and imaginary—on any celebrity they could.

Prue and Jaylee were chatting, big, fake smiles on their faces, big fake gestures, and mock shock as they outed Auntie Annalie's face and identity to a gazillion viewers ahead of her publisher's schedule.

"Oh, no," Annalie breathed. "This wasn't supposed to happen for another week, at least."

Samantha felt her aunt go slack with shock so she tightened her arms around her, practically holding her up.

"Oh, Auntie."

On the screen, Prue looked past the camera. "Hey, Ted, can we get a visual? Do we have a...okay, great."

The screen changed to a still photo of Annalie sitting across from Bette in a restaurant, having what looked like a deathly serious conversation.

Bette caught Annalie's eye. "That was the day you told me they were outing you. Those sons of bitches *knew*...they followed you."

"That's her," Prue continued, "talking to Bette Collins. Can we do a close-up? Great. Take a good, long look folks. That's the face of terror right there. Annalie Givens."

Samantha prepared to help Annalie to the couch, maybe grab a glass of water and possibly some smelling salts.

And then her aunt did something totally badass.

She straightened up, clenched her jaw, and proceeded to badmouth the publisher who outed her for the publicity, using every swear word in the book. She went to her tote and pulled out a phone to call him and chew him out.

But that wasn't the badass part, in Sam's opinion. No, the badass part was Annalie going toe-to-toe with Man Mountain Malcolm over what a terrible idea that was, and how it was exactly what her publisher wanted her to do. He had a point, and Annalie finally saw the light when Murray agreed with Malcolm. Grandpa Murray worked his magic further, convincing Annalie that this was a good thing and they could turn it around and work it to their advantage.

Samantha loved the gentle smile Murray gave Annalie. "Accentuate the positive, kid."

She smiled back and nodded. "All I want to do is write my books and communicate with my fans—my real fans."

"Only thing that's changed is now you get to do it in person." Murray looked at Malcolm. "While this fellow keeps you safe."

"Speaking of safe, we're about to have a situation," Eric said, and Sam's attention snapped back to him. He glanced at her and she felt thoroughly assessed as if she were a prop.

"I just texted with Gina and Lachlan back at HQ," Eric continued. "The paparazzi are on the move and headed our way, probably to get Bette's opinion and ask if she knew Annalie's identity already."

Great. Jake was right. He'll really be insufferable now.

Eric frowned as he looked at Annalie. "I'm sure some of them have figured out where you live and are headed for your home too, Annalie. From here on out, your place is off-limits to you."

She huffed. "Good thing Gina grabbed some of my things, huh?" She reached into her tote. "Including this." She pulled out her nine mil.

Total and complete badass. Sam had no idea her sweet little aunt carried.

"Where's the thirty-eight?" Malcolm asked.

Annalie smirked up at him. "Already wearing it."

Sam's jaw hit the floor. And the way Malcolm was looking at Annalie now... *Go, Auntie!*

"If they find you here, Annalie, all hell is going to break loose," Eric said. "We need to get you out of here ASAP without you being seen."

"What's the plan?" Malcolm asked.

Eric's eyes darted to Sam, then Jake, then back to Malcolm. "Decoy."

Suddenly, the wig on Sam's head felt heavy. *Oh, shit, no way.* Her heart pounded. *Yes!* This was where she'd prove herself.

Jake damn near exploded. "Oh, no you're not."

Eric totally ignored Jake, which made Sam's heart do a little happy dance. "She looks just like her right now," he said. "We might as well take advantage."

Samantha couldn't help it. She fist-pumped the air. Her mother groaned and Jake swore.

"Yes! I can do this. I'll take off on my bike—"

"No, you won't." Eric cut her off.

Whoa. Excuse me? Sam's formerly dancing heart stopped mid-pirouette and looked around for a rock to throw at him. *Just...don't hit his face. It's way too perfect* she told her stupid heart. *Go for the chest where it'll bounce off like a cotton ball.*

Eric's eyes narrowed as if he could hear her deranged thoughts. "If this is going to happen, you will listen to me and do exactly what I tell you. You're not going out on your own—"

"She's not going out *at all*." Jake grabbed Eric's arm. Samantha barely recognized her brother. As much as he teased her and played the overprotective big brother to a fault sometimes, he seldom ever lost his temper like this, and never with a teammate. Totally verboten.

What the actual hell is going on with you, Jake?

Eric pulled back and glared at Jake. "This is my operation, not yours." The growl in his voice sent involuntary shocks up and down her spine.

Jake stood his ground. "We are under my mother's roof, which means it damn fucking well *is* my operation. I'm in charge of security here while this is happening and I say *she's not going.*"

I don't know who this stranger that only looks like my brother is, but I've had enough.

"I *am* going, Jake." Samantha stared down her brother. "I'm an adult and you can't tell me what to do."

Eric put his hands up. "Hear me out. Samantha, you, me, and

Blaze will take the SUV and make a show of leaving. The papps will see us and think it's Annalie, and follow us like a swarm of hornets." He looked at Jake. "They'll forget all about talking to your mom, I guarantee, which will take the heat off her and make your life a hell of a lot easier. I'll lose them and we'll double back here when it's safe to do so. They won't be waiting for Samantha Collins to return because they won't care." He looked at Malcolm. "Meantime, you wait until the coast is clear and then head out with Annalie and Murray. Annalie, you stay disguised as Samantha, just in case. Throw off any lingering tails."

Sam held her breath. The plan sounded solid to her, but now it was up to everyone else.

As usual.

"All right," Malcolm finally said.

Sam took a breath. She was actually doing this. Her mom waved her over. Gone was the face of a psychopath, replaced by her mom's worried eyes.

"Be careful, sweetheart."

"I will, Mom," Sam answered, hugging her.

Jake glared at Eric. "If anything happens—"

"It won't." He signaled to Blaze to heel and the dog obeyed instantly. Samantha adjusted her wig, mentally went over how Annalie walked, and followed Eric out to the drive and the waiting SUV.

Here's where it begins she thought excitedly. *The rest of my life.*

She wasn't wrong...but her timing was.

TWO

Samantha swung herself up into the passenger seat of the SUV. Eric was around the back getting Blaze settled into a kennel. She listened to his soothing voice as he spoke to the dog, and crossed her legs. One minute he was all fire and sternness, the next, soft and gentle. And that back-and-forth contrast was doing...things...to her body that she wasn't used to. Not since her last college boyfriend, the one with the amazing tongue but no personality to go along with it, sadly. His only ambition was to be seen with her as it turned out, and when she realized it, she dumped him, then found a thousand ways to distract herself from picking up another guy just like him.

Eric walked past her window and glared in at her. All thoughts of thanking him for trusting her to do this shriveled and died. That look was anything but trusting. He stalked around the front of the SUV and got in.

"I would've held your door open and helped you in," he said. "If you'd given me a minute."

"Oh." Right; that's what Annalie would've done—wait for him. But Sam was not one to wait, ever.

You aren't Samantha Collins, you're Annalie Givens for the afternoon and don't you forget it.

"Sorry about that. You're right; Annalie would've waited and if anyone was watching, they might not believe the ruse."

He paused from starting the engine and studied her, looking impressed. "Good point." Then it was as if a cold, invisible wall slammed down between them. "But, that's not the one I was making."

"No?"

"No. I just wanted to show you that I can be a gentleman." He turned the key in the ignition. "I heard what you said to me inside and I'll respect your privacy as requested. We don't even have to say a word to each other—"

"Wait. What did I say inside about you respecting my privacy?"

Eric side-eyed her. "You don't even remember," he said, his voice flat. "Bit ironic."

Now he was being a jerk. Sure, all the handsome ones were in this town. The difference was, she was used to them trying to kiss her ass. Her first instinct was to turn away, but he looked genuinely upset. Was Eric being a jerk to be a jerk, or did she really say something that offended him?

"Come on, Alanis Morrisette, tell me what I said."

That got her a surprised-sounding chuckle. He touched a screen on the dash that pulled up a map with real-time traffic and started driving down the long drive to the front gate.

"What?" she continued. "I'm Jake's sister. You think the music references end with him? I can quote songs and lyrics just as fast."

The icy wall he'd put up cracked just a little. "Maybe I misheard you in there."

"I think you must have. What'd I say?"

"I said to get ready for Blaze to forget you exist if there's a threat, and you said, 'If only that were true with some people.' Which I took as you wanting me to leave you alone."

Now Samantha laughed. "Oh, my dude, yeah, you totally misunderstood. I was meaning my own little party of freaks online, not you." No wonder he'd stepped away from her so quickly.

Color rose up his neck. "Great. Now I'll never convince you I'm not a bad dude."

"*Au contraire*, my friend. I think you're awesome." She rolled down her window.

"What are you doing?" He hit a button and her window started up again.

"I can already see cars gathering out there past the gates and these windows look pretty dark. I want to make sure they can see me and think I'm Annalie."

"They can see as much of you through the tint as they need to. Do not roll the window down again. The glass is bulletproof." His tone was a delicious mix of the stern and the sweet. "We don't know if there's a hostile in the crowd and I don't want you hurt."

She grinned. "Because my brother will kill you?"

That side-eye again, which turned to a quick sweep over her body—like, blink-and-you-missed-it quick. "No. It's because I just don't want to see *you* hurt."

Sam suppressed a delicious full-body shiver. She never reacted this way with any guy, especially not right after meeting him. Maybe it was his absolute air of confidence and no-bullshit way of treating her.

The gate opened ahead of them. They went through, turned, and drove past a gathering of cars

The only vehicle that concerned Sam was the motorcycle.

Back for more, huh, Anderson?

"I see him," Eric said as if reading her thoughts. "He won't be a problem."

The papps getting out took one look through the passenger window and got back in their vehicles. The chase was on. Eric roared through the neighborhood, then sped away into traffic and quickly lost the other cars due to Eric's evasive maneuvers.

Impressive.

Sam's phone buzzed. Jake's name came up on her screen.

Everything ok?

She frowned at the text. It had been what? Ten minutes?

Just fine, thanks she texted back.

Five minutes later, another text came in from Jake asking for a status report. Sam ignored it and he texted another one a minute later. She practically growled as she punched in her reply that nothing had blown up yet, so please, stop with the texts.

But, Anderson was still on their tail long after the others disappeared in the rearview mirror. Twice, he jumped out of the lane and sped between cars, almost catching up to them and getting a good peek in the window, but Eric used a combination of skill and brute force to switch lanes in time to block his view.

"You want to shake him completely, turn off at the next exit," Sam said. "We can gain some speed there if you don't mind breaking the law. Let him get behind us going a minimum of fifty then take a sudden left. He tends to doubt himself and brake mid-corner. Put on more speed after that, do your evasive dance, and boom, we've lost him."

She expected the usual pushback. Instead, Eric nodded and switched lanes to exit, Anderson not far behind and closing in. When they hit surface streets, Eric let him get closer until he was just behind, then he put on speed. Like a replay from earlier that morning, as soon as they hung a fast left, Anderson hit the brakes on the turn and nearly laid his bike down. *Idiot.* A minute later, they'd lost him.

"Told you." Sam couldn't keep the pride out of her voice.

Eric chuckled. "You did."

"Thanks for actually listening to me," she said, and meant it.

Eric only nodded.

Buzz. Another stupid text from Jake. *Jesus.*

She texted that she was now putting her phone on 'do not

disturb' for the next half hour and would respond after that. Then, she looked at Eric.

"Actually, why *did* you listen to me? No one else does."

"Well, you sounded like you knew what you were talking about. That's the most confident I've heard you sound all day."

That took her aback.

"Can I ask you how you knew he'd do that?" Eric added.

Sam smiled and relaxed in her seat. "I've known Ron Anderson a long time. He's hounded our family for years, even when we were kids. Especially then, when Mom and Dad tried to shield us from publicity. He just loves getting photos of people who want to stay out of the public eye, especially if they're on the vulnerable side. Annalie had to be catnip for him."

"Definitely," Eric agreed

"He's gotten a few good ones of me, but not as long as I was on my bike."

Eric looked over at her. "You mentioned a bike earlier. You ride?"

"Oh hell yeah I ride. Dad taught us all, starting when we were young. It might not be my dad's Indian—he gave that to Jake, dammit—but I know how to handle both my Kawasaki Ninja and my Harley. Every time I've gotten into a race with Anderson on the Ninja I've smoked his ass." She almost added, *This morning, I beat him on the Indian* but stopped herself just in time. She couldn't believe how at ease Eric made her feel.

Eric laughed and smacked the steering wheel. "But today, he might have had the advantage over the SUV since I couldn't weave in and out of traffic the way he could on his bike. Good thing you knew his weakness." He turned again and gave her a beaming smile.

Resistance is futile.

She smiled back.

Eric turned back to the road just as his phone rang through the stereo speakers.

"Eric here."

"It worked." Malcolm sounded pleased. "That first group all took off after you. Some got footage of the SUV leaving and after they posted it, the next group left."

"Excellent."

Sam figured Eric would start back toward the house now that they'd lost Anderson and it sounded like no one was interested in talking to Bette. She was glad Annalie had avoided any trouble, but she was also sad that her time as a double was over so quickly.

It had nothing to do with riding with Eric, who listened to her and trusted her opinion. Nothing at all.

Yeah.

"If you don't mind, I'm going to keep driving around a while, just in case any stragglers decide to turn around and see if maybe Annalie didn't leave after all," Eric told Malcolm.

Really? Sam's heart lightened.

"Sounds like a plan," Malcolm said. "I'm not comfortable leaving with Annalie for the safehouse yet anyway."

"And my mom's told you that you're staying for dinner, hasn't she?" Sam interjected.

Man Mountain Malcolm actually laughed. "Busted. That is indeed the case."

She grinned at Eric, who gave her a much warmer side-eye.

"She'd like you two to join us."

Sam rolled her eyes. "More like she demands, I bet?"

Malcolm grunted. "Also, your brother is pissed that you put your phone on do not disturb."

"Sucks to be him then. Tell him I'll text in," she checked her phone for the time, "seven minutes."

"Make it six and I'll give you a hundred bucks," Malcolm said, sounding exasperated.

"Nope." She crossed her arms as if Malcolm could see the gesture. Eric chuckled.

Eric and Malcolm made a plan to meet back at the safehouse with Annalie later, then Eric disconnected.

"Figures my mom would insist they stay for dinner. She tends to dictate everything that everyone does. And my brother lately," she huffed. "Well, you work with him, so you know."

Eric's small grin disappeared. "Did you want to go back home right away?"

Shit. "No, not at all. I can use the break from my family." *I need to stop talking about myself.* "Sorry about you and Jake fighting."

"It's all right."

She looked out the window at the businesses and neighborhoods flying by. "Where we going? Still just random driving?"

"Where would you like to go?"

Good question. For a year, she'd gone almost nowhere but to the gym, then the other gym, then occasionally the beach or for a long ride in the canyon, then back home, all in the name of training.

But Annalie would not go to a gym.

"Well, there's where *I'd* like to go, then there's where Annalie *would* go, and since I'm Annalie," she gestured down her body like a gameshow host showing off a prize, "I have to think of where she'd go." She tapped her chin. "Which is home to write, because that's all she ever does. So that won't work." She laughed.

"I like this dedication to the mission. You might consider a career with Watchdog."

That made Sam laugh even harder. "Work *there*? Oh, hell no." All she needed was for her brother to boss her all day.

"Yeah, right. Dumb idea." Eric grimaced. "You're gonna be an actress."

That felt like a punch to the gut. "Who says?"

He raised his eyebrows. "Um, everyone?"

Another punch. "So that means I should be one, huh?"

They came to a stoplight and he turned his head and studied her. "You...don't want to act?"

Uh-oh. Danger zone. She flashed briefly to her meeting with Quincy.

"I didn't *say* that. Exactly."

The light turned green but Eric didn't go. "So, what do you want to do?" He looked completely intrigued.

She pretended to misunderstand. "Do? We can keep driving. Light's green, by the way."

His face fell and she hated that. Hated even more that she'd made it happen.

Eric drove. Silence crept in. Uncomfortable silence. She texted Jake back telling him they were okay, then put her phone back on do not disturb.

"I'm not like Bette," Samantha finally said.

"Mmm?"

Well, that was marginally better than silence, so she continued. "My mom has loved acting since the moment she was born. She was set up for it though. Named after an actress."

"Bette Midler?"

Sam grinned. "No, Bette Davis, even though my mom's name is pronounced *Bet*. It's her eyes. They reminded my grandma of Bette Davis from the moment she looked at them."

The corner of Eric's mouth quirked up. "Like from the old eighties song? 'Bette Davis Eyes'."

"Ha, yeah, but that was a little after Grandma's time. My grandma used to say that when my mom was a baby, she would look around to make sure she had an audience before she'd start crying. And then when she got older, she would organize all the neighborhood kids into doing skits. But she was always the star."

"Why am I not surprised?"

"Exactly. She's got to be at the dead center of the spotlight at all times. That's who she is."

"Okay, but who are *you*?"

She paused. "What do you mean?"

"I know who your mom is, the whole world does, but who are you? She's a separate person. Tell me who you are."

That stopped her. No one had ever asked her that question before. Anyone who met her assumed that because she looked so much like Bette she must be exactly like her, that she must crave the spotlight too, that she was planning on going into the movie business, just like Eric assumed.

I am going into the movie business, but not the way they think. She couldn't tell him that though and risk it getting out before she could break the news. Could she?

"Who am I? I'm just...me." God, she sounded so unsure.

"Sounds like you need to figure out who that is."

"What?" His question had totally thrown her off and she wasn't used to it, wasn't used to people challenging her.

"You need to figure out who Samantha Collins is."

"I know exactly who I am." She folded her arms.

"Then who is that?"

"Not Bette Collins."

Eric laughed at her.

"What?" She was definitely not used to being laughed at.

"You're telling me who you *aren't*, not who you *are*."

Sam didn't say anything.

"Tell me what you like." He'd softened his voice, and she kind of hated that. She was used to people trying to manipulate her and one of the ways they did it was to change their tone when they knew they weren't getting through.

"You mean like, what's my favorite color, or favorite ice cream?"

He shrugged a shoulder. "If you want to start there, sure."

She rolled her eyes. Why was she finding him so infuriating? "Those are questions you ask a five-year-old."

"I love butter brickle when I can find it. And blue. My favorite color is blue. Your turn."

Is he making fun of me? "What's butter brickle?"

"You've never heard of butter brickle?"

"Um, no. It sounds like a kid's shoe. With butter on it."

Eric guffawed. And damn if she wasn't trying not to laugh herself.

"Seriously! Like, a little English kid's shoe from, I don't know, *A Christmas Carol.*" She put on a terrible British accent. "'Oh, no, Mummy! I've gone and spilt butter all over my best brickles and now I can't go to the Christmas *pahty.*'"

Now Eric roared with laughter, so hard she was afraid he'd drive off the road. "Well, it doesn't taste like a kid's shoe with butter on it." He wiped a tear from his eye.

"So what does a brickle taste like?"

"Nope. You tell me first what your favorite ice cream is." He grinned at her.

"Easy. Moose Tracks. Salty-sweet chocolate ribbon for the win."

"Mmm. Good choice."

She watched as he actually licked his lips and dammit, now she needed to cross her legs again. *I shouldn't like him this much* she reminded herself. Especially when he was being so irritating.

"Okay, so color. What's your favorite?" he asked.

"Red. All shades. Except pink." She winced at a childhood memory of Bette having her room painted and decorated all in pink.

"Yeah, I didn't take you for a pink girl." He turned back onto the highway. "What's that flinch about?"

"What flinch?"

"You actually flinched when you said pink."

"No, I didn't."

"You did."

She huffed. "Maybe I did a little."

"Any particular reason?"

She scoffed and shook her head. "Nosy."

"Very." He glanced over at her. "I find you interesting."

"Why? You know nothing beyond my favorite ice cream and color."

"Oh, I found out more than that just now."

"What, that I hate pink?"

"Sure, that. But also that you're funny as hell and strongly opinionated and private. Good conversation," he added without a trace of irony or teasing in his voice.

Sam got quiet. "You think I'm funny?"

"I know you're funny. I damn near laughed us off the road, didn't I?"

She resisted the urge to ask him if he liked funny women.

I'm not on a date or trying to pick up a guy she reminded herself. And no way would she pick up a guy like Eric. Way too bossy. She had enough of that at home. Not to mention he was one of her brother's co-workers and that way lay madness. Jake had always been super-protective of her, even more so than their oldest brother, Grant Junior, who'd been on his way out of the house by the time she was born.

Bette liked to tell people that Samantha had been born with champagne bubbles in her blood, which was a Bette-like way of admitting that Sam was an oops-baby conceived after celebrating one of her Oscar wins. So, while Grant loved his little sister, Jake was the one who herded her around like he was a sheepdog when they were growing up and still acted like a damn mother hen.

Like today. She gritted her teeth, remembering the scene at the house earlier.

Eric must have misread her expression. "I wasn't laughing *at* you, Samantha." Eric sounded almost condescending, which really put her off.

"I know you weren't."

"Then why are you acting so angry right now?"

She pressed her lips together and looked heavenward. "I'm not angry."

"You are so angry."

"Maybe a little angry. But, it's not at you. It's...nothing you need to worry about."

"Of course I need to worry about it. We're out together and it's my job to keep—"

"So help me, if that ends with the word safe..."

He laughed again. "Well, it is my job to keep you," he paused, "*that* word. Even if you don't think you need it."

"I don't."

"Samantha—"

"I want to be a stuntwoman," she blurted out. *Shit.*

Eric's eyes widened.

"You think it's a bad idea."

"No. I don't." That infuriating grin played at his mouth, telling her that he was humoring her.

"Of course you do. It's okay to say it, I need to get used to hearing that once I tell Bette."

"Your mom doesn't know?"

"Nope. God, no." She crossed her arms, more out of the need to comfort herself than from anger.

"What does she want you to do with your life instead?"

"What do you think?"

"Act?"

"Yup, she'd be fine with that." *Just like everyone else.*

He rubbed his chin. "So she wants you to follow in her footsteps instead of your dad's?"

"Something like that." *She'd want that if she knew that was my plan.*

"Huh."

"You sound surprised."

"I guess I am."

"Why?" She purposefully jabbed. "Is it because of what happened to her?"

Eric got quiet for a minute and she could practically hear the gears grinding in his head. She'd unfairly set him up to ask about

Bette's wheelchair. Sam readied her collection of neutral responses, honed over years of being asked about this very topic. Everyone wanted the 'secret' scoop on Bette, and Sam had been confronted by reporters since she was a kid, people who didn't mind asking a little girl the most private and personal questions they could about her mom. She'd long since gotten used to people cozying up to her just to ask things like *Does your mommy cry when no one else is around?* And *Does she drink a lot of grown-up drinks since she got hurt and needed the wheelchair, or take medicine that makes her sleepy or act funny?*

Now that she was grown the insulting questions were more like *Does she ever get jealous of you since you look like a younger version of her?* Or they poked in the opposite direction of *Is she encouraging you to take her place in younger women's roles?*

So from a young age, Sam and Jake and even Grant had been extensively coached in giving neutral responses whenever the topic of Bette Collins came up. But Jake and Grant never got questions like Sam did, as if Sam were merely a physical extension of her mother.

Eric was no different. She put a mental bet on him asking some version of the second question—did Bette want a carbon copy of herself as a living vanity project?

Because that's what everyone assumed at this point.

"I am a little surprised she'd encourage you to go into acting, yeah," Eric finally said. "I mean, she was physically attacked for going against a powerful producer, and she strikes me as very protective of you. Of everyone in her family."

Oh. That was...different. "She *is* protective, actually. My mom would roll herself in front of a speeding bus if it meant someone she loved didn't get hurt."

"And that bothers you."

What are you, my shrink? She almost—*almost*—spat that out before she realized he really wasn't interrogating her. He was actually making a legit observation. Because it did bother her.

Stop being a bitch to him.

"Of course it bothers me. I'm the baby of the family and yet I could kick my brothers' collective butts. My family will never see it that way though. They think I need to be wrapped in bubble wrap and put on a shelf." That wasn't entirely fair, but dammit, she was still angry over Jake and her mom's behavior.

"They love you. That's..." He trailed off.

"Surprising? Because why exactly?"

"I was going to say that's obvious. And awesome. It's a good feeling to be loved by your family."

Oof. "Yeah. It is. But it can also feel smothering when they don't want you to be who you are."

"And who are you, Samantha Collins?" This time he gave her a full-on dazzling smile, one that went straight to her lady bits, dammit.

"I am a woman who would love some ice cream right about now, thanks to someone who shall not be named bringing up the subject."

"Okay, now we're getting somewhere." Eric took the next exit. "I know just the place."

"You still haven't told me what a brickle tastes like."

He laughed again, much to her delight. *No, no, no. Do not be so happy about that.*

"I'll do you one better. I'll buy you a scoop of butter brickle."

"What if I hate it?"

"You won't hate it."

THREE

"I don't hate it," Samantha said, then licked the last bit of orgasmic, toffee-flavored ice cream off her spoon. "I do believe this is my new favorite ice cream."

"Told you." Eric grinned at her across the frilly little metal table in the frilly little ice cream parlor. They'd taken a table in a rear corner, Sam's back to the shop and Eric's back to the wall so he could observe everything. Blaze lay beside the table, happily licking a bowl that formerly held a little scoop of doggie ice cream and a couple of bone-shaped biscuits. Luckily, the shop was empty, so they could relax and enjoy themselves.

"Did you have to surrender your man card at the door the first time you came in here?"

"Yes. Yes, I did. And it was worth it for this. Can't get the real stuff anywhere else in this town." He nodded solemnly as he held up his own spoonful of butter brickle, then plunged it into his mouth. The overly air-conditioned parlor suddenly felt a lot warmer.

Oh, to be a spoon.

Sam knew she'd been staring at his lips a little too long when

Eric's expression suddenly changed, becoming dead serious. She looked away and tried to focus on her ice cream again when he suddenly grabbed her arm and pulled her up with him. Her spoon clattered to the table.

"Wha—"

He pulled her close, then turned her around and walked her backward until he pinned her against the rough wall. He caged her into the corner and her knees melted like her ice cream.

"Eric—"

"Sorry. Can't be helped."

Wow. Yeah, okay. Let's just go with this. This is good.

His face was inches from hers, his rich, sweet, toffee-scented breath so tantalizing. Her lids dropped to half-mast and she prepared for a kiss when he said, "I think they found us."

Wait? What? Her eyes flew open. "Oh. Right." She wasn't Samantha, she was Annalie.

"Can't be sure, but I wanna play it safe. So, forgive me for this."

He leaned down, and his gorgeous, perfect face came closer. His big hands cupped her cheeks like he was about to take a drink of clear, cold water on a hot, dry day.

Limes and crushed green leaves. Water splashing on rocks. His skin smells like a cool oasis.

Eric tilted his head one way and she automatically tilted hers the other. Her eyelids dropped to half-mast again as he stared at her intently. His lips parted and she readied herself with a quick swipe of her tongue.

Then his thumb was suddenly between their lips and he was kissing it, not her.

Yep. He was giving her a stage kiss.

But at the same time, their bodies were pressed close enough together that she felt every one of his abs. There had to be at least eight of them. Possibly ten. Oh hell, an even dozen.

And something else—something down much lower—pressed against her as well.

Only briefly though, as Eric quickly pulled his lower torso away.

But Sam knew what she'd felt. And that was definitely not a thumb.

He kept at the fake kiss until Sam felt herself fighting off a giggle. *Nope, not a thumb.* This was absolutely ridiculous.

"Don't make *me* laugh," he murmured against his thumb. "You'll give us away."

Which of course only made it worse. Now she snorted.

"Samantha," he growled.

"What? I can't help it," she whispered. "No one can see me behind you anyway. Your chest is huge."

And that's not all that's huge. She blushed even harder as she snickered.

He kissed his thumb harder. His lips brushed hers—the worst, the best, the most frustrating tease ever. She ran her nails slowly down his back and felt him shiver.

"Samantha." This time, he whispered her name, soft and sweet.

"Just playing my part."

"You're playing it a little too well, baby."

She listened as people ordered ice cream. They sounded uncomfortable. A couple minutes later, minutes that felt like an eternity, she heard retreating steps and the bell over the door jingle as they left.

Eric pulled away. Cool air rushed between them like a chaperone. He looked flushed as he studied her face.

"Are you all right?" he asked.

"Yeah. Fine." *More than fine. Wow.*

"Sorry to do that to you. It was just a false alarm," he said, deflating her.

Joni Mitchell lyrics from one of her sadder songs. Damn, she couldn't help it. *Jake, brother, get out of my head. Right. Now.* She pushed past Eric and dropped back down into her seat.

Eric walked around the table and sat back down. He didn't

meet her eyes as they finished their melting ice cream. The parlor turned orange as the setting sun shone through the front windows.

"I should get you back home," Eric said. "I've had you out too long."

"Yeah, I guess so."

"Hey." She looked up. He was smiling softly at her. "Just so you know, I think you'll make a kickass stuntwoman."

"If I can get it past my mom."

"Samantha. Don't let anyone tell you how to live your life. Not even Bette Collins."

"Easier said than done." She looked down.

"Don't argue with me."

Her eyes snapped back up. "Wait, did you just tell me what to do right after telling me not to let anyone tell me what to do?"

"Maybe?" He leaned over the little table. "But I'm serious—don't let anyone treat you like a child, because you aren't. Stick up for yourself without losing your cool, and you'll have the life you want because you've got this. I believe in *you*, Samantha Collins."

She smiled wider. "Want to skip dinner and drive around some more?"

His eyebrow quirked up. "Only if we can follow dessert with dinner. I know a good burger joint..."

***

I believe in you, *Samantha Collins.* She carried those words like a shield that night when Eric brought her home. Jake actually met them at the door as if she were a teenager coming back late from a date with the high school bad boy.

"You missed dinner. Everything all right, Samantha?" he asked her while his eyes never left Eric.

"Copacetic," Eric answered. He nodded to Samantha, turned, and left without another word. Jake closed the door.

Sam wheeled on Jake. "Can you be a bigger jerk next time maybe?"

His eyes narrowed. "*Next* time? He didn't ask you out, did he?"

She ripped the wig from her head. "Like that's *any* of your business."

"He's too old for you."

Sam was about to snap back that Eric was only Jake's age which was hardly a problem when she stopped and took a deep breath. She softened her voice. "Jake? Seriously, what is going on with you?"

He opened his mouth, then closed it again. "Nothing, why?"

She rolled her eyes and turned to go to her room when Bette came around the corner.

"Oh, good, you're home." She stopped her chair and looked back and forth between her son and daughter. "What's wrong?"

Grant came around the corner a moment later and laid his hand on Bette's shoulder. Her dad's gaze immediately went to Samantha.

"Nothing," Sam said. *Except that Jake's being a Neanderthal again.* She was just about to voice that opinion when Eric's words came back to her. *I believe in you.* She took a deep breath instead to calm herself.

"Samantha's apparently dating Eric now," Jake said.

Her eyes went round. "What? No, we're not. I never said, never even implied that."

"You said 'next time' and you didn't deny it, which totally implies that you'll be seeing him again."

"Yes. I'm sure I will." She gestured at Bette. "At one of Mom's Bashes along with the rest of your co-workers who I'm also not dating."

"Kids," Bette held up her hand, "it's been a long day for everyone and emotions are running high. Jake." She fixed her gaze on him. "I say this with all the love in my heart. Chill the hell out. You've been on high all day."

"*Thank* you," Samantha said.

"As for you, daughter mine, you haven't been yourself either. Walk with me, loves." She touched her husband's hand and turned her chair. They followed in her formidable wake. As Sam moved down the hall, the smell of fresh-baked chocolate chip cookies grew stronger. Sure enough, there was a plate stacked high waiting on the kitchen island and a sink full of mixing bowls and spatulas. Bette always made cookies as a stress reliever. The kitchen layout had been modified so that Bette could easily bake to her heart's content from her wheelchair. She went to the sink, turned on the hot water, and grabbed a sponge; she wasn't about to leave a mess for her staff to clean up overnight.

Jake and Grant immediately snapped up a couple of cookies. Sam still had the taste of butter brickle—she hid a grin at the word —and the barest whisper of Eric's lips on hers in her mouth, and as good as her mom's cookies were, she wasn't about to sacrifice that lingering sweetness.

"Is Auntie Annalie okay?" Samantha asked in an attempt to forestall an interrogation.

"She's just fine, thanks to Eric's plan." Bette's eyes flickered to Jake, who scowled, then back to Sam. "And I take it you weren't discovered?"

"Nope. All went according to plan." The memory of Eric's abs...and more...caused her to touch her stomach as if to see if they might still be there.

Bette arched her eyebrow and tilted her head, a sure sign she knew Sam was holding back.

"He's really good at his job," she added. "Total professional." Then since she had nothing to lose, she added, "I was a total professional too, if I can say so myself. Ron Anderson was on our tail, but I told Eric how to shake him."

"Ron Anderson." Her mother spit that name out like she was ridding herself of venom she'd sucked from a snakebite.

Her dad grinned. "Let me guess; he was on his bike."

"Yup, he was." Sam. returned her father's smile.

"He still brake mid-corner?"

"How do you think we lost him?"

They fist-bumped. "Atta girl."

Her mother pursed her lips in thought as she dried one of the bowls, then set it aside. "Something else is going on with you that has nothing to do with today's fun. What is it?"

Ugh! She hated how good her mom was at interrogations. A freaking bulldog. And the more she resisted, the harder Bette's jaws would clamp down. Sam snagged a cookie but didn't bite into it. She turned it over and over in her hand like a coin.

"Well, I did get some news today." She searched their faces for their reactions. "A job offer that I'm going to take. On a set."

"Darling, that's wonderful!" Bette exclaimed. "Tell me it's Jodie Foster's new one."

"Nope, not Jodie." *Oh, boy.*

"Oh! Ava DuVernay's upcoming project then. I *knew* it. Good job, Samantha."

"It's Quincy Torrent."

Dead silence.

Grant looked at the tiled floor as he rubbed the back of his neck.

"Quincy. Torrent." If Ron Anderson's name had been venom on Bette's lips, Quincy Torrent's name was pure acid.

"It's a smaller production," Sam started to explain. "Independent. It's—"

"It's not for you, dear." Bette's tone brooked no shit. "You aren't taking that job."

"Mom—"

"You will not be starring in *any* of his films."

"Okay, you're right. I won't be starring in his film."

"Glad you see reason." Bette picked up another bowl to dry. Her dad looked up.

"I'm not starring in it because I'm going to be the lead's stunt double."

"Excuse me?" Bette blanched as she covered her heart. But she recovered quickly. "I think something's wrong with my ears because you couldn't possibly have just told me you're going to be a *stunt woman.*"

"All right, Mom, let's do this." Sam set the cookie down. "I want you to get every single one of your objections out in the open right now. Let's hear them. Do your worst."

Bette raised her eyebrows. She carefully placed the glass bowl on the counter and tossed the dishtowel over one shoulder. Sam scoffed inside—this was her mother's favorite game. In an instant, she went from Bette the Mom to Bette the Actress. There was a good deal of her stone-cold and calculating serial killer character in her expression and controlled movements.

"This is the movie about the motorcycle gang, do I have my projects straight?"

"Yup."

"Good. I know all about it then. Let's start with the broadest problem and work our way down, shall we? It's a non-union production."

"Hardly the only one out there. And one of the reasons why I'm able to work on it." She blew out a breath. "You and Dad have worked non-union jobs."

"And they were fine, but Torrent will be able to push you all past your limits, make you do whatever he wants. You won't have twelve-hour turnarounds between set times. Just ask your father how much your body needs to rest between stunts, and that's without getting injured. If you're tired, you'll make mistakes."

She was more than ready for this argument point. "I'm up for it. I've been training hard for this for a year. I know my limits. And Ken is the second unit director. He's fantastic. He'll look out for us." Ken Adams was one of her dad's friends. They'd met toward the end of Grant's stuntman career and the beginning of Ken's.

Grant had taught him everything he knew. "I couldn't be in better hands, Mom. Present company excluded." She nodded at her dad and he tipped an invisible hat.

Bette looked back and forth between the two. "Did you know about this?" she accused Grant.

"This is news to me, too."

Thanks, Dad.

Then he dropped the next bomb. "But, Sam did ask me to talk to Ken about getting her onto his next project. Luck of the draw that it was Quincy's, my love."

Bette's eyes narrowed the tiniest bit and Sam knew she was trying hard not to roll them. She also knew Ken would be quietly uninvited from Bette's next Bash.

"Grant, Ken can only do so much. I've worked with Quincy one time—*only* one time—because I didn't appreciate the way he manipulated his set. Of course, directors have their little power trips, but Quincy had a way of smarming up the production crew and talking them into pushing their people too hard."

Grant shook his head. "Ken's a total pro and he's no pushover. He'll have Sam's back, Bette."

Whoa. Her father adored his wife, so Sam had very rarely heard that warning tone directed at her mom. Directed at Sam and Jake and even Grant Junior, yeah, more times than she could count when they were rambunctious kids, but at Bette? This was practically a first.

To her credit, Bette hid her shock, doubling down instead. "Oh, really? I can feel Quincy's influence already, just by the fact that Ken suggested her." She turned her attention to Sam. "Mark my words, he won't be satisfied just having you as a stuntwoman."

"What are you saying?" Sam bluffed. She knew exactly where her mother was going with this.

"He wants you as his star, Samantha. They all do. How many unsolicited offers have you gotten to read? Or do they even bother asking you to read?"

Yup, that's exactly where she thought Bette would go. It felt like every production out there wanted to be the first to cast Samantha Collins in the lead. She was a guaranteed box office draw—but only because of her parents, her mom especially. Sam wasn't naïve enough to believe otherwise. Her talents didn't lie with acting, they were in high-speed motorcycle chases and jumping off tall buildings with a CGI explosion behind her. Why couldn't her mom see that?

At least her dad did. Enough to stand up for her.

"I already met with Quincy Torrent and he didn't say a single word about me starring. It was all about the stunts."

Crap. Why did Bette suddenly look like she'd scored a point?

"The very fact that *he's* meeting with you instead of Ken doing the interview tells me he's after you as his star."

"No, he's talking with everyone, down to the Best Boy."

"Then he's only gotten more controlling."

Great. She was referring to the controversy surrounding Quincy's last giant summer blockbuster.

Jake jumped in. "Is this the same Quincy Torrent accused of inappropriate behavior on the set of *Invincible Gods, Part Four—Balefire's Revenge?*" He held up his phone.

"Surprised you hadn't heard," Bette said.

"Music's my jam, Mom, not movies."

"It's the same man, yes."

"No one's submitted a formal complaint," Sam said.

"Darling, two actors were hospitalized for exhaustion. Twice."

"Right, twice, which means they came back to the set. Publicity stunt, he told me. A huge superhero movie like that, they were all under enormous pressure, even Quincy, which is why he's taking a break and doing this smaller passion project."

Bette just shook her head. "A Quincy Torrent passion project just makes it worse."

Sam ignored that. "Besides, like Dad said, Ken's got my back. I'm doing this no matter what."

Bette swallowed hard. "Grant." She gestured at Samantha. "Please. Tell her this is madness."

"Honey, Ken is one of the best in the business. I raised him up myself. He's not going to let anything happen to Sam."

Bette shook her head. She turned her chair and rolled down the hall toward the master suite.

The look on her dad's face broke Sam's heart. Enough that she considered telling Quincy she'd changed her mind.

"Sorry, Dad," Sam said quietly. "I can tell him no and wait for the next opportunity."

"Sweetie, don't. I'm proud of you. I trust Ken. And it's about time you did your own thing." Then he took off after Bette.

Which left Sam alone with Jake.

He scowled at her. "Great job, sis. Just fucking great."

"Jake—"

But her brother had already turned and stormed off toward the suite he shared with Rachael when they spent the night.

Fucking wonderful.

Sam sighed and blinked back tears. "I should just say no," she told the plate of cookies. "Mom's right, I can't do this."

I believe in you, Samantha Collins.

She touched her lips. Eric hadn't actually kissed her, not for real. Which was fine. Which was great, because the last thing she needed was one more person in her life to disappoint.

She bit into her cookie.

FOUR

Two months later

Eric pulled up in front of the Collins estate and parked beside half a dozen other cars. Today was one of Bette's Backyard Bashes, though it was smaller than the usual ones, made up of Eric's coworkers from Watchdog and their spouses—not a director in sight and the only actors were Bette and Grant. The day promised to be a fun one, and a big surprise for Annalie.

All the same, Eric wished he could be anywhere but there.

Annalie's agent Murray Ackerman rode beside him in the SUV. The two had become fast friends over the past two months on the book tour. Eric had come to adore the little old man. Hell, he'd come to think of him like a father—certainly a more encouraging one than the flesh-and-blood father he had back in Montana.

"What's the matter, kid?" Murray asked. "You look a little peaked. I thought I was the one with the health issues."

Eric grinned. Murray had had a serious health scare on the

book tour—and considering what he and Annalie had just been through, 'health scare' was the understatement of the year.

"Don't you worry about me, Murray. Remember our cover story for today?"

The man fixed him with a droll stare. "Of course I do. I'm not exactly drooling into my Wheaties these days."

Now Eric laughed. Murray was one of the only people who could make him laugh like that. He tried not to think about the other one.

Samantha Collins.

Just thinking her name sent the blood racing straight to his groin. And that was exactly why he didn't want to be here.

He had a good-sized text string from Samantha on his phone, spanning back to the beginning of the book tour. Nothing serious, mostly funny memes she forwarded, interspersed with messages like *I hope you found some butter brickle in Idaho* with a shoe emoji. Her personal messages actually made him laugh harder than any jokey memes she sent. He went to war with himself, wanting to answer her immediately—no, if he was being honest, he'd wanted to call and hear her voice—and hitting delete on a relationship that could never happen. He took the middle path and mostly replied with laughing emojis, but every now and then he couldn't help himself and asked how she was doing and if she was a stuntwoman yet. Regret hit him every time he hit send and she answered quickly with an optimistic response. He had no business even communicating with her, so once Eric was back in town, he stopped replying until her messages slowly dried up. Only later did he learn there was a term for what he'd done—ghosting—and it was considered a deeply shitty thing to do. He couldn't blame her if she wanted nothing to do with him at the party. Truth was, she'd probably forgotten about him and moved on.

Embrace the suck. You're here to surprise Annalie and celebrate with your friends, not see Samantha. She's probably not even here, and if she is, she's certainly not thinking about you.

"Where'd you go, kid?" Murray asked.

"Just thinking about what you said earlier today, about my screenplay."

"It's a good one, and I especially like the heroine. Still needs work, but I think you'll be ready to shop it in a few months."

"Are you just being kind?"

"Do I look kind?" Murray gave him an exaggerated scowl like only an old-school, native New Yorker could manage. Eric laughed again.

"We'd better get in there before Malcolm chickens out," Eric joked.

Murray waved him off. "As if that big man doesn't already drink Annalie's bathwater."

Eric snorted. "Where do you come up with this stuff?"

"Frustrated author. Those who can't, teach, edit, or become agents." Murray give him an all-is-well wink and opened the SUV door.

Eric hurried to open his. "Wait, I'll help you out."

"Oh, stop hovering like a mother hen. I'm fine."

Sure enough, Murray had jumped down before Eric was even halfway around the SUV. The man was still spry. Eric retreated to the back of the SUV to let Blaze out. She sensed the other dogs there and was eager to play, but she obeyed Eric's command to heel. When they walked in, Eric heard cheers coming from the back patio. He and Murray exchanged looks.

"He wouldn't...not without us there, would he?" Murray asked.

"Of course not," Eric said, though just like Murray, he was wondering what the heck was going on. They went straight to the French doors leading out to the backyard. As planned, everyone was out on the expansive patio overlooking the lawn, where Blaze quickly joined the other dogs.

Before he could stop himself, Eric scanned the group, looking for Samantha.

Annalie and Malcolm were sitting with Eric's co-worker Elissa.

Gina, one of his bosses, sat at the table next to theirs. Elissa's fiancé Nash sat beside her with his arm draped over the back of her chair. His thumb stroked her opposite arm. Eric's other boss Lachlan stood behind Gina's chair. Eric sensed a definite vibe going on there. He could almost see invisible strings attaching the two. He wondered if anyone else noticed.

Tina sat in Bette's lap beside a table while Tina's parents Camden—another co-worker—and Elena stood beside Bette with Psychic and his fiancée, Jordan. Elena and Jordan were hugging while everyone watched them, still clapping.

And there she was, sitting behind Elena and Jordan at a table beside Jake, Rachael, and Grant.

Eric's breath caught in his chest.

God, if it were possible, she was even more beautiful now than she'd been the first time he'd laid eyes on her. She was wearing a gorgeous sundress that showed off her toned body. He'd always been a sucker for an athletic build, but Sam's was perfect—not too muscular but well-defined. Her skin glowed. His body reacted as he remembered how she'd felt in his arms as he'd pressed her against the wall.

Shut it down, now.

Her lips were curved into an enticing smile and her eyes danced as she watched Elena and Jordan hugging.

Stop staring. Stop staring. Stop staring.

Eric turned his attention back to Jordan and Elena. For sure, it looked like he and Murray just missed something important. The women stopped hugging and sat down, their fiancés hovering protectively over them. Elena placed her hand over her belly, emphasizing the baby bump there.

"Not quite how or when we wanted to announce it," Psychic said, looking at Malcolm. He sounded like he was apologizing for stealing Malcolm's thunder. This confirmed the rumor Eric had heard from Nash—Jordan was pregnant too.

Annalie frowned when she heard Psychic's words. "What's

that about?" she asked Malcolm. He shrugged and then cleared his throat. She looked over at Elissa, who appeared just as confused. Samantha looked like she was hiding a smile—like she knew exactly what was going on and couldn't have been happier for her aunt. Jake must have let on at some point.

"Mal," Annalie chided. "What?"

"I—" Malcolm looked past her to the French doors where Eric and Murray still stood. "Hey!" The man looked relieved that they were finally there.

Showtime Eric thought.

Annalie turned, surprised. "What are you guys doing here?" she asked. "I thought you were busy brainstorming the screenplay."

Samantha looked up and her eyes immediately locked with Eric's, sending electricity through his entire body. She studied his face before her gaze moved slowly down his chest, lingering on his abs, dipping down farther before traveling back up.

Did she just look me up and down? Could it be that she'd forgiven him for ghosting?

Eric couldn't help the grin that spread across his face.

Samantha's eyes widened and her gaze quickly snapped to Murray, but Eric couldn't miss the pink flooding her cheeks.

Mercy.

"Hey, Annalie!" Murray said as he crossed the patio, Eric at his side. Malcolm was already standing and offering him his seat. Murray looked around, eyebrows raised. "I didn't miss some excitement, did I, kiddo?"

"You did. Jordan and Elliot are pregnant," Annalie confirmed. She kissed Murray on the cheek.

Eric caught Samantha's gaze again and he gave her the brightest, happiest smile he could manage. Her returning smile lit up her eyes like sunlight on the water.

Dazzling. Perfect. And he couldn't believe it was aimed at *him*.

First, it didn't matter that he was a former SEAL—in this town, in the crowd he ran with now, he was nobody. Just a bodyguard. A guy with a dream about selling a screenplay. That made him like every single other dude who'd come to L.A. Nothing special.

Second, she was *the* Samantha Collins. Enough said.

His smile faltered.

Samantha quickly swallowed her smile, lifted her chin, and pointedly looked at Annalie and Murray instead. It felt to Eric like the sun going behind a bank of clouds.

"Pregnant? Wonderful news!" Murray told Annalie. "And a great plot twist for the day."

"Plot twist?" Annalie asked.

And that's when Malcolm dropped to one knee in front of her.

Elissa gasped while Nash chuckled. "You all *knew*, didn't you? See? You *guys* gossip way worse than we do."

Annalie covered her mouth. "Oh, you have got to be kidding. How did I not see this coming?"

Then Malcolm proposed marriage.

With tears in her eyes, Annalie answered, "Yes, I want nothing more than to marry you."

He placed the ring on her finger, then pulled her out of her chair. Her feet left the ground as he hugged and kissed her. Eric cheered with the rest, happy for his two friends who'd found love.

But he couldn't help himself. He stole another look at Samantha.

Stop dwelling on how amazing she looks today.

So his thoughts dove into the past instead—straight to the 'kiss' at the ice cream parlor—an image that popped into his head all too frequently. The way she looked up at him when he pressed her against the wall—surprised yet willing. The feel of her heart and her breath speeding up as he leaned forward. The smell of her skin. The brief softness of her lips past his thumb, the way his body reacted to having her in his arms, craving her. He'd never been so hard—

Samantha's eyes darted back to Eric. From the way the blush

climbed her throat past her hard swallow, he thought he might be reminiscing too.

No, you're imagining things. It was nothing. Nothing at all. Just a weird, shared moment brought on by the excitement of that day and needing to keep Annalie safe. I was just doing my job and she was playing along because it was fun. A diversion.

And so was he.

Samantha suddenly stood up, crossed the patio to her aunt to congratulate her, then quickly made her way back into the house.

Fuck. Did I just misread everything? Maybe she hadn't forgiven him for ghosting after all. He deserved her anger. It was a shitty thing to do. He'd never been good at communicating but that didn't excuse his behavior.

Eric thought of following her inside to apologize, then shoved that impulse down deep. *What am I, a stalker?* Despite the smoldering look she'd given him the moment he walked outside with Murray, he didn't want to push her.

He'd learned that pushing Samantha Collins about anything was a terrible idea.

So was entertaining any thought that there could be something between them. Even if she wasn't *the* Samantha Collins she was only in her mid-twenties and life hadn't tested her yet. Too young for him. At least that's what he told himself.

Then there was Jake. Eric hadn't seen much of him since coming back but when they did cross paths at the office, Jake acted wary. He couldn't imagine how the man would react if Eric asked Samantha out.

Dating Samantha Collins. Yeah, right. He glanced at the door where she'd retreated. Samantha couldn't have made it clearer that she didn't have time for him, even if she did like what she saw. Any real connection he thought they'd made was an illusion.

A shocked voice jolted him out of his thoughts.

"What do you mean you already got married?" Elena's eyes darted back and forth between Jordan and Psychic. That shushed the crowd.

Psychic shrugged in his cool, unaffected way. "As soon as Jordan confirmed the pregnancy with her doctor, we went to the courthouse." His gaze turned tender as he looked at Jordan. "I want our baby to know he or she has a father who loves their mother and loves them and will always be there. I never had that."

"You *went to a courthouse?*" Bette shrieked. Her wheelchair zoomed across the patio. "I did not give anyone here permission to get married without allowing me to butt in and tell them how to do it."

Whoa! Eric had never seen Bette act so dramatic.

But if Eric was surprised, Jordan looked downright shocked. Eric didn't know her well, but he did know Jordan was a bit of a recluse, preferring her gardens to people sometimes. Right now the poor woman looked devastated.

Until Bette reached out and gripped her hand. "Honeybee, I'm only joking. I'm sorry." Her voice was back to a normal tone and infused with warmth. "But I would be honored if you'd let me throw you a congratulatory party." She held up her hand. "At your discretion, of course."

Jordan's smile looked slightly forced.

"A small one. Only close friends, like today," Bette added.

Jordan visibly relaxed. "Thank you. That sounds fun. As long as I get to choose the flowers."

End scene Eric thought as he made mental notes about their interaction. And who better to study than Bette? Though he didn't doubt her sincerity—she'd shown her generosity time and again with Watchdog—she couldn't help but be 'on' all the time, or so he suspected. Watching her was like getting a masterclass on how an actress can take some simple lines from a screenplay and infuse them with emotion, turning a flat character into a person an audience could relate to.

And at the same time, he was beginning to understand exactly where Samantha was coming from. Bette got what Bette wanted.

"I know that look," Murray said beside him. "Seen it with Annalie a million times when she's knee-deep in writing a novel. You're studying those two," he subtly pointed at Bette and Jordan, "and thinking about your screenplay."

"Guilty," Eric said. He was in the practice of studying any room for threats, escape routes, things like that. But he was still learning to picture how things would look through a camera lens.

"I also didn't miss you studying someone else here," Murray continued.

Eric started to deny everything, but when he turned to see Murray's knowing smile, the lie died on his lips. No way was he going to slip anything past his mentor and friend.

"Okay, you caught me. I was thinking about...someone, yeah. But there's nothing there, as you can see when she retreated."

"Kid, what I see is an interesting little dance going on between you two. I've known Samantha since she was knee-high and one thing I've never seen her do is retreat." He winked. "*That* was a dance move." He leaned closer. "And it's gonna be up to you to decide which one of you leads the dance."

Eric chuckled good-naturedly. "I'll sit this one out, thanks. She's too young for me, for starters." *And way out of my league* he added silently. Still, his gaze drifted to the French doors. He got up and crossed the patio to a cooler and pulled out a beer.

When he straightened up, Jake Collins was standing next to him. Eric braced out of habit.

"Jake." He gave the man a chin lift and hoped he could leave it at that.

"Eric." The warning tone told him Jake was spoiling for a fight. "Was just thinking of the last time you were here at the house. Now, let's see, what went down that day?" He tapped his chin, pretending to think.

"Jake—"

"Oh, yeah. You took off with my little sister into a dangerous situation."

Okay, now the man was pissing him off. The tension in the office was bad enough, he didn't need this outright bullshit today.

"She was never in any danger, Jake, you know that. She was a decoy to throw the press off Annalie's trail, and everything went as planned."

As far as anyone here knows.

"All I know is she's acting different now."

"Different?" That bothered Eric.

Jake went on. "Yeah, ever since you were willing to put my untrained sister in danger for a mission."

"Okay, that's taking things too far." Rage flooded Eric until felt a cold dog nose nuzzle into his hand. He glanced down to see Blaze at his feet. The German Shepherd looked up at him as if to say *Keep it cool, but if not, I'm here for backup, partner.*

Eric took a deep breath to center himself. "Jake, at no point was Samantha ever in danger. When I got word that the papps were on their way over here to scoop Bette about Annalie, I did what any of us would have done—evaluated the situation, looked at the resources at my disposal—"

"My sister is not a *resource,*" Jake said through gritted teeth.

"Of course she isn't and that's not what I meant. She was in costume, looking like Annalie. She offered to be a decoy. I wasn't forcing her to do anything. We drove off, the paparazzi followed, we lost them, Annalie and your mom weren't harassed that day. Mission accomplished."

Jake's eyes narrowed. "What happened on that drive?"

Shit. He knows about the kiss. No, the almost-kiss.

"I drove. We talked. We got hungry and when the coast was clear we stopped for ice cream, then burgers. I brought her home, safe and sound. End of story."

Hardly the end of the story. Though all technically true.

"Bullshit," Jake growled. "That's not all."

Fuck. She told him. Eric had offended Samantha at the ice cream parlor after all and she told her brother.

Jake narrowed his eyes. "What did you *talk* about?"

Talk? He wants to know what we talked *about? Not a word about the kiss.*

Eric watched Jake's shoulders tense as he shifted his weight to one foot. *Goddamn, he's getting ready to punch me.* This wasn't the Jake Collins everyone knew, the guy who was quick with a joke or a bit of music trivia, the man who kept his cool under all circumstances. *What gives?*

Eric thought about all the things he and Samantha had talked about. Ice cream, favorite colors, nothing serious except—

I want to be a stuntwoman.

Shit. Eric suddenly realized Jake knew—or at least suspected—that she'd told Eric first. Eric had said nothing to anyone about it. As far as he was concerned, it was no one's business. But Jake seemed to have taken offense. His gut clenched.

"We talked about her, mostly. All right? That a crime?" He shook his head. "Jake, what the hell are you implying? This isn't you."

"Well, my sister hasn't been herself either since she got back from that little joyride. She's always been defiant but now she..." He trailed off. "She's gone and done something absolutely rash and it's tearing this family apart."

Jake jabbed his finger into Eric's chest. "So, I'm asking the source right now—what the hell happened on that car ride? What did you say that encouraged her?"

Jake made a fist. Eric shifted his weight and wondered if he could catch his hand midair when over Jake's shoulder, Eric watched Lachlan approach them.

"What's going on over here?" their boss asked. "Someone take the last beer?" He pretended to look over the cooler. "Nope, I see plenty of good ones in there. So, it's gotta be the bathrooms."

That stopped both of them. "Bathrooms, Boss?"

"Yeah, Shep," Lach answered Eric. "Must be all the bathrooms are occupied because now that I'm here up close and personal, this looks like a pissing contest."

He looked from one man to the other, his furrowed brow as craggy as a Scottish landscape. So far, he hadn't lifted his voice—which often boomed through the office—probably out of respect for Bette. "Is that what I'm seeing, gentlemen? A pissing contest?"

"No, sir," Eric answered. Jake glared at him.

"Jake?"

"Just a friendly discussion about the weather. Sir."

Lach lifted a brow and his nostrils flared. "Eric, stop by my office first thing tomorrow morning. New assignment."

"Yes, sir."

Lach didn't move. His stormy eyes shifted from Eric to Jake, assessing the threat level. Finally, he bent and scratched Blaze's ears while he grabbed a beer.

"Keep an eye on these two jackasses for me, lass," he told the dog, then stood, turned and practically stomped away.

"I'll leave," Eric told Jake. "Gotta check on the dogs anyway." Not really; Marc had everything under control at the kennel as usual and besides, half of the dogs were here and the other half were out on assignment. He gave Blaze the signal to heel and walked away before Jake had a chance to speak.

Fuck him.

Eric hated this. He and Jake had always gotten along before that day. He was beginning to understand the full weight of what Samantha had confided in him. At the time, he'd felt honored that she'd shared, but now, he was in the shit.

Then there was that almost-kiss that he couldn't get out of his mind.

Just leave. Just walk out. Hopefully, Lach's assignment is an away mission that'll give everything a chance to cool down. It would be just like his boss to separate them that way.

Eric stopped briefly by Bette's table and told her thank you. He was halfway to the French doors when he remembered that Murray had ridden with him.

Fuck.

He turned to approach Murray, but the man was waving him off. "I'm covered, kid. Go do your thing."

Eric nodded to cover his annoyance. Was every single person here watching him? Speculating?

He went inside, and as his eyes adjusted from the sunny day outside, he saw her.

Samantha stood between him and his escape route.

A small smile played around her lips. She looked uncharacteristically shy. He thought about the moment they first met. That day, he had to admit, she'd initially struck him as a bit of a brat, especially when he'd misunderstood her, thinking she wanted nothing to do with him. But the texts had changed his mind. And after the way Jake reacted outside, he could see where she was coming from that day.

Samantha took a step forward. "I was just, uh, going back outside. Hi." She started to bite her lower lip then stopped herself.

"Hi." He tried to focus only on her face; not a hardship. Since working up close with actresses and musicians, he'd found that what looked like flawless skin and flowing hair in photos was often highly manipulated, and in person, they had the same pimples and split ends as everyone else.

Not Samantha. She was perfection. Flawless. The spitting image of her mother's youth combined with her father's athletic build. *And, here I am looking below the chin.* Eric's gaze quickly snapped back to her face.

Stop it right now.

"Are you leaving?" she asked casually.

"I am, yeah. Gotta check on the dogs."

"Always working, huh?"

"Always."

Samantha nodded as if contemplating something. "I figured

maybe when you stopped texting me back you were busy." She gave him a smile that was pure essence of fake. "Well, I'll let you go."

"Samantha, wait. I owe you an apology. I didn't mean to ghost you like that. It was rude."

Her fake smile was replaced by an honest frown. "Yeah, actually now that you mention it, it was rude. I thought...never mind."

If I stay a second longer, I'm only going to make this worse. He started to move past her.

Samantha's hand landed on his arm and he stopped like he'd hit a wall. Her touch flared like she'd palmed the sun and pressed it against his skin. They both looked at her hand and then into each other's eyes.

After a beat, she broke the silence. "But, I just wanted to thank you for listening to me in the car that day. And your texts meant a lot when you said you believed in me. I just wanted to let you know, I'm going to do it. I'm going to be a stuntwoman. So, I'm sorry if I was a problem that day, and I apologize for being pushy with contacting you."

"No, don't apologize. You weren't pushy at all. I enjoyed every single text. Some days, it was my only laugh."

Her beautiful eyes went soft. She was killing him with that look. "I'm glad. That's what I wanted."

"I've seen how everyone underestimates you, Samantha." He glanced over his shoulder hoping no one could see in. "It's not fair to you."

Her eyes lit up like a flare—one signaling danger.

Nope, don't look directly into the sun. Shut this down, now before you end up kissing her for real this time.

"I'm the one who should apologize," he said, hating how husky his voice sounded almost as much as he hated what he was about to say. "And not just for ghosting you."

She doesn't need me around to cause her more problems.

"Apologize for what then?" She licked her lips. Her eyes flicked over his face and he felt flushed.

She's out of my league anyway.

"That kiss in the ice cream parlor. I never should have coerced you into something you weren't ready for."

Her eyes flared again, only this time, angry heat sparked in them. "Not ready? I—"

She stopped when they heard footsteps approaching from the patio. Probably Jake still spoiling for a fight. The hurt on Samantha's face and the way she braced herself when she turned that way stabbed his heart. All his resistance flew out the window.

He touched her jawline and gently turned her face back to his.

"Confidence looks good on you. Make your stand against your mom and your brother and anyone else who gets in your way and pursue *your* dreams. Take care of yourself, Samantha."

Eric moved past her. He and Blaze started toward the front door.

"I always do," she said. "Don't need anyone to do it for me."

He turned to respond, not caring if anyone saw them, but she was already gone.

FIVE

Eric stopped by Malcolm's office Monday morning to congratulate him again on his engagement before heading into Lach's office to discuss his new assignment with Lachlan and Gina. His bosses hadn't been very forthcoming with the details in the email he'd gotten the night before, and Eric was eager to find out why. He'd spent the last month working in-house with Marc in the Watchdog kennel, and while he loved the dogs, he was finding the kennel to be a bit, well, boring. It was too well-run and there were no surprises. Eric found himself missing the excitement of guarding Annalie on the road.

His thoughts went back for the hundredth time to evading the paparazzi with Samantha.

And like every other time, he caught himself shaking his head and grinning, despite his encounter with Samantha the day before.

Just shut that BS down right now, bud.

Eric knocked on Lachlan's door.

"Come in," his boss called in his typical, booming style. He opened the door to find Lach and Gina waiting for him. Gina was standing while Lach was behind his desk. Sam, Lach's old dog, was in his usual spot in the corner snoozing on a pile of blankets. Fleur was curled up beside him, her golden eyes watchful.

Eric sat in the chair opposite Lachlan and cut to the chase. "So, new assignment?"

"Brand new," Lach said. "But let me ask you a question first. How happy are you here?"

The question took Eric aback. Was he referring to yesterday's argument with Jake? He'd be doubly pissed if the man cost Eric his job.

"I'm...very happy, sir. Is there something wrong with my performance?"

"You scared him, Lach," Gina said as she began to pace. "You're fine, Eric. Excellent, even."

"Which is *why* I'm asking if he's happy here," Lach said, eying Gina. "Don't want to lose him." He looked at Eric. "I know you love the dogs, but you seem restless lately."

Eric blew out a breath. "Okay, yeah, I am." He held up his hand. "The kennel is great, the dogs are amazing, Marc's got the place running smoothly. I guess I'm feeling...redundant. Like backup."

"You liked being out on the road?"

"I did. It was a challenge. Exciting." Eric nodded. "I liked it a lot."

Lach smiled. "Great, just what I wanted to hear. I think you're the right man—no—I think you're the perfect man for this assignment." He hesitated.

Gina's pacing brought her back to the desk and she stopped. "We're just afraid we might lose you to this assignment."

"Lose?"

"As in, you might like this one a little too much and jump ship on us," she said. "Lach just wanted to be prepared if you did."

Now Eric was really confused. "Like I said, I enjoy my job here. I can't imagine what would tempt me away from it."

"This might." Lachlan pushed a folder across his desk to Eric.

He picked it up and opened it.

No way. No freaking way.

Eric looked up in shock at Lachlan, who turned to Gina. "See? I was right to worry. He's already gone."

She folded her arms and rolled her eyes. "He's got to be employed by us for this assignment, Lach, so he's not gone." She turned her amber gaze on Eric. "At least not yet."

Eric dropped the folder on the desk and put his hands up. "I will sign any additional contract you want, pledge myself to continue working for Watchdog for however long, if I can have this assignment."

Lachlan laughed. "He'd sell his soul for this one."

"Damn near!" Eric said. "Seriously, working with dogs on a movie set? You already know I love dogs. I'm a huge movie buff, too. It's why I'm here in L.A." He stopped when he realized he was damn near babbling. "Okay. Come on, what's the catch? I'm good with animals, but there are plenty of others more qualified than me. I don't belong to a union. I—"

"You won't be the only animal handler. Let's say the animal handling part is secondary to your actual job there."

"Oh. Got it. Undercover work." He was kicking himself inside. Of course, this was a bodyguard job because that's what he did. *I must sound like a complete jackass.*

Gina chuckled. "Lach, I think we have our man. His enthusiasm alone will convince them he's legitimately apprenticing."

"Okay, so who am I supposed to be guarding? Or watching? Or...what? How did this even come across your desk?"

"Seems we can't go to a party at Bette's without picking up a new client," Lach said.

"Wait, how? That was just us. Unless." He looked back and forth between Gina and Lachlan for confirmation.

Gina walked to Lachlan's office door and turned the lock.

"Bette is hiring us for this one. This does not leave this office, understand?"

"Not even Jake?"

"*Especially* not Jake." Gina paced back to the desk. "Can you do this?"

"Seriously? I'm going to be working on set with Bette Collins? Of course. Yes, I'm your man."

"Slow down," Lach said. "Not with Bette."

"Not Bette? Then who?"

"Her daughter, Samantha."

Eric schooled his features. "Sounds copacetic. When do I start?"

Oh boy. This should be interesting.

When Samantha had told him the day before she was going to be a stuntwoman, he'd thought she was still talking in the abstract, not that she'd gotten an actual job.

She did it. Good for you, Samantha. He felt her success as if it were his own.

"There's more to it," Gina added. She tapped the folder. "Samantha can't know about it ahead of time."

"I don't like that."

"Knew you wouldn't," Lachlan said. "But, it's part of the deal. Bette doesn't trust the first thing about this production, starting with the director, who has totally won over Sam."

"Who is it?"

"Guy named Quincy Torrent."

Eric's eyes widened. "*The* Quincy Torrent?"

Lach snorted, picked up his cut-down pen, and shoved it in his mouth. "Oh good, you've heard of him."

"Are you fucking serious? He just directed *Invincible Gods, Part Four—Balefire's Revenge*, which no one thought he could handle. He's done so many art films, they didn't think he could direct something so commercial, but he knocked it out of the park. Biggest summer blockbuster in years, but they can't get him to do the next one. Guy's a legend." Eric trailed off as he watched Gina and Lach exchange looks.

"Lost him already," Lachlan growled. Gina smirked.

"No, seriously, I love it here," Eric insisted.

"Mmm," Gina said, sounding unconvinced. "Well, first thing you're going to do is meet with Mr. Torrent this afternoon. Think you can handle that without fanboying the entire time?"

Holy. Fuck. "Yeah, of course I can."

"Because here's the deal." Gina leaned down into his face. "We're not sending you in to be buddies with Torrent. He's the reason why Bette is not happy with Sam's life choices."

Eric felt the back of his neck prickle with irritation. *Could it be that Bette is being overprotective?* The words were almost out of his mouth but he stopped them at the last second. He gave something away though, from the way that Gina studied him.

"What does Bette have against him?"

Gina straightened and began pacing. "Quincy is very charismatic. His crews worship him and he rewards them by using them over and over on different projects. That's been fine on his smaller ones, but the scope of this last movie and the deals already in place meant he had to work with a much bigger cast and crew than what he's used to. At first, he won everyone over. But according to Bette, the set became...well, she heard it was almost cultish. That despite the union rules, people were exhausting themselves trying to please him. People ended up in the hospital."

"I heard that was just a publicity stunt."

"Bette says that's how they spun it."

Eric frowned. "And the actors went along with the spin?"

Gina shrugged. "They refuse to comment. Or talk to Bette. She tried."

"And if Bette couldn't get them to talk," Lach said, "they aren't gonna say boo to *anyone*." He winked at Gina. "No offense."

She rolled her eyes. "Stuntpeople too," Gina continued. "There were injuries. One lawsuit."

"I hadn't heard about this," Eric said, feeling uneasy.

"No one has. It was settled out of court and out of the spotlight. But there's one less stuntman working because of it."

Eric considered this.

"I see I have your attention now." Gina smiled.

"Yeah, you do, Boss."

Lachlan shifted in his chair. "So, Torrent's staying out of the spotlight, too. He's gone back to making a smaller picture, we think, until this all blows over. He's hired his old friends, but he's needing new people too, so he's meeting with every person on the crew, and that's gonna include you today. Torrent's never had animals on his set so the animal handler he's hired is new to him. So are you."

Eric paged through the folder until he found the name of the animal handler. "Does this Tim Bakker know the score?"

"He does," Lachlan said. "He's an old friend of Bette's."

"Who isn't in this town?"

"Quincy Torrent."

Eric nodded. "Do I have any other allies?"

"Yeah, Ken Adams. In this case, he's a friend of Grant's and Bette's. That's the stunt coordinator. Grant asked him to keep an eye on his little girl."

"She sounds covered then. And Bette still wants me?"

Lach nodded. "Ken's also friends with Torrent. And he worked on *Invincible Gods*."

"Where the stuntman was injured."

"Now you're getting the picture." Lachlan took the pen out of his mouth. "Have fun meeting your hero today." He leaned forward. "But don't forget who you are and who he is."

Eric straightened his tie for the thirty-fifth time as he waited for Quincy Torrent to call him into his office. Blaze lay curled up and snoring at his feet. Showbusiness meant nothing to her. Eric was trying to follow her example.

Of course his first priority was Samantha's safety. He'd do anything to protect her. That was his job.

He told himself it was *only* his job, not his personal interest in her.

But meeting Quincy Torrent. That was something he never imagined doing.

"Quincy will see you now." Torrent's personal assistant Cinnamon—who insisted that Eric call her by her first name 'like a big happy family'—smiled at him from behind her desk. She gave him the once-over when he stood up. Blaze came awake immediately and stood at attention, then heeled as they headed in to meet the director.

Quincy Torrent was already out of his chair and heading around to the front of his desk before Eric and Blaze even got through the door. He was a head shorter than Eric, wiry, and full of energy. Before he even greeted Eric, he was down on his knees and petting Blaze.

"Hey, pretty girl, hey! I heard you were out there and I wanted to meet you." His voice was high-pitched, a dog-greeting voice, and he ran his hands over Blaze's fur. She in turn lapped up all of the attention from the stranger, which was totally unlike her.

So much for being the model of professionalism Eric thought. *You're letting me down, girl.*

Quincy looked up at Eric. "It's Blaze, right? That's what Cinnamon said."

"Yup, that's her name."

"Pretty, pretty girl." He finally stood up. "Sorry, man, couldn't help myself." He offered his hand to shake. "I love animals. Dogs are the best. So glad I finally get to work with some."

Quincy's friendly gaze bore right into Eric's, which set him at ease and put him on alert at the same time. He was expecting the director to act slick, show a little fake politeness maybe. He wasn't expecting the guy to be so overtly friendly, enough to win Blaze over.

"So, Eric, nice to meet you, too." Quincy laughed. "Take a seat."

"And you." Eric sat down as Quincy circled the desk. "I'm a fan."

Quincy waved him off. "Don't need to do that, man, you've already got the job." He laughed again as he sat down, then he bounced right back up as if he'd sat on a nail. "Shit, my manners suck. Let me get you a bottle of water. We all need to stay hydrated." He jogged over to a credenza that concealed a mini fridge and pulled out two bottles of expensive water. He set them on the desk and sat back down.

"No, I mean it, I'm a fan of your work. *Brutal Honesty* was a masterpiece," Eric said. He was testing Quincy's response, but it was also sincere.

Quincy covered his heart. "Thanks, man. That's my personal favorite. But we aren't here to talk about me, but for me to get to know you." He folded his hands on the desk and opened his eyes wide to listen.

The guy's good, I'll give him that. He genuinely seemed interested in whatever Eric had to say. So Eric dove right into his cover story, handcrafted by Gina herself. The best lie was always based on a half-truth, so they'd kept his real name, his tenure working with dogs as a SEAL, but wiped his employment with Watchdog, replacing it with a post-Navy career training dogs for service and the entertainment industry. Everything would check out online and Tim would vouch that he'd worked with Eric for three years and that he was an outstanding trainer looking for his first break in the movies.

Quincy was such an enthusiastic listener that by the time Eric was done talking, he half-believed his own bullshit.

"Man, I am so glad I have you on board," Quincy said as he leaned back in his chair and covered his heart with both hands.

"That's what this picture is all about, giving new people their start and my old friends a fresh start."

Eric saw his opening and took it. "Yeah, I heard that the latest *Invincible Gods* was a bear to make."

Quincy turned serious. "Lots of pressure for that one. Insane budget, lots of special effects, big egos, unbearable producers. It took a lot out of all of us. Too much. That's why I've gone back to something smaller and out of the spotlight. Give my family a chance to rest and heal, man." He squeezed his eyes shut as if he were in pain.

"Your family?"

"Yeah, my crew. They're my family. I spend more time with them than I do with anyone I'm related to." He smiled sadly. "Blood family just doesn't get it sometimes."

An image of Eric's dad scowling at him popped unbidden to his mind. "Yeah, I can relate." *Shit. I did not mean to say that.*

Quincy nodded. "I thought so. Us creative types, huh?"

Eric shook his head. "I'm not creative."

Quincy scoffed. "The fuck you aren't! You're a SEAL, you guys have to be creative to survive." He nodded slowly. "I have a feeling about you. A good one. You're gonna thrive on my set and I'm gonna like having you around, my man."

Eric grinned. "Thanks."

Quincy turned serious again as he leaned in across the desk. "So, tell me the truth."

Oh, shit. He'd slipped up somehow. "Truth?"

Quincy laughed and clapped his hands together once. "Yeah, man! Come on, you have a script, don't you?"

Eric laughed with relief. "Damn, you are perceptive, aren't you?"

Quincy pretended to buff his nails against his chest. "Naw, I just know all you military guys have fucking incredible stories, and since you're wanting to break into the movies I just figured you've got a manuscript up your sleeve."

Don't. Don't. "Yeah, I'm kind of working on something." *Shit.*

"Ha! Knew it. Well, tell you what. I'd love to take a look. I could really get behind a project like that."

Eric blinked rapidly. His oldest, craziest, most out-there childhood dream of seeing one of the stories in his head on the screen, and Quincy was offering to help it along into reality. "Um, that's... I don't know what to say."

"Don't say anything, just send it here." Quincy pulled a card out of his desk drawer that had nothing on it but an email address. "That's my private one, so no sharing. You're a SEAL though, so I trust you."

"Thanks, Mr. Torrent." Eric put the card in his pocket.

"Dude!" Quincy cackled. "How many times I gotta say it's Quincy?" He reached across the desk to shake Eric's hand.

"Welcome to the family, man."

Eric felt welcomed.

And as the meeting went on, covering the details about Eric's job on set, he understood more and more why Samantha was so adamant about working on this project.

SIX

Samantha dreaded dinner with her family the night before she left for the set.

Just like every other dinner—no, every *interaction*—since breaking the news that she'd taken the stuntwoman job on Quincy's new movie. The interview with him had been totally surreal. She kept waiting for Quincy to try and convince her that she was mistaken and that he wanted her as the lead—not the stunt double.

I mean, what director at his level talks to the stuntpeople, anyway? That was Ken's job as stunt coordinator.

But Quincy had been adamant that he respected what she wanted to do, and after watching the videos she'd sent him—the ones she'd made at the parkour gym and the motorcycle stunts Ken had filmed on the racetrack—he'd told her she was the only woman who could double for Lacey Grey. Lacey was a relative unknown, but Quincy believed she would blow up after this film—yeah, his ego was that big—but that after *Invincible Gods* he was on a different path now, and that he wanted to go back to his early roots of making smaller films that revealed new talent.

And he wanted Samantha Collins to debut as a stuntwoman—exactly what she wanted to be.

By the time he was done talking to her, Samantha would have flown to the moon to make a movie for Quincy Torrent. Instead, her destination was a small mining town in Arizona. The movie, *Wheeler, Dealer* was set in the 1970s, and Quincy described it as 'A pulp movie, *Romeo and Juliet* meets *True Lies*, meets *Breaking Bad.*'

It was the *True Lies* part that made Sam's heart go pitter-patter. *The stunts in that one...*

Sam had gone over the script, which was heavy on motorcycle stunts, and couldn't wait to get started. She talked to Ken about expectations—and was glad that he avoided any talk of her family—until she was confident that she could handle anything.

Eric Armstrong was to blame for that confidence.

Not that he cared about that, apparently.

The image of Eric turning his back and leaving her at the party had morphed into a gif on permanent repeat and played in her head every time she closed her eyes. And his remarks about their not-a-kiss at the ice cream parlor...that was its constant soundtrack.

Always working. Just doing his job that day. I was an idiot to think otherwise.

Sam braced for a fight as she headed down to dinner. She was leaving first thing in the morning, and she was getting flak for deciding to ride her Harley the entire way instead of flying to Tucson, Arizona then renting a car and driving south to the little town of Sagebrush. But she wanted to clear her head and there was nothing better for that than a nine-hour ride that would take her through Joshua Tree. She craved the feel of hot wind and burning sun, dry air, and the road flying under her bike. She told herself it would help get her into the mindset for the movie and provide her with some additional practice on the bike.

What she really hoped was that the long ride might scour off some of her residual doubt and trepidation, the disappointed looks from Bette, and the guilt she carried for causing an ongoing fight between her parents.

Bette and Grant were not as lovey-dovey these days and it broke her heart.

At least Jake wasn't around to make her feel even worse. If anything, he'd been avoiding coming over, and now he was away with Rachael at a music festival.

Sam walked into the kitchen. The smell of lasagna—Sam's favorite—filled the room. *Wow, Bette's really rubbing it in.* Her parents were already on the small patio just off the kitchen where they liked to eat when it was just family. Normally, their voices would drift in, filled with laughter, but lately, their meals were nearly silent. Tonight was no exception.

"There she is," Bette said as Sam stepped out onto the porch. Her mother's smile put her on guard even as she cringed at the tone.

"Thanks for making lasagna. It smells amazing." She bent to kiss her mom's cheek.

"You have a long ride ahead of you tomorrow, so I figured a mix of protein and carbs tonight would give you a good start."

Sam looked at her dad for any hint as to why Mom was suddenly so accommodating. He gave her a friendly look that said *hey, just take the win* and forked another bite of cheesy lasagna into his mouth. He smiled across the table at his wife, who sipped her wine.

Sam did her best to take his silent advice. She cut into her generous square of lasagna and ate. She took a swig of the red wine that went so well with the meal. They ate in silence and passed polite smiles around until she was absolutely ready to scream.

God, she's devious.

Sam finally broke. "So, can I ask why we're having such a *pleasant* dinner?"

Bette dabbed at her mouth with a napkin. "Why wouldn't we? It's a beautiful night, I'm here with my handsome husband and beautiful daughter. By the way, your hair looks amazing," she added, referring to Sam's new darker color that matched Lacey's. Bette picked up her wine glass and raised it in a brief toast. Grant did the same. Sam eyed him like he'd been taken over by an alien.

"You do know I'm leaving tomorrow and where I'm going, right?" Sam asked her pod-parents.

"Of course." Bette gestured at Sam's plate. "Would you like more? I made a whole pan, and with just your father and me here, I'll end up freezing most of it."

"Okay, what is it? What's up?" Sam asked, her gaze darting between the two of them.

"Sweetheart," Grant said, "we're just proud of you, that's all." She studied his face and saw nothing but sincerity.

"I've perhaps been a little...difficult," Bette admitted. "But your dad and I talked. He's confident that you can handle anything that Quincy throws your way, and I feel better about the whole thing now." She smiled warmly at Sam.

No use in trying to read into Bette's expression. It looked true enough, but Sam could never quite be sure.

Something in her gut told her not to trust it.

Sam was up before the dawn packing the last few things she needed into her bike's saddlebags—not a whole lot since she'd mailed her larger items to the hotel already—when her dad came out to the garage.

He patted the bike's fender. "You checked the oil?"

"Yup." Sam tightened a strap.

"And the tire pressure?"

She tilted her head. "You think I'm an amateur?"

He laughed and ran a hand over her head. "No, of course not."

Sam straightened up from where she'd been crouching beside the bike. "So. Dad. What's Mom trying to pull?"

"Sam. I just talked with her and reassured her that she raised a smart daughter who won't let herself be taken advantage of."

Sam crossed her arms. "Really?"

"Really. Besides, you've got Ken there."

Maybe that was it. Maybe they expected Ken to babysit her. He'd hardly have the time for it with all the motorcycle stunts, and not just hers. And she had no plans to give Ken any excuses to show her preferential treatment.

"Ken won't have any problems with me."

"Of course not. But, I'm telling you, you'll need to really prove yourself to them, Sam. I mean the whole crew. This is a tough job, and half of it is getting your fellow stunt crew to trust you."

He ruffled her hair. "I've seen what you can do, and I'm confident you'll be able to handle yourself whenever the camera's rolling. It's what happens between scenes though that makes or breaks your chances of getting your next job. Gotta know when to stand up for yourself and when to be a team player."

Sam looked down and nodded.

He tipped her chin up. "You have any concerns or worries, you call me, all right?"

"I will."

Grant smiled. "Now give your old man a hug."

She huffed out the breath she'd taken in anticipation of any further argument and hugged her dad instead.

The miles flew by as she knew they would. She rode through dry desert, some places barren as the moon, and tried to get into the right mindset. Riding through Tucson reminded her that yes, there was still civilization. South and east of the city, the landscape went from desert to dry hills and canyons as she neared Sagebrush, an old mining town and the on-site location of *Wheeler Dealer*. The sun was beginning to set, sending pink and orange light across the landscape. She drove past the turnoff to a now-abandoned open-pit copper mine. The town's main drag still retained old stone buildings from the turn of the century. From a distance, it looked really cool, but as she got closer the numerous boarded-up windows told her Sagebrush had seen much better days.

Sam pulled up in front of the biggest building on the street—an old three-story hotel—her new home for the next several weeks. Quincy had also insisted that the cast and as much crew as possible stay in town at the Sagebrush Inn or in a motel from the fifties along the interstate just before the turnoff to Sagebrush, so he rented out the whole inn and the motel. He didn't want anyone staying all the way back in Tucson and 'breaking out of the Seventies mindset.' That was fine by her, since it would save two lengthy daily commutes on top of a twelve- to fourteen-hour day.

Score one for her against Bette's argument that she'd be dangerously exhausted. Quincy took care of his cast and crew.

She parked her bike at the end of a long row of motorcycles and wondered how many of the crew rode, or if these were some of the movie props. Sam stepped off her bike and stretched. She'd get her gear after checking in. Right now she just wanted to get out of the wind, wash the grit and sweat off under a muscle-pounding hot shower, and fall into bed. As she walked up the steps to the front doors, Sam couldn't help but smile to herself knowing that she'd finally made it, and made it all on her own.

She opened the doors into the dim lobby and waited for her eyes to adjust. Only a few glass-shaded table lamps provided light here and there. The lobby was full of people talking and laughing as they caught up with each other. She loved the excited buzz in the air. Sam looked at the crowd, hoping to find Ken since he was about the only person here she knew personally.

And that's when she saw him and all her optimism dried up.

Eric Armstrong.

No, Eric *Fucking* Armstrong.

He stood beside another man who was in the middle of telling him something, but Eric's full attention had snapped to Sam's face as if he'd felt her looking at him.

Maybe it was the daggers shooting straight from her eyes.

Now she knew why Bette suddenly seemed so calm about Sam taking the job.

She'd hired a babysitter after all.

And the guy who had inspired her to strike out on her own had apparently raised his hand for the job.

Traitor!

SEVEN

I'm in trouble now Eric thought.

Samantha Collins looked like she was ready to ride her motorcycle right over his sorry ass.

"Hey, you still with me?" Tim Bakker, the lead animal handler for the set asked. He'd been telling Eric some of the details about one of the dogs when Samantha walked in.

"Yeah. Sorry, I need to head off a situation." Eric gave Tim a tight smile and turned to face Sam, who was already stomping across the polished stone floor. Damn, even furious she was sexy as hell. Maybe more so. He started walking to meet her and heard Tim say something about wrangling a bull. He didn't think the man was referring to anything they'd be doing on-set.

Improvise. Adapt. Overcome.

The three directives he'd learned as a SEAL went through his mind as they drew closer to each other. He'd definitely have to improvise because he'd never been on a mission quite like this one or faced such a beautiful opponent.

She's not your opponent, she's your principal. She is the mission. Only it was getting harder to convince himself she wasn't about to attempt to throw him over her shoulder the closer she got. Righteous fury burned in her beautiful eyes. She clenched her jaw and he could practically hear her teeth grind.

"I know why you're here." She said the words almost under her breath as she looked him straight in the eye.

"Samantha—"

"How *dare* you?"

"It's not what it looks like." He cringed inside.

Her eyes widened. "Not what it looks like? You're here on Bette's command to babysit me."

"It's not like that."

"Oh, really?" She put her hand on her hip. "You mean to tell me that you just happened to be in town and decided to check into this hotel today?"

"No, of course not. I'm the assistant animal handler."

Fuck. Lachlan had counseled Eric on what to say the minute Samantha saw him. Eric had the rest of the cover story queued up in his head. All he had to do was open his mouth and let it flow out.

No, I can't mislead her. That was all kinds of wrong, even if the cover was true. First of all, she'd see right through it anyway. Second, he flat-out respected Samantha. She deserved the truth. The problem was, he really did need to stick to the cover story, at least with the rest of the cast and crew.

"Assistant animal handler," Samantha said flatly. "What, do the dogs need a body—"

"Samantha."

She stopped at his warning tone. At first, he thought he'd scared her, but no. She wasn't about to let anything intimidate her.

"Please." He darted his eyes around the full lobby. He could tell they'd already caught a few people's attention by the way they quickly looked anywhere else but at Eric as he scanned the room. "I'll explain later."

"There won't be a later because you're leaving. I will out you to the rest of the crew that you are not an animal handler."

"Actually, I am."

Sudden movement caught Eric's eye. A man jumped onto the oak reception counter and Eric automatically moved to stand between Samantha and the potential threat. His shoulders relaxed as he recognized Quincy in a navy blue baseball cap, Rick Nelson Record Store tee, and khaki cargo shorts. His designer kicks probably cost Eric's salary.

Three other people stood behind the counter, two men and a woman. The poor woman tried not to look horrified as she eyed the director standing akimbo and looking like he might accidentally kick the old-fashioned landline phone right off the counter. The man standing next to her was covering his shock better, but only marginally.

The third man in a suit looked downright pleased.

"Welcome, ladies and gentlemen!" Quincy shouted.

Everyone started clapping.

Quincy gave them a self-conscious smile and shook his head. "No. No, that's not right. Let me start over." Now his smile turned warm and indulgent. "Welcome, *family*."

The room erupted with cheers.

"Are we ready to make a movie?"

If the other outburst was loud, this one was deafening.

Eric looked around the lobby and felt the enthusiasm infuse him. Their argument temporarily forgotten, Samantha's smile stretched from ear to ear. Eric wished Bette could see her daughter now, see the joy and confidence shining on her face as she shouted *yes*.

And then she was suddenly in his arms as she stumbled and he caught her. His body remembered the ice cream parlor faster than his brain and reacted accordingly—if embarrassingly. An overly enthusiastic guy had bumped into Samantha as he made his way closer to the counter and Eric kept her from falling forward.

"Steady," Eric said, making sure Sam had her footing. She looked up at him and he thought he caught a moment of heat before she narrowed her eyes and pulled away, settling her attention back on the director.

"I am so psyched to be here with everyone right now I can't even *tell you*." Quincy's voice rose on the last two words.

"So you're gonna shout it instead, huh?" That was from a guy standing across the room who looked to be in his forties with salt-and-pepper graying hair under a dusty cowboy hat. He had a craggy face and a few scars marring the sleeves of tattoos covering his crossed arms and a good-natured smile. Eric recognized Ken Adams from his briefing at Watchdog.

Quincy laughed. "That's right, Ken. Everyone, that's your new Uncle Ken standing right there. Ken Adams has been in the stunt business since I was a little kid watching him defy death on the big screen and I am truly...you know, I don't think it's an exaggeration to say that I am truly blessed to be working with him again as my second unit director on this project today, as are we all. Ken is the absolute master when it comes to designing and capturing longer stunts and doing them safely. You'll see. Ken Adams, everybody."

Quincy pointed at Ken and everyone turned and clapped. Ken tipped his hat and looked down, still with a good-natured smile but obviously not used to such attention.

"Let's see, who else we got here?" Quincy looked over the crowd. "Well, we've got *everybody* here."

And everybody obliged with a laugh.

Quincy pointed as he talked. "Terri, hey, she's in make-up. And Smithy over there is handling props. We've got Sparky—bet you don't know what he does." The crowd laughed and clapped for the electrician. "And I couldn't do any of this without the greatest assistant director in the world, Cassidy Andrews." He paused while people applauded and whistled at a young woman standing next to the front desk just below Quincy.

"She's my bullhorn. My Hand, if you're a *Game of Thrones* fan." More laughter. "One day she'll be a director in her own right, but in the meantime, be nice to my gal on the set when she's telling you what to do, huh?"

Quincy turned a little more serious. "But I do want to point out a few faces in particular. People who are new to all this and I couldn't be happier to have them here."

Sam straightened up beside Eric. She surprised him with the look on her face. She'd gone from happy to wary as she glanced around.

Eric elbowed her. "Think he's going to mention you?"

She whipped her head in his direction. "God, I hope not."

Quincy named a few people, then pretended to shade his eyes as he surveyed the crowd. "Where is she? I just saw her..."

He looked in their direction and now Sam actually took half a step behind Eric.

Quincy's face brightened. "There she is! In her first film debut, let's welcome—"

Eric felt Sam brace.

"—our lead, Lacey Grey!"

All eyes turned to a spot just behind Eric and Samantha to see a young woman whose height and build were remarkably close to Sam's. With Sam's new color, their hair matched perfectly. Lacey smiled and blushed as she acknowledged everyone around her, especially Sam, then she looked back up at Quincy when he started talking again.

"I was super happy when Lacey signed on and you'll see why as soon as the cameras start rolling. Now, I do have some other old friends here. Tristian, where are you? You here yet?"

Everyone looked around. Eric couldn't spot Tristian St. Paul in the crowd. Maybe the seasoned actor had already gone up to his room, not wanting to mingle with the rest?

Quincy waved it off like it was nothing. "So, as you may have heard, I just got done directing a little-known movie last year. Something about a superhero."

People laughed.

Quincy turned serious. "That was a tough one. I lost my way a little bit there. A few of us did. So, I needed a break and I went on my sabbatical. I drove around, just breathing the air and contemplating my next move. It was so freeing, just to get in the car every morning, point it in a random direction, and explore." He looked down and nodded to himself, letting just enough time pass that people leaned closer to see if he'd continue.

"Maybe it wasn't so random. Because when I found myself in Sagebrush, something inside me just said, yeah, this is the place. This is where you're gonna get back to your roots. I knew I was destined to make a movie here. So I asked around, and now here we are." His brightness returned.

"So, while I've got you all here, I want to introduce you to the most important person in this town. Without him, none of this would be happening." Quincy turned to the man in the suit. "This is Zachary Fischer, the mayor of Sagebrush." Quincy offered the mayor his hand. "Don't suppose you want to come up here so the family can get a look at you?"

Mayor Fischer smiled while he shook his head. "No, I'm afraid not. But you can expect a bill for climbing on top of my hotel desk there." The joke fell flat with the 'family'.

Quincy laughed it off. "Put it on my tab." He turned back around. "Mayor Fischer has kindly allowed us to rent out this historical hotel as well as use it for several scenes, both inside and out. That goes for most of the town."

Most of the town consists of less than a dozen buildings Eric thought. At least the area was relatively small, and very isolated.

"So, I want everyone on their best behavior while we're here. This is a living town, not an empty back lot. That's what I wanted for this film. A place that was lived in. I want *realism*, and this place is *real*. So be nice. Show respect. And we'll get respect in return."

Quincy bowed, prompting a final round of clapping, then dismounted. The woman behind him quickly took her position behind the counter as she returned to the chaos of checking people in.

But checking in wasn't the only chaos Eric faced.

"Tell me you are not staying in this building," Samantha said, "and that Quincy's got you in that motel down by the highway."

"I could tell you that I'm staying at The Cactus Tree Motel, but I'd never want to lie to you."

Samantha rolled her eyes. "There is want and there is need, and I think even if you don't *want* to lie to me, that's all you've been doing—"

"Hey, excuse me." Lacey tapped Samantha on the shoulder. She turned, the pissed-off look on her face quickly replaced with a warmer smile.

"Hey, Lacey."

"I'm just so glad to meet you, and it looks like we're roommates, and I..." She looked back and forth between Sam and Eric. "My timing is terrible, isn't it?"

Sam's smile grew bigger. "Not at all. I wasn't talking to anyone." She turned her back completely on Eric. "I think I need some fresh air. It's gotten stuffy in here, so let's go outside and I'll check in once the crowd's thinned." At that, she looked over her shoulder and shot Eric a look of pure annoyance.

Which at this point he shared completely.

Eric knew Samantha would be upset, but he didn't quite expect this level of hostility as he watched her back grow smaller. He needed to stay close—his job officially began the moment she got there. Eric took two steps forward, then broke into a run the minute they opened the hotel doors.

A crowd of locals stood outside chanting, "Go home, Hollywood!"

So much for mutual respect.

The rest of the indoor crowd turned to face the doors, confusion on their faces. Eric pushed past several people and reached Samantha and Lacey just in time to see Sam catch a rotten tomato square in the chest.

He grabbed both women and pulled them back inside.

"Stay here," he ordered before rushing back outside. The crowd started booing and Eric dodged another tomato. He burned the man's face into his memory.

Mayor Fischer joined him on the landing at the top of the stairs.

"Everyone, please! What kind of message do you think you're sending?"

"Go the fuck home!" A man shouted.

The mayor eyed Eric, sizing him up. Looking resigned, he said, "You want to tell all that Hollywood money to go home too? We all stand to benefit by being good hosts."

The townspeople continued to boo.

"Elvin," Mayor Fischer addressed the man who threw the tomato. "Creative way to use up the last of your bumper crop, but come on. You stand to gain, right?" He gestured out past the crowd. "Some of the filming's taking place on your acreage and you're going to be compensated. You, Jeannie." He pointed to a woman at the front. "You think these good people won't be coming around to your store? Just try and stop them. Unless you don't want to fill your cash register."

The crowd quieted.

"Folks, go on home. Trust me when I say I've had the pleasure of meeting these fine people, and I can assure you, the rumors are not true."

Rumors? Eric wondered.

"But, I'm not going to try and convince you. I'm going to let them show you. Mark my words, by this time tomorrow, you're going to wonder why you ever had a problem. Now, go home. Elvin, you find something else to do with those tomatoes."

And to Eric's surprise, the crowd actually listened to the mayor and dispersed. Eric turned to Mayor Fischer.

"Rumors?"

Fischer studied him. "Nothing important."

"I beg to differ." Eric gestured at the last of the crowd.

"You're the animal handler, aren't you?"

"Assistant animal handler, yeah."

Fischer gave him a dismissive nod. "I suggest you stick to *assisting* with the animal handling and let me handle my town."

With that, the mayor started down the stairs.

"Eric?"

He turned at the woman's voice and saw Lacey standing behind the open door, using it as a shield. "Thank you." She smiled and closed it. When Eric climbed the steps and went in, She was already gone.

And so was Samantha.

EIGHT

"So, this is our room," Lacey told Samantha as she opened the door to their third-floor hotel room. The first thing that hit Sam was the musty smell underneath the sweet stink of cheap air freshener. Obviously, this place didn't see much business. "I already picked the bed closest to the window, but we can trade if you like."

"No, that's fine," Sam said. She grimaced, thinking she sounded angry at Lacey, when really, all her fury was directed at Eric. Sam crossed the room to the window and looked down. It was dark enough now that the streetlights had come on. Their light reflected off her bike's chrome. She inspected her motorcycle for any damage, but it looked like the crowd had left it alone. She looked up and down the street but there was no sign of anyone.

"I should run down and get my things now that the crowd is gone," Sam said, looking down at her leather jacket and the stained shirt underneath.

"Oh, yeah, can I help you carry anything up?"

Sam turned to look at Lacey and tell her she didn't need any help. But the woman looked so nervous underneath her smile that Sam changed her mind.

"Yeah, sure, that'd be great, thanks."

Lacey immediately brightened. "Cool. And I promise not to snoop into your things."

Sam laughed. "Not worried at all."

As they brought everything up, Sam wondered how on earth this quiet, nervous woman had managed to land the role of a hardened biker chick.

After they brought Sam's things up and she showered and changed into clean clothes, they sat on their beds facing each other.

"What do you think that was all about outside?" Sam asked.

"I have no idea. I haven't really wandered outside since getting here. Not sure if I want to now."

"We'll be okay once they realize we aren't here to cause trouble."

Lacey smiled. "You sound like Shawna Reeves." They both laughed—Shawna was Lacey's character. She rolled her hand in the air, gesturing for Sam to finish the line from the script.

"Trouble only starts when they find out the truth."

More laughter.

"You should be the one saying the line," Samantha said.

"That was perfect. I'm surprised you didn't get this part." Lacey's eyes widened and her cheeks turned red. "I mean..."

Sam waved her off. "I didn't want it. I wanted to be the stunt double."

Lacey cocked her head. "For real?"

"For real. I'm not actress material, trust me."

Lacey looked at her hands. "I was both excited and terrified when I found out I was working with you. But you're really cool."

Sam snorted. "I'm a nerd, seriously. And once this movie's out, you'll be saying, 'Samantha who?'"

Lacy looked up at her. "You think this movie's going to do that well?"

"Of course I do. Quincy Torrent directing, Tristen St. Paul

starring as Jesse, Ken Adams designing the stunts, and introducing Lacey Grey as Shawna Reeves? It's gonna slay."

Lacey chuckled and waved her off, then said, "We really do look alike."

"That's the point." Still, the way Lacey said that, Sam wondered what she was getting at.

"Do you know Tristen?" Lacey asked.

"Only in passing. You read with him during your audition though, right?"

"No, actually." Lacey looked thoughtful. "I haven't met him yet. I was hoping he'd be downstairs."

Sam shrugged. "You'll meet him at the table read tomorrow for sure though." She leaned forward and lowered her voice. "Truth is, you aren't missing much."

"The table read," Lacey said in a wistful voice like she was talking about Camelot. Sam basically had the next day off while the cast sat around a big table and read through the entire script, working out the kinks and getting the characters to play together. Though she'd never admit it, Sam would have loved to be in the room just for the nostalgia. When she was younger, Bette brought Sam along whenever she did a table read for an animated movie by Pixar. *Call it bring your daughter to work day* Bette told the director. Sam sat quietly in the corner with a bagful of toys that she never touched, enraptured by her favorite characters' voices coming from real people, knowing that she was in a special place behind the scenes watching the magic being born.

Sam's heart squeezed at the memory. She wished she wasn't fighting with Bette. *But sending in Eric was a low blow* she reminded herself, and the anger rushed back in along with a sense of betrayal—from both of them.

Lacey brought her back to the room. "Who was that guy in the lobby? The one who pulled us back in the door."

"What? Why?"

"You look as angry now as you did talking to him downstairs. So, who is he?"

Sam made a raspberry. She almost said *nobody* but couldn't quite get the word out. "He's one of the animal handlers."

"And?" Lacey prompted, grinning.

"And a complete ass." *Who shouldn't be making my heart race like this.*

Lacey nodded. "A complete ass who had our backs."

"Yeah, he did." But when it came to Sam, he was only doing his job—his words.

"*And*...you totally have a thing for him."

Sam picked up one of the little decorative pillows on her bed and tossed it at Lacey who caught it with a laugh. "I knew it!" she said.

"Don't make me throw another one," Sam warned, grinning. But Lacey had already picked up a pillow and tossed it back. Pretty soon, laughter filled the room as pillows flew.

Someone knocked at the door.

"Oops, we're already being evicted for being noisy," Lacey said as she stood up.

"Wouldn't be the first time for me." Sam reached the door first and opened it.

Eric stood in the hallway looking like he did the day she met him—bossy and serious. *And delicious, dammit.*

"What are you doing?" he asked.

Sam smirked. "Pillow fight. What are *you* doing?"

She watched his eyes dilate and his lips twitch and enjoyed both reactions just a little too much.

"I'm checking on you after what happened downstairs."

Yup. It's just his job.

"Seriously? You think a rotten tomato scares me?"

"No, but an angry crowd might."

Sam shook her head. "I've dealt with sketchy crowds all my life. Or do you need to put something in your report to Bette?"

Eric's gaze flicked to Lacey and then back to Sam. "Can we talk alone?"

Lacey nudged Sam. "Need a stunt double?"

That made her smile. She was liking Lacey more and more. "No, I got this." She pointed at the hallway behind Eric. He backed up and she followed him out. Eric turned and started down the hall.

"My roommate's out," Eric said. "So we'll talk there."

"Won't my mom be upset when you tell her I was alone in a room with a boy?"

Eric whirled around. She was expecting him to look pissed. No, not expecting—hoping. But instead, he was trying not to laugh.

"Hey, I might even give you a beer."

Thank goodness he'd already turned back around before he caught *her* attempt not to grin.

No, no, no! I'm angry. Right?

How dare he try and disarm her before she'd even thrown the first punch?

"This is me." Eric opened a door across the hall and three rooms down. He closed it behind them. Sure enough, two long-neck bottles of beer sat on a nightstand. "I woulda gotten a pint of butter brickle but they are sadly short on ice cream parlors in this town. There is however a roadhouse just past the main drag."

"This'll do. Thank you." Sam grabbed one of the frosty bottles, took out a plastic lighter, and used the bottom of it to pop the cap off.

Eric looked surprised. "You're a smoker?"

"Oh, God no." She took a swig and held up the lighter before pocketing it. "But these have a million uses besides lighting up."

"Have a seat." Eric gestured to one of two chairs.

"No thanks, I'll stand."

"Alrighty then, we'll stand." Eric twisted the cap off his beer and took a long pull.

"So, you're going to patronize me?"

"No, Samantha. I'm going to do two other things, okay? First, I'm going to listen to you tell me what a horrible person I am. Go ahead and rant, rail, whatever you need to do." The corner of his mouth turned up. "Throw pillows at me if you need to."

Infuriating! "I wouldn't give you the pleasure of a good pillow fight." And damn, if her voice didn't betray her with the hint of a purr. Not to mention her body, specifically her tingling nethers as she looked at Eric standing there with his cocky smile and his tight tee and windblown hair.

I need to get out of here before I do the dumb. "I have nothing to say to you that I haven't already said."

And then there was the casual way he shrugged, amused. "Have it your way. I'll do the talking then." He set his beer down. "Last time I saw you, I told you I believed in you, that you should stand up to Bette and pursue your dreams. And then I go and show up here as your babysitter."

"Yup." She popped her P.

He spread his arms, palms out and up. "I suck."

Whoa. Now *that* she was not expecting. Gaslighting her that she had him all wrong, yes. A defense of his shitty actions, absolutely. But admitting that what he'd done made him suck—no way. Which immediately put her on the defensive.

"Yeah, you do suck."

He smiled. "All right, awesome, we agree on something. Now we're getting somewhere."

Sam had no idea what to say to that.

Eric took advantage of her silence to say more. "I suck because when my bosses told me that they had a dream job for me, I said yes—"

"Your dream job was to babysit me?"

"—I said yes before asking about who I'd be guarding, and if I'd done that first and found out it was you, I'd have turned down the job," he finished.

Sam crossed one arm over the other holding the beer and tilted her head. "So...you didn't know I'd be here?"

"Not until after I was committed to the job, no. I actually thought I'd be guarding your mother on a set, not you."

"So...guarding my...*mom*...is your dream job?"

Eric laughed. "Not exactly, no." He started pacing. "Look, I'm a movie buff, and having the opportunity to work on an actual set? I jumped immediately."

"Ah, I see." Sam nodded.

"Officially, I'm the assistant animal handler. Like an apprentice, really."

"But you have no experience. How did you get—"

"Gina. And probably Bette."

"Ah, yeah, duh, okay. But, what happens on set when you don't know what you're doing?"

Eric stopped pacing and fixed her with his stare.

Zing! That got him.

"Who says I don't know what I'm doing?"

"Did you even read the script?" Sam set her beer down. "The biker gang has two ways of making money—manufacturing crank and dogfighting. You don't strike me as someone who has a lot of experience with either."

His good humor evaporated. Eric leaned back against the wall. "Then you don't know anything about me."

When he left it at that, Sam raised her eyebrow. "You can't just let something like that hang in the air."

"I can, and I will, for now." Quick as lightning, he darted forward, swiped his beer off the nightstand, and drained it.

All of a sudden, making Eric feel like shit didn't feel so good. It felt awful.

"Hey, I'm sorry. That was pretty bratty of me. You're right, I don't know anything about you."

The corner of his mouth quirked up but the smile didn't come anywhere near his gorgeous eyes. "Thanks. I appreciate that."

"I do know your favorite ice cream though, so...that's a start?"

No dice. His eyes failed to lighten. "Look, I'm sorry I'm the one who ended up with this job."

That stung when it shouldn't have.

Eric softened his voice. "I know what it means to you to be here, so I'm not going to sit on you, okay? So, think about it. You could have gotten someone who *would* babysit you. So please, for both our sakes, don't blow my cover, okay?"

"Sure." She toed the frayed rug, vaguely wondering if it was original to the hotel.

"I'll keep out of your way as much as possible, Samantha. But I am here to stay. All right?"

"Yeah, all right. And I'll stay out of yours."

Eric nodded slowly, studying her in a way that should have made her skin tingle. Okay, it did make her skin tingle—it was like Eric's gaze was full of little electric sparks that liked to dance over her—but this time, it left her cold.

Sam didn't like being cold.

"I should go."

Eric's chin nodded toward her half-empty beer. "You aren't going to finish that?"

"No. Thanks, though." She turned toward the door to go. Just before she opened it, she looked back. "Both for the beer and for your honesty."

"I owe you nothing less." He toasted her. "And I'll respect your wishes. If that's what you want."

"Great. That's absolutely what I want, yes. Good night." She smiled.

And turned away quickly before he could see that no, that was not at all what she wanted.

NINE

Eric sat straight up in bed, covered in sweat and shaking. It took him a moment to remember where he was. Then it came back to him—the set, the old hotel, listening to the air conditioning unit humming away in the window as he drifted off, trying not to think about his conversation with Samantha. Trying not to think about her at all...

...Then he was back in Afghanistan, back in the stink and the moon dust, hearing the high-pitched whine of the dogs, the men shouting, goading them on...

And the boy's voice shouting in heavily-accented English: *Friend! Help me catch him, friend!*

Then he was awake and shaking with the memory of what happened next.

It wasn't a sound that woke him, but the sudden lack of one. The air conditioner unit was dead. The temperature in the room was cool, but if the unit was busted, the south-facing room would turn into an oven by mid-day.

He ran his hands over his face. Then remembered he was

sharing the room. He blinked as his eyes adjusted to the dim light coming in from around the shades.

The other bed was empty.

Thank God. He didn't want to explain the way he woke up. He wasn't sure if he'd shouted or not. Wouldn't be the first time. The first time, he'd had a woman over, and when he woke up fully, he found her standing beside the bed, brandishing a table lamp just in case he 'lost it with the PTSD' as she so kindly put it.

No woman had spent the entire night since, even after years without nightmares.

It was talking about dogfighting that triggered the dream. Fuck.

Maybe he couldn't do this job after all.

"No," he told the darkness. "I can do this."

Steps drew closer in the hall and the door opened. Tim Bakker, the lead animal handler, stepped inside.

"Had to piss. Did I wake you up?"

"No. Was the air off when you left?"

"All the power's out. Happened when I was in the bathroom down the hall. The hallway's like walking through a tomb."

"Shit." Eric got up and walked to the window. He pulled the blind back and looked outside. The whole street was dark, the only light coming from the gradually brightening sky. "Wonder how often this happens."

"Good question. Since we're up, wanna check on the dogs?"

"Yeah." Eric turned. "I was just gonna suggest that." No way he was getting back to sleep for the hour or two left before morning.

They didn't bother changing out of their sweats and tees, just threw on their shoes and headed for the hotel basement. They used the flashlight apps on their phones to find the stairs since the elevator was out of the question, then climbed down four flights to the basement where they'd set up a kennel in a spare storage room the day before.

Neither Tim nor Eric had liked the arrangement at first and neither did the rep from The American Humane Association, until they'd put into place safe escape routes for the dogs. The room had a couple good-sized windows near the ceiling at street level, so they'd set up two folded flights of mini-stairs the dogs could run up easily, then they tested the system repeatedly, much to the dogs' delight. Running up the stairs and out the windows was all just good fun for them, but if the hotel caught fire, God forbid, they'd have a way to escape quickly.

Eric noted the room's temperature on a wall-mounted gauge. It was comfortably cool down here, better than the stuffy stairwell. If the power was off for any extended period of time, he thought he might just set up a bedroll beside the kennels and sleep in comfort.

The dogs—a mix of pit bulls, German Shepherd Dogs, Huskies, and Rotties—were eager to see the men. They danced excitedly at the front of their kennels, tails wagging, paws scraping at the doors. Eric missed Blaze.

"Hey, boyos," Tim said, his voice flooded with affection, "sorry about the dark. Let's get you fed and outta here." He used an app on his phone to remotely open the kennel doors which could also open the windows—another safety precaution. Eric had the same app just in case. It was customized, designed by one of Gina's many tech-savvy friends once they knew the dogs' set-up.

The dogs—eight in all—calmed down and trotted out of their enclosures, though their tails never stopped wagging. Tim and Eric set up their food then checked and topped off their water dispensers while the dogs chowed down. The light from outside grew brighter.

"You think the schedule will be updated or changed?" Eric asked Tim. The first few days, he and Tim would mostly be helping the crew move sets and props—since it wasn't a union production, it was all-hands-on-deck and Eric was expected to do a number of different jobs until filming started with the dogs. He hoped to use the opportunity to get to know everyone, including the townies. After last night, he was convinced something bigger was going on in the town.

Tim shrugged. "With the power out? We'll see. Probably the first thing we'll be setting up are the generators." While they'd be shooting some outdoor footage in town, the main set was located on an old ranch several miles outside of town in the desert near a canyon. Eric had checked it out briefly the day before and met with Ken, who was already scouting the area where most of the stunts would take place.

After the dogs ate, the men leashed them and prepared to take them upstairs. Eric joked that it would be easier just to let them run up the stairs and out the window. Voices and footsteps grew louder above them as cast and crew awoke to discover they had no power.

Tim looked at the ceiling and laughed. "You might be right. But, it's time to do some education." He looked at his dogs—five belonged to him and three to one of his friends also in the business —and added, "Don't scare the folks, boyos." Eric handled the three while Tim took care of his five. They were good dogs, well-behaved and used to each other, but because of their sizes and breeds, they often made people around them uneasy.

When they got upstairs to the lobby, sure enough, it was already full of guests complaining about the power outage while the poor woman behind the desk repeatedly said there was nothing to be done.

"It's the whole entire street, folks," she said, her voice on the edge of impatience. "Yeah, the utility company has been called. Again. Got 'em on speed dial."

Tim shook his head and smiled at Eric, then gestured with his chin toward the front door. The crowd parted like they had crocodiles on leashes instead of big dogs while Tim tried to assure everyone that they were safe. Eric couldn't help but look for Samantha among them, but there was no sign of her or Lacey.

They took the dogs across the street to a small park and gave them a chance to run, exercise, and do what dogs do, then loaded them up into a couple of vans in the pre-dawn light and headed for the set. Dust kicked up behind the vans as they drove past the roadhouse—Rafferty's—where Eric had snagged the beers. He had a feeling they'd be spending a lot of time there in the coming weeks, and he wasn't so sure it was the safest place in the world. When he'd walked in, heads turned, many belonging to leather jacket-covered men whose bikes were lined up outside. The bartender, Mags, flirted with him, but also did her best to get Eric served and out of there as quickly as possible.

The set looked even more realistic in the dim light. The ranch house was authentic, but a lot of the other buildings scattered around were barely a month old despite their peeling paint and weathered wood. As they pulled into the flattened, hard-packed earth surrounded by a split rail fence that served as a parking lot, Eric couldn't help but notice the two motorcycles parked next to each other. He didn't recognize one, but the other was Samantha's. His stomach decided it was a great idea to do jumping jacks at the thought of seeing her and he groaned.

She's going to think I'm stalking her, right after I told her I'd stay out of her way.

Welp, this was an impossible assignment. He hated the fact that he would also be reporting her movements to Lach, starting with whatever she was doing here at the set first thing in the morning on what was supposed to be a day off.

And who the hell is she with? He felt an irrational stab of jealousy as he looked at the other bike. It wasn't Ken, who he'd spotted in the crowd at the hotel, also looking around.

Shit. Looking for Samantha, probably.

So, who's she with?

Eric parked the van, killed the ignition, and got out to unload the dogs who were getting restless. He felt another pang. Yup, he missed Blaze, who was staying back at Watchdog. But, outside animals were discouraged from coming to the set and he'd have to sign a ton of waivers to have her there, especially since she was a female surrounded by male dogs—not that his girl couldn't handle herself with any of them.

Well, he'd probably end up warming to the set dogs anyway.

Tim and Eric unloaded the dogs and let them run within the fenced confines of the set. The more comfortable the dogs were with the territory, the easier they'd be to handle once the cameras were rolling. They kept an eye out for snakes and scorpions that might still be coming home after a night's hunt for insects. The scorpions weren't much of a problem—mostly little Arizona bark scorpions with milder venom than the ones Eric had encountered in Afghanistan. But a scorpion bite on a dog's sensitive nose could still be a problem.

Eric scanned the area for signs of Samantha. He'd spotted a couple of her footprints in a patch of softer sand around the bikes but didn't see a second set, which was curious. The hardpack kept him from tracking her, but he suspected now that she and whoever she was with had gone toward the nearby canyon, which made him uneasy. He knew from the script that she'd be performing a few stunts there. They were all crazy, but one was absolutely insane, in his opinion.

He shook his head and focused instead on the bikers he'd seen at Rafferty's. From what he'd observed, there was cause to worry.

"Something on your mind?" Tim asked.

A woman's laugh carried across the property, ticking Eric's heart rate up. He turned his head toward the sound and saw a head of dark hair emerging from between two boulders on a path leading through a stone outcropping. He strained to see the second person moving beside her.

"Or maybe some*one*?" Tim added.

Eric's attention snapped back to Tim, who was staring at him, eyebrows raised.

"Yeah, no...I—"

"Give it up, dude." Tim slapped Eric's back good-naturedly. "No shame in that game. She's a show-stealer." Tim's gaze followed Eric's.

"She is."

Two women emerged from behind the second boulder—Samantha and Lacey. No wonder Eric thought he only saw Sam's prints—Lacey's feet were the same size and they wore identical boots—easy enough to think he was only seeing one set of prints when he was looking at two.

"And her stunt-double's not half-bad, either," Tim added.

What?

"I'm not thinking about Lacey," Eric quickly said before the women came within earshot.

"Well, you look like you're thinking about someone." Tim winked at him. In the meantime, the dogs had decided to check out the new humans and were quickly swarming the women, who reacted by laughing and dropping to their knees, raining pets and kisses down on furry heads.

"Come," Tim shouted and clapped his hands. The pack turned and approached them as one.

"Aw! No fun!" Samantha said, laughing. She looked up and stopped laughing when she saw Eric. Which cut surprisingly deep. She and Lacey got to their feet and walked over to the guys.

"Love the dogs," Lacey told Tim. "I'm eager to work with them."

"Good," he replied. "I hope they didn't overwhelm you just now."

"Not at all. I grew up with huskies. I'm not afraid of these big guys." She ran her hands over the furriest of the pack, a German Shepherd-Husky mix. Then she grew serious. "I don't really want to watch them fight though. You sure they're gonna be okay in those scenes?"

"It's against American Humane Society guidelines to let animals fight or even get aggressive with each other, so all those scenes will be one hundred percent simulated in post. My boys here will be filmed separately barking and acting aggressively, then the footage will be put together to make it look like they're ready to attack each other. The rest will be CGI."

Both women looked relieved. "Good. I'd hate to see them get hurt, even by accident," Lacey said.

"No way," Tim said, scratching one of the pit bull's heads. "These are my boyos. That's how I got this gig; I had a big enough dog pack that gets along well, so there's no chance of aggressive behavior. Otherwise, they could shut this whole production down."

Samantha looked thoughtful and Eric wanted to ask what she was thinking. Instead, he asked her, "So what are you two doing out here so early?"

"I wanted to get a good look at the canyon where most of the stunts will be. Lacey wanted to tag along."

"Actually, I'm jealous of what Sam gets to do," Lacey added, grinning. "She gets to do all the fun stuff."

"That's right," Samantha said, beaming. She turned her attention away from Eric and it felt like the sun had gone behind a cloud. "So, you ready to take the bikes up there?"

"Wait, you're doing a stunt now?" Eric resisted the urge to grab her arm.

She pinned him with a look that said *don't be stupid.* "God, no. Quincy would probably murder me if I got his lead killed." She winked at Lacey. "We're just riding a little, getting a feel for each other's moves so that we're synched when the filming begins."

"You ride?" Eric asked Lacey.

She gave Sam a look that said *Can you believe this guy?* "It's how I edged out the competition. I've been riding since I was small."

"And, she inherited *her* dad's bike. Me, I had to settle for buying one, since Dad gave Jake his Indian," Sam teased.

Samantha and Lacey turned and walked to the motorcycles. From behind, they could have been twins. Eric noted how Sam watched Lacey and adjusted her walk until they were mirror images. They mounted their bikes the same way. Then they were off, up the dirt path to the canyon.

"If we load the dogs in quickly, we can drive up and watch,"

Tim said.

"Let's do it."

***

Eric watched from the top of the steep canyon wall, his heart in his throat. "Not doing any stunts, my ass," he muttered as he watched Samantha and Lacey zigzag through the canyon, going up the walls and back down, making small jumps and something called stoppies where they went up on their front tires.

And of course that was the time Lach called for an update.

"How's our principal on the first day?" he asked without preamble, his gruff voice coming in loud and clear over the van's speakers.

"Could you have waited for the sun to come up?" Eric joked back. *Or is this a trick call, seeing if we're sharing a room?* he couldn't help but wonder. But with Watchdog's history of romantic entanglements, Eric could hardly blame Lach if that was exactly why he was calling so early.

"I could wait, Bette could not," Lach grumbled. "Sam didn't bother calling her last night when she got in, or this morning, either. Bette says to send along her thanks for reporting that her daughter made it to Arizona alive and in one piece."

And so the babysitting begins. Only, Eric wondered which woman actually needed the sitting—Samantha or Bette.

Just then he hissed as he drew in a quick breath—Samantha had just come close to laying her bike down on a sharp turn.

"She *is* still in one piece, Eric?" Lach asked.

"Yeah, yeah, but that was a close one just now. I'm watching her practice with the lead on their bikes and she damn near laid the thing down."

"Shit. I don't envy you." Lach paused. "I probably shouldn't say that. Gina's been lecturing me on being more upbeat with you assholes. So, uh, keep up the good work."

Eric stifled a laugh, imagining the taciturn Lach trying to lighten up at Gina's suggestion. "Thanks, Boss. That sounded heartfelt and means a lot to me."

"Shut up, fucker."

This time, Eric did laugh. He heard Lach suck in a breath and could imagine him chomping on his cigarette substitute.

"So, am I to tell Bette that her daughter is being, well, her daughter, which means foolhardy?"

Eric felt a sudden protectiveness toward Samantha flare up in his chest. The truth was, even when she almost stopped his heart a couple of times watching her, she never looked like she was out of control. Yeah, the riding she was doing was risky, but it wasn't careless. It was calculated, skilled. She was already a pro in the making. Bette needed to see how well Sam was doing. See it and acknowledge it.

"No, actually she's doing great. I haven't seen her do one foolhardy thing." Eric scratched his chin. "Relatively speaking, of course. The entire profession is a risk. But less risky than what we do, right? So, no, she's not being foolhardy in the grand scheme of things."

Lach chuckled. "Nice philosophizing, there, Shep. Or, is it rationalizing?"

"Nope, not at all, Boss. She's not the only professional here." Damn, he hated how defensive he sounded. So he plunged into a generalized report about his observations so far.

"One thing bothers me. Saw a bunch of bikers at this roadhouse outside of town. No one started any trouble, but they were none too friendly and made the bartender nervous."

Lachlan grunted. "You get a look at their vests?"

He thought about the logo he'd seen on the backs of a couple jackets. "Yeah. The Red Hands. I haven't seen them in town. Hopefully, they were just passing through."

"I'll have Elissa see what she can find on them. How's the town?"

"Honestly, the town is not so friendly, either. We had an issue last night with a group of townies protesting the movie."

"Anyone get violent?"

"Only if you consider throwing rotten tomatoes violent."

Lach harrumphed. "What's the problem?"

"A tale as old as time. Money. Some people are benefiting from this, some not so much, or at least that's their perception. The mayor simmered things back down."

"What's he like?"

"He's a politician, Lach."

"Yeah 'nuf said." Eric heard him suck on the fake cigarette again. "Torrent?"

"Torrent remains charismatic. I like him." Eric surprised himself by saying that. It was true, but something in his gut still nagged at him. "He seems like he really wants to create a family here with the cast and crew, not the type to overwork someone."

"Careful, Shep. You sound a bit starstruck."

Shit. "Don't worry about me. I know the rumors."

"Be sure that you remember that I trust Bette's judgment here a thousand percent."

"Right. Yeah." Now he was feeling a little annoyed. *Which one of us is on the job, and which one of us is maybe a little bit overprotective?*

No. He needed to drop that attitude right now. Samantha was getting to him. He needed to be objective about Quincy Torrent, too. He'd liked what the guy had to say last night, but this was show business, after all.

"Eric? Do I need to send someone else?" Lachlan asked, as if he'd been reading Eric's mind.

"No, sir. You're right, I need to be more objective when it comes to Torrent."

And Samantha.

Yeah, tell that to his heart, which flipped when she did her next wheelie.

TEN

Sam fanned herself as she stood in the hotel lobby. The morning hadn't been so bad, but now the place was sweltering without air conditioning. She was hoping that after being out in the sunny canyons all day, she could come back to a cool room and shower off. Instead, she'd come back to a lobby full of crew hanging out in the—relatively—cooler space. At least she'd had a chance to meet everyone who she'd missed the night before. All anyone could talk about was how great it was to be working with Quincy again now that he was away from *Invincible Gods*.

My mom is totally wrong about him.

Sam wiped the sweat off before it could trickle into her eyes. Power or not, she needed a shower. She walked to the front desk. Poor Edna the desk clerk was still there. Sam half-believed the woman lived behind the counter.

"Hi, Edna. Are the showers working?"

"They are," Edna said. "Good news is, you can take a nice cold shower since we don't have hot water."

Sam laughed. "Great, thanks." She saluted Edna and headed

upstairs. A cold shower was probably a good idea anyway. Anything to wash away the day.

And cool down her inappropriate thoughts about a certain bodyguard.

Lacey had gone back to town for the table read after they'd had some fun on the bikes while Sam met up with Ken and the rest of the stunt team for the first round of going over the stunts. Most of them were honestly pretty standard. Things like getting hit by cars, jumping from a motorcycle to a car, or even jumping from a car to a motorcycle. And there were explosions, of course. Even though he said otherwise, this was, after all, a Quincy Torrent movie and that meant action. Though he said he'd wanted to scale down the action for this one and focus on character development instead.

Yeah, sure, whatever that means in a movie like this.

He did have one showstopper of a stunt and Sam was the one to pull it off.

She was very excited about performing it. Okay, honestly, she was equal parts excited about performing it—and scared to death.

Sam headed up the dark back stairs to her room. The higher she climbed, the hotter it got. By the time she reached the top of the stairs, she was covered in sweat despite the dry desert air. Lacey wasn't back in the room yet, so she went ahead, stripped down, and jumped into the ice-cold shower. As refreshing as it was, the minute she stepped back out the heat clung to her. She quickly toweled off, then pulled her hair up into a messy bun, got dressed, and went back downstairs.

By now the cast had returned from their table read. They didn't look wilted so they must have used one of the trailers on set. Quincy stood in the middle of the cluster and—wonder of wonders —the elusive Tristian St. Paul was present as well.

He'd grown his hair out into a shaggy mop and changed its color since Sam last saw him at one of Bette's Bashes, probably for the part of Jesse, but he looked meticulously groomed otherwise.

Tristian and Quincy were engaged in a private conversation surrounded by the rest of the cast.

As Sam approached the crowd, she spotted Lacey on the edge. "Don't even bother asking about the power. It's still off," she told her.

"That's what we figured," Lacey said. "But when we passed that roadhouse the beer signs were on, so I think we're all going to head down that way." She linked her arm with Sam's. "I could really go for a beer right now," Lacey added as she eyed Tristian and Quincy. Sam noticed now that her new friend seemed anxious.

"Something the matter?" she asked her in a low voice.

"Yes. No." She laughed lightly. "Can we talk about it later?"

"Of course." Sam looked over again to see that Quincy and Tristian were done talking. She caught both men's eyes and they smiled. Tristian gave her the elevator eyes—once up and down her body. *Yuck.* She wished she could shower again. Sam didn't care how attractive he was—and he was one of the most gorgeous men she'd seen in real life—she did not care for his quick assessment of her as if he were looking over a steakhouse menu and deciding on which cut of meat he wanted.

Quincy and Tristian started walking in their direction and Sam felt Lacey flinch against her. Things obviously did not go well at the reading. Neither man gave Lacey a second look—all eyes were on Sam.

"There they are," Quincy said. "Our stars. Aren't they lovely?" Tristian smiled back, though the man's eyes never left Sam's body. "I can barely tell them apart. Can you?"

Sam felt Lacey go even stiffer next to her. Her smile was so fake it could have been on a mannequin's face.

"I can, actually," Tristian said. He held out his hand for Sam to shake. "I know your mother, but I don't think we've met yet." Sam tried not to roll her eyes. He'd just been at one of her mom's parties a few months ago. "I'm Tristian St. Paul."

Yeah, as if I wouldn't recognize him. Nevertheless, Sam took his hand and shook it. He had one of those awful limp fish grips with a soft hand. *Yuck again.* Obviously, Tristian wasn't a method actor, or else he would have crushed her hand. He was supposed to be playing a character named Jesse, the leader of a vicious outlaw motorcycle gang and in love with Lacey's character, Shawna. That was the Romeo and Juliet portion of the movie. But as she watched the two of them together, her heart sank. This movie was never going to make it if it was based on their romance. There was zero chemistry between the two.

No, I take that back. There is negative chemistry between these two. What in the actual hell?

"Of course I know who you are, Tristian." Sam wasn't in the mood to play any games. "We probably won't be seeing much of each other, though. I don't think you're performing your own stunts, are you?"

A quick sour expression passed over his features before they settled back into his stunning, almost trademarked grin. "If it means I get to work with you, I may have to brush up on my stunts." His voice held a slimy quality to it, at least to her ears. He actually threw his head back to laugh, a fake chuckle. So Sam gave him her own patented, *did someone just fart in the room?* look.

And of course that was the moment when she caught sight of Eric across the room—who was studying her right back. His smile though was absolutely genuine. Actually, she could tell he was trying to hold back a laugh. He did that so often that she wanted to tell him *just go ahead and laugh, Eric. It's okay, really.* But he had his job to do. A big, tough, burly bodyguard who was there to babysit her. He wasn't supposed to smile, right? He was supposed to look grim and tough and intimidating. *Ugh.*

OK, be fair. That's not what he's like at all. As much as Sam wanted to dehumanize Eric, she just couldn't.

In the meantime, Quincy was actually chatting up Lacey. "You did a super job today, kid. I was really proud of you."

Kid? Did he just actually call her kid? But then again, this was

Quincy and he had his whole, just-a-big-happy-family thing going on, so maybe this was his way of making her feel accepted. If it was though, it wasn't working. Lacey might have been smiling, but Sam still felt how nervous she was as she tightened her arm around Sam's.

"I think we all need to head down to that roadhouse. It looked like the power was on there," Quincy said.

"Sounds good. I just showered and I'm already sweating like a pig," Sam said. Tristian actually took a step back.

"Women don't sweat, you *glisten*," Quincy said. "Right now, you're shining like a star. No, like the entire Milky Way galaxy across the sky. Precious little dew drops of starlight—"

By now, both women were cracking up at Quincy as he swept his arm through the air.

"—that shine—what? Stop laughing, I'm serious! That shine only for you and maybe grace us mortals with their essence—"

"Stop, stop, stop!" Sam practically snorted. Lacey was losing it, all her anxiety seemed to be gone. Everyone around them had stopped talking and started laughing along.

"—if you but shake your head—" Quincy demonstrated like he was in a slow-mo shampoo commercial—"and bless us with your holy water."

"Jesus, stop!" Sam could barely get the words out past her laughter, which had doubled her over. It had to be the heat and the excitement that was making her delirious, and had allowed Quincy to cast his spell again over everyone. Because now, people were clapping at him, even if—she was sure—they had no idea what he was talking about.

Then Quincy put his arm around Lacey and pulled her close until her arm slipped from Sam's. "And you, my dear, are exceeding expectations."

Now the smile on her face looked genuine. Until her gaze flicked back to Tristian, who still looked like he'd swallowed a lemon.

"All right, people!" Quincy clapped his hands in the air. "Nothing to do but head down the street to Rafferty's. I hear they have cold beer and hot food and...air conditioning! I don't know about the rest of you but that's all I need. Everything's on me tonight."

Cheers filled the lobby.

"Tomorrow, we really get started and I want you all fat and happy." Arm back around Lacey's shoulders, he made a beeline through the crowd to the front doors and everyone followed in his wake.

He's like the Pied Piper.

Sam felt Eric sidle up next to her before she looked up. Even in the crush of people, she felt his presence, smelled his skin over the heat, dust, and sweat permeating the air. Her body responded by heating up further, as if the blowtorch of the day wasn't hot enough.

No. You are not allowed to feel this way. You saw him this morning, watching you from one of the vans and talking to someone. No doubt making his report and probably telling everyone how irresponsible you are.

Sam pushed ahead to catch up with Ken. And pretended she couldn't feel Eric right there with her. *So much for staying out of my way.*

Sam walked through Rafferty's front door into the dusty, smoky, high-raftered room and took it all in. Dartboards to the left, a couple of pool tables to the right. Banged-up wooden tables and chairs in the middle. A dancefloor near the bar at the back was presided over by an ancient jukebox. Rough wood walls decorated with flickering neon signs for beer brands from decades past. The air was thick with heat and the smell of beer and greasy burgers.

She fell in love with the place instantly.

"Thought it was supposed to be cool in here," Tristian complained.

Locals looked up from their drinks at the newcomers and frowned before going back to them.

"Okay," Quincy said. "So, maybe I wasn't quite honest about the air conditioning, but look." He pointed up. "High ceilings. Heat rises. And beer makes one forget about the heat, and I know the beers here are ice-cold." He strode ahead of the pack toward the bar, threading between the tables and chairs, smiling and addressing patrons by name, which seemed to go a long way toward making them friendlier, at least toward him.

Sam couldn't help but notice Eric sizing up and cataloging everyone in the room. One group especially seemed to catch his eye, a tableful of bikers with red hands on their vests. She had no doubt that as Quincy walked through the crowd calling people by their names, Eric would memorize them. Or even better—cross-reference their names and faces with the Watchdog files her brother had undoubtedly compiled on everyone and their dog who lived in town.

Why am I watching him? I should just ignore him. I'm walking away right now.

"See anyone dangerous?" she asked instead, keeping pace as they walked to the bar.

He smirked down at her. "I'm looking at her right now."

She almost—*almost*—stuck her tongue out at him. "I knew exactly what I was doing at the canyon today."

"I know you did. That's what makes you so dangerous."

Her heart fluttered like she was back in the canyons. How could he make her feel like this with just a few words and a look?

"If you think *that* was dangerous, you haven't seen anything yet."

Did he just flinch? Sam decided to push it. "Yup. Did you see them putting up the nets in the gorge? That's about a three-hundred-foot drop. I can't wait." She suppressed her own shudder. And was pretty sure he was hiding one, too.

"When does that stunt happen?"

"Toward the end of filming. Quincy wants to get the other stunts out of the way first. Work our way up to that one. The *True Lies* stunt, he's calling it."

"I'll be there for it. For all of your stunts."

"Why? It's not like you can guard me when I'm hanging three hundred feet in the air."

He flinched again. Eric did not like the idea of her in danger, that was for sure.

"No. But I also know you're talented and you've got that part covered."

"Then why do you flinch every time I mention my stunts?"

"No, I don't."

"You do!" She grinned. "You're worried about me."

"No, it's all the other things going on—"

Lacey jogged up to Sam's side. "Hey, what's up?"

"Just talking *stunts*." Sam winked at Eric, who pretended to glare back—while his eyes did that magical sparkle like light dancing on a swimming pool.

"Cool," Lacey said. "Or, are you nervous?"

"More excited than nervous." She glanced at Eric. "But, yeah, maybe a little nervous about the last one."

They reached the bar. Eric gestured for her and Lacey to order first. But Tristian butted in.

"I'll autograph anything you want if you give me a Pumpkin Spice Porter from that one Phoenix brewery."

The bartender, a woman with two iron-gray braids framing her face, glared at him as she wiped a glass.

He smiled.

She glared harder.

"Um, I'll take a Stella Artois instead?"

Her eyebrows went up.

"Any pilsner from this decade?"

Her mouth twitched and she reached under the bar. She pushed a warm can of Pabst at him with two fingers.

"Retro." He rolled his eyes as he walked away with his beer.

"Asshole," she murmured, then looked at Eric. Her expression softened the tiniest bit. "What can I getcha, T, B, and H? Same as last night?"

T, B, and H? Sam watched Eric's face flush. *Damn, he's cute when he does that.*

"Pitcher of beer to start, Mags, thanks." He looked at Sam and Lacey for confirmation.

"Perfect." Lacey nodded.

"Oh, so we're sitting together?" Sam asked Eric.

"I'm sitting with a pitcher of beer that I'm happy to share," he shot back as he helped himself to the three frosty beer mugs that Mags set out. "You can sit anywhere you'd like."

Mags snorted and filled a pitcher from one of three taps. She gave it to him with a wink. "If she's not warming the seat next to you, I'll be happy to on my next break, T-B-H."

Grinning, Eric tipped an imaginary hat to her and she laughed before turning to take someone else's order. The place was filling up fast so Eric led them to an empty table near the dancefloor.

Lacey leaned close and whispered to Sam, "I can sit elsewhere if you'd like a little private time with him."

Sam grabbed her arm. "Don't you dare abandon me."

"You sure?"

"Positive. Besides, you need to tell me how today went."

Lacey's good humor evaporated. "Later."

Eric pulled out both Lacey's and Sam's chairs for them before sitting down. Sam took the one directly opposite—and farthest—away from him.

"What's T-B-H mean?" Sam asked as Eric pushed a full mug across the table to her.

Lacey laughed. "You can't figure it out?" She gestured at Eric, her arm moving up and down to indicate his entire frame. "Tall, Blond, and Handsome."

Sam rolled her eyes. "Of course."

Eric shrugged. "It's ridiculous, I know."

She took a drink and then pressed the cold mug against her temple. Prickly sweat trickled down her spine. At least there were a couple of box fans blowing across the empty dancefloor. The slightly cooler air reached their table and offered a smidgen of relief. Eric had chosen the best seats in the place. She studied him over the rim of her mug as he looked everywhere but directly at her. The moment he did, it was her turn to let her eyes roam the room.

Cast and crew sat in groups at separate tables, but that was based mostly on tradition and old friendships, and she didn't sense any animosity—at least between them. Between them and the townies, well, that was another story.

Quincy sat at a table in the center of the place, holding court in the round as it were. He acknowledged anyone who walked past with a smile and a word. Ken sat at his table along with Tristian and Caleb Chaney, who was playing the villain, the vicious rival club leader named Rage. That cracked Sam up. In real life, Caleb was a softie, but on the screen, he could freeze your blood with his dead-black stare. She glanced at Lacey, who should have been sitting with them as the lead actress.

I've been selfish, expecting her to be my support system. She was about to tell Lacey that if she wanted to switch tables, she could, when Tim walked up.

"This seat taken?" he asked as he was already pulling out the chair beside Lacey's.

Lacey's face lit up. "Not at all."

Tim set his bottle of beer down. "I like this place," he announced.

"I do too," Sam said, eager to fill the table with any conversation that didn't involve her talking directly to Eric. "It reminds me of somewhere, but I've never been..." Then it hit her.

"Where?" Eric asked. "Looks like you've remembered."

"Not so much remembered as heard it described to me. This is like The Hideout, where Jake took Rachael when they met. It was the first place where she ever sang in public, too."

"I read all about that," Lacey said, leaning forward. "She has such an amazing voice."

"I'll introduce you once this is over and she's back from her tour."

"Thanks!"

"*That's* what's missing," Eric said. He stood up and walked across the dancefloor to the jukebox. After perusing the selections for a minute, he looked up and waved Sam over. She took a fortifying swig of beer before joining him.

"What's up?" she asked.

"Check it out." He gestured at the clear glass displaying their choices. "It's The Jukebox That Time Forgot."

The machine was ancient, housing forty actual 45 records stacked up horizontally. She'd never seen one like it in real life.

"Wow, it sure is." Sam studied the song titles typed out on the white squares lining the front. "Heavy on The Eagles. And Journey. Oh, here's 'Baker Street.' Gerry *Rafferty*."

Eric looked toward the bar. "Hey, Mags. Does this baby work?" he shouted.

"You bet it does, sugar," she yelled back. "Need dimes?"

"Ha! Dime a dance," Eric chuckled.

Mags was already out from behind the bar and approaching them. "I got twenty dimes if you got two dollars."

Eric was already reaching for his wallet. "Hell, yeah. I'll give you five for twenty. Keep the change."

"Why so much Eagles?" Sam asked.

Mags smiled. "Because back when Don Henley and them were just the backup band for Linda Ronstadt they played this very place one night when they were passing through on their way to a show at Disneyland. That's where they decided they were a band all on their own. I'll never forget it. Don's got a voice like an angel. Linda, too." She sighed and pointed to a yellowed photo above the jukebox. "We're big fans here."

Sam stood on tiptoes to lean in and get a closer look. It looked like them, and sure enough, it looked like they were standing on the dancefloor of Rafferty's.

"How cool is that?" She couldn't wait to tell Jake.

"They played *this* place?" Tristian had sneaked up behind Sam. "Their bus must have broken down. And they were high, right?"

Mags wheeled on him. "You know, you can drink somewhere else."

"Wouldn't dream of it. The Eagles played here." He laughed.

"Eagles, not *the* Eagles," Mags snapped.

"Old farts," Tristian said.

"Nope. Masters," Eric countered as he dropped a bunch of dimes into the jukebox and hit several buttons. A mechanical arm carried a 45 to the turntable and a guitar riff tore through the bar, stopping all conversation. Don Henley's voice growled the opening lyrics to "Victim of Love" and Eric smiled and close his eyes. "The best."

"Jake would agree," Sam admitted reluctantly. She turned and stalked back toward the table.

"Hey." Eric caught up to her. "I'll let you sit down for now, but we're dancing to the flip side of this one."

She stopped and bit her lip at the sudden lurching of her stomach. Then her entire body agreed that yes, yes, they would be dancing to the next song and that it had better be a slow one. She shivered despite the heat as memories of how good his arms felt around her flooded her brain and shut down all rational thought.

Nope, nope, not gonna happen.

"We are, huh? What happened to staying out of each other's way?"

He leaned in close until his lips were almost brushing his ear.

"Oh, well, that's on the set," Eric said smoothly. "This is not on the set. Though, I have to admit, it sure feels like I'm in a movie right now." The shiver his voice created threatened to bring her to her knees. "Do you even know what the flip side is?"

"Huh? Flip side?" Damn, she was having a hard time concentrating on anything. *It's the beer and the heat and the letdown after a long, exciting day* she told herself.

"The record," Eric's voice purred. "The song on the other side. It's a good one. My favorite Eagles song. Do you happen to know what it is, music buff?"

Sam shook her head. "I...don't." She laughed nervously. "Jake would tease me. He'd know."

Why do I keep bringing my stupid brother up?

Eric leaned back and studied her.

Oh, because it makes Eric back off and I can think clearly again.

She missed his closeness immediately.

"I'll give you a hint," he said. It's a slow one."

And, I'm a dead woman. The last notes of 'Victim of Love' played and Sam looked around wildly, hoping to escape without looking like she was running for her life.

Too late—Eric's arm went around her shoulders and he took her other hand to pull her up as the first notes and guitar chords of "New Kid in Town" trickled out of the jukebox and drifted over the dance floor.

And that was it. She was his for the next five minutes while the song played.

The world shrank down to nothing but the music, the heat of Eric's hand against the small of her back, the dusty air, and their swaying bodies as Glenn Fry sang about fickle love quickly found and quickly lost to the next new kid in town. Eric sang the lyrics low and soft, tickling the fine hairs along her forehead. She wanted to run her tongue along the salty trail a bead of sweat left as it ran down the side of his neck and into his shirt. God, he smelled good this close—fresh and cool and clean. Her oasis in the prickly heat of the desert. She could stay here forever, just swaying to the music.

Sam pulled away slightly as she tried to shake herself out of the spell of this perfect moment.

"Who's flinching now?" Eric growled softly.

"Not fair," she purred back. "And besides, you can't possibly want to hold me close. I'm filthy."

Eric grinned as one eyebrow shot up. "So am I."

"Stop it."

"Stop what?" He turned them slowly on the floor just as she looked over Eric's shoulder and caught Tristian watching them.

"We should stop dancing. We shouldn't be doing this."

He dipped his head until his lips were close to her ear, bringing on full-body shivers.

"No. We definitely should be doing this."

Yes, yes we should.

So she leaned back into his body with a soft growl of surrender.

His chuckle vibrated in his chest and her head was suddenly filled with visions of his perfect body suspended over hers as they strained and sweated in bed. The idea of his cock filling her nearly brought her to her knees. She pulled him even closer.

Eric maneuvered her toward the edge of the floor as other people surrounded them in pairs. She hadn't noticed them at first— she'd been too busy looking into his eyes and drinking in his clean oasis-smell of lime and crushed leaves. And thinking how right the world felt when she was in his arms. Was he trying to get her back to the table? She could grab her purse and jacket and they could go back to the hotel together. His room or hers, it didn't matter.

No. I can't do this. I'm losing my focus. I'm here to prove myself, not fall in—

"Jake thinks you're too old for me," she blurted.

Where the hell did that come from?

That broke the spell. Eric straightened as the heat seeped from his eyes and he turned serious. "Tristian has designs on you and I don't know what they are, but I know they aren't good."

"Tristian is just being Tristian." Anger swept every last bit of weak-kneed fascination she had for Eric right out of her. "I don't appreciate—"

"He's messing with Lacey's head, too, if you didn't notice already." Eric was suddenly all business. "I needed to talk to you about it without either of them around and this was my only chance."

Wow. Right. It's the ice cream parlor all over again. Just a job. Fake.

But, that's what I want, right?

Her body said otherwise.

Body, you are not the boss of me. That's not how stunts get done, and right now this is a stunt, plain and simple. I have to be in control.

Sam pulled away until there was a mile of open space between their bodies. "So why are you telling me this? Shouldn't you be dancing with Lacey instead, warning *her*?"

"I wanted to warn you first. And get your impressions. I need your help, Sam."

My help? That's different.

Eric went on. "What are you seeing? Has she told you anything?"

"No, not yet. Something's bothering her though. I don't think the table read went well today."

Eric nodded. "I know it didn't, but thanks for confirming that. I appreciate it."

So now he appreciates me?

Focus. He doesn't want you, and that's the way it should be.

"What do you think it is?" she asked. "Or rather, what does my mother tell you it is?"

That made him wince but he recovered quickly. "She still

suspects Torrent wants you for the lead and that he doesn't care who he manipulates to get his way."

"Yeah, just what I thought. Well, the next time you snitch on me, tell her he hasn't mentioned a word about it."

Eric started to respond when he looked up. Tristian had sidled up to them.

"My dance now, buck," he told Eric, and grabbed Sam's arm.

ELEVEN

Eric narrowed his eyes at the asshole trying to cut in.

The last thing he wanted was anyone getting between him and Samantha. Holding her, dancing with her, smelling her salty skin, and feeling her pull him closer had put him into a dream he never wanted to awaken from.

Jake thinks you're too old for me.

That brought him right out of the dream, gutting him, but she was right. What would she want with someone like him, when she could have anyone she wanted—even this good-looking schmuck.

Except...not right now.

Never thought I'd be squaring off against Balefire from Invincible Gods. He's a lot shorter than he looks on screen. They must fix his height in post.

"What are you smirking at?" Tristian said, squaring his shoulders.

"You're not cutting in," Eric told him. "Not for this dance."

"Sam?" Tristian wheedled. "Are you going to let this caveman tell you what to do?"

"I'm not going to let either of you tell me what to do," she said, looking back and forth between them. "I need to get going anyway. I have stunts to perform tomorrow." Samantha shook her arm out of Tristian's hand and stepped out of Eric's arms. She turned her back on them and headed for the table.

Tristian trotted after her. "Sammy sweetie! Let me escort you back to the hotel."

Now Eric was pissed, mostly for letting her get into this situation. He caught up to Samantha.

She glared at both of them. "No one's escorting me. I rode my bike." She picked up her purse and looked at Lacey, who'd been talking to Tim. "I'll see you back at the room."

"What time do you want me to be on set tomorrow for your stunts?" he asked.

She actually looked like she was considering his offer, wonder of wonders. "No, I'll be fine. I'm sure you have dogs to look after." Samantha turned to head for the door, but Eric wasn't about to leave her side. He heard Tristian behind them, but one look over his shoulder stopped the man in his tracks and sent him walking backward.

"I mean it, Samantha. I'll be there." He held the door open for her.

"Thank you," she murmured as they went outside.

The air was cooler than it was in the bar now that the sun had set. She slowed her walk until they got to her bike. He expected her to toss one last snarky remark at him, then roar out of the parking lot and back to the hotel. Instead, she stashed her purse in a saddle bag and let him help her put on her leather moto jacket—heavy-duty leather for protection, not meant for fashion—and grabbed her helmet. Then she paused as she looked out across the road to the desert.

"What is it?" he asked. She turned her gorgeous face up to his and he caught his breath the way he did every time she looked at him.

"Do you know how to ride?" she asked out of nowhere.

"I do, actually. Why?"

She blew out a breath. "Just the thought of going back to a hot hotel room makes me claustrophobic, especially when faced with a winding road like this one with no one else on it. Just open space and wind and freedom. Sound good to you?"

Jesus, it sounds like heaven.

"Yeah. I could go for that. But there's just one problem." He tapped his head. "No helmet."

"Ah, but you're wrong." She opened a bulging saddle bag and pulled out a second helmet. "I brought two, just in case Lacey didn't have one. They're wired so we can talk to each other." She patted her bike's seat. "What do you say?"

"As long as I'm not riding bitch."

Sam laughed. "As long as you promise to never say that again, I'll let you drive."

Fuck yes!

"Don't get all excited though. This is really just for practice. I have to ride double for the movie and I wasn't about to ask Jake if I could practice with him back in California."

Eric chuckled. "No? I can't imagine why not."

She handed him the second helmet. "Full disclosure—this is his helmet. I swiped it when I left."

"Oh, shit," Eric laughed. "If I put it on, will it shrink around my neck until it decapitates me?"

Sam grinned. "Next month on Netflix—The Haunted Helmet. Starring Eric Armstrong as "Decapitated Guy Number One.""

"Number One? Oh, so you plan on replacing me with some other sap right after, huh? Decapitated Guy Number Two?"

"Yeah, I'm thinking Tristian." She slapped her hand over her mouth. "Wait, that sounded wrong."

"Just get on the bike, Collins."

Her eyes practically clicked in her head as she blinked slowly.

Glad she's riding behind me and not in front. Because there was no way he'd be able to hide his physical reaction to the tantalizing smile she gave him next, right before putting on her helmet.

They got on her bike and disappeared into the night.

The ride was just what they both needed. He felt her body relax against his as the miles disappeared. They didn't talk much; they didn't need to. Their bodies spoke for them. She held him tighter than she needed to as they leaned together into the turns. And when the turnoff came up that would carry them up an outcropping that would overlook the highway, he didn't need her to say yes to take it.

Up they rode along the twisting path between the rocks until they came to the top of a cliff. Eric cut the engine and stepped off. He offered his hand to help Sam and she surprised him when she took it. They removed their helmets and sat down close to the edge to enjoy the spectacular view. Up here, the air was cool and crisp enough that Eric thought he could bite into it like an apple. They looked down at the black ribbon of road unwinding along the pale blue desert under the moon.

Samantha sighed. "The whole world is perfect from up here, isn't it?"

"How so?"

"It's quiet and calm. No one around for miles. And I can think of a million ways of descending this cliff that would probably make your hair stand on end to watch."

That cracked him up. "Samantha Collins, destroyer of my peace and well-being."

"That almost sounds like a movie trailer," she said, then deepened her voice. "In a world full of nighttime tranquility, one woman will shatter it all just to watch a man lose his shit."

Now he was roaring. Little night creatures skittered away in the brush beside them.

Sam watched him, her smile growing wider. "There we go."

"What?"

"I've watched you fighting back your smiles all day. No, actually, I've watched you do that since the day we met. It's good to see you just let go."

"I don't do that," he said, surprised.

She crossed her arms. "You sure as hell do, bud. I watch people as closely as you do, even if it's for different reasons. And you are a man who doesn't like to let his laughter go. Why is that?"

Eric grew quiet. Was he like that? He thought of himself as easygoing, but that was only while he wasn't working. But when wasn't he working? He buried himself in his job. Being around Samantha though, he realized that he was laughing more, even as she drove him crazy.

"I shouldn't have asked," she said softly. "I ruined your mood."

"You didn't. You just made me think, is all. Maybe I am a little...reserved."

"Sometimes you're downright scary. The day we met when you thought I'd insulted you."

"I apologized after realizing I misunderstood you." He turned his head and looked at her. "Were you still afraid of me after that? It didn't seem like it."

"Not as." But her tone sounded unsure. "I was a little afraid of you tonight when Tristian interrupted us."

Again, she surprised him. "How?"

"You should see your face when you're pissed. Your eyes. They go...somewhere else...when you're angry."

Her hand was in his grip before he realized it. "I don't want you to be afraid of me, Samantha. I'm here to make sure nothing happens to you. So when a threat comes close, yeah, I imagine I do look a little scary." He ran his thumb over the back of her hand and could almost imagine sparks coming off their touch. Flint and steel.

"He's not a threat, not to me. The man has a grip like a dead fish. If I'd given him a proper handshake like my dad taught me I think I would have broken his twee little bones." She grinned.

"There you go trying to hide your smile again. Are you back on the job?"

Damn, she was right—he was trying not to smile again. "I'm always on the job."

Samantha gave him a curious look. "You keep saying that, and I keep believing you. But you know what? It's not true."

"It's not?"

"No. You weren't on the job a minute ago." She scooted closer to him. "And you weren't on the job when we were riding, either." She looked deeply into his eyes. "Were you?"

Do not put your arm around her. Do not pull her in close for a kiss from those impossibly soft lips. Do not tell her you can't stop thinking about how she'd feel moving under you. How badly you want to feel her nails scraping your back while you bring her to ecstasy. Stand up right now, pull her up, and go straight back to the hotel.

Eric dropped Samantha's hand. He got to his feet and watched her face fall. He offered his hand to pull her up and she took it again.

That's where their touch should have ended. Instead, Eric pulled her close and she didn't hesitate to put her arms around him.

"Why'd you invite me out here, Sam?"

"You know, I think that's the first time you've called me Sam and not Samantha."

"You're avoiding the question, *Sam*."

"Because we never got to finish our dance." Her voice was soft and teasing as she tilted her chin up to look at him.

"No, we didn't, did we?" His voice came out rough and low.

They started moving together, close and slow. She never let her gaze drop from his. He could have danced with her like this all night, except his body wanted more. And judging by the way her pupils dilated, she was feeling the same thing.

The bike was right there. They didn't have to go back to the hotel in Sagebrush. They could go to another and no one would ever know.

Their feet slowed until they were only swaying together.

"We're not dancing anymore," Samantha whispered.

"We aren't." He dipped his head and hesitated only a fraction of a second before his lips claimed hers. And God, they were so soft and she tasted so good.

Samantha ran her hands down his back to his ass. His cock jumped, jealous of the attention. He ran his left hand through her long dark hair. His right thumb found her nipple and flicked over it, which made her gasp. He groaned in response.

He broke their kiss only to say, "We could find somewhere—"

"No," she said quickly. "First stunts are tomorrow."

"I'd have you back well before then."

"I know you would, but probably not well-rested." She pressed her forehead into his chest. "As bad as I want this..."

So did he. "I'll take you straight to the ranch. Tim's got the dogs tomorrow while I'm setting up props there—"

She pulled away, looking disappointed. "No." She shook her head as she searched for the right words. "This was great tonight..."

"But?" He could already feel her pulling away mentally.

She gave him a faint smile. "You asked me who I am. I'm the woman who used to watch my dad's movies with him when I was little and I'd clap and cheer during all his stunts. I've wanted to be a stuntwoman ever since I watched Trinity in *The Matrix* and realized that women can do this, too.

"I can't be distracted by you tomorrow, Eric. I can't make a single mistake. I'm not even talking about the stunts themselves, but the attitude that people have about me. I have to prove myself every single time I go out there. Every time I come near that motorcycle, I'm going to have to prove I can ride it better than any stuntman here. This is a crew that doesn't know what I can do. They know me for my name, for my mom, for my dad. They don't know *me*.

And if I make a mistake, that will follow me like a ghost wherever I go."

She pressed her hand against his chest. "And you, my friend, are a huge distraction." She sighed and smiled up at him, but it was a sad smile. "Especially that sexy ass of yours," she added through gritted teeth.

Eric chuckled despite the situation.

"So...maybe you should just help Tim with the dogs tomorrow."

Oh hell no. "Sam. You know that's not why I'm here."

"*Please*, Eric. Just give me space tomorrow morning. At least until I get my bearings." She sighed. "I wish...I wish we'd met under other circumstances, Eric. Because I think we might have something."

That hit him hard. But he thought about what she'd said earlier. Jake told Samantha Eric was too old for her. But it had nothing to do with Eric's age. It wasn't so much that Eric had a few years on Sam, it was that those years carried some serious weight. She didn't need to be around someone who'd seen so much. He wanted her, and he hated to admit it—but she'd be better off with someone not so haunted. Someone who wouldn't wake her in the middle of the night from a nightmare.

The thought didn't ease his ache.

But they could do this for now, couldn't they? Have fun as long as the filming lasted. Nothing permanent. Just...fun. Then go back to normal—whatever that was—once it was over.

Eric ran his thumb over her cheek. "You're gonna be great, you know."

"I *don't* know, that's the thing. I might get out there and choke. Lose my nerve."

Eric shook his head. "You aren't going to lose your nerve, Sam."

"How can you be so certain?"

"Because that's not who you are. You show me every time I ask you, that you are a brave, determined, and courageous woman."

She rolled her eyes. "Just like my mom, right? You forgot to add that part."

"No, Sam, I didn't forget because I wasn't going to say that. You're brave all on your own." He brought her fingers to his mouth and kissed them. "I want a raincheck on our dance, back at Rafferty's."

He bent and kissed her, long and lingering. "And when your stunts are over tomorrow, I want more."

TWELVE

Sam was the first one on the stunt team to show up on set the next morning. The power was still out when she and Eric got back to the hotel, and she'd been unable to sleep, both due to the heat and her own excitement.

Not even going to think about Eric she told herself. *Or wish he was here. Why did I tell him not to show?*

She'd spent the day before practicing, and now she was leaning into her anxiety. *I'll sleep when I'm dead* she'd told Lacey when she got up before the light. This was finally—finally!—her chance to shine.

Sam had already helped herself to the wardrobe trailer and found her costume. She checked to make sure her stunt bumpers were firmly in place on her elbows and on her knees under her skinny jeans. The flesh-colored soft padding would allow some protection in case she banged an arm or leg. She wished that her character wore more clothing. That was the advantage stuntmen had over stuntwomen—more clothing equaled more padding.

At least she'd be wearing a helmet later during the semi and motorcycle chase, and then again in a few days during the *True Lies* stunt. Sam tried not to think about it. *One day at a time.* Today would be relatively easy. They'd do some work with a stunt jump air bag for a scene where she had to jump from the top of a three-story building, then she had to do a car hit where she rolled off the front of a car as it 'hit' her. They'd do several takes for that one, she figured.

The morning was cool at least, thanks to the dry desert air. Sam traced lines in the sand beside the stretch of road while she thought about dancing with Eric at Rafferty's...and their second dance later. It was just as wonderful as she knew it would be. Turning him down had been one of the hardest things she'd ever done. She knew at the time she wasn't going to get any sleep anyway, as keyed up as she was.

Maybe she shouldn't have turned down his offer to spend the night. They could have had fun, but something inside her said it would be more than that. He'd gotten under her skin in a way no one ever had before. She found herself thinking about him constantly—and his question, *who are you?*—which no one ever asked her.

Everyone else takes one look at my face and they stop right there. They expect me to be a star and only because I look like Bette Collins.

Eric saw...more. Expected more.

And he certainly wanted more.

So did Sam.

She just wasn't sure how she could handle all of it at once.

Sam didn't have to wait long before the rest of the crew showed up with the stunt bikes, the cars, and the cameras. After that, two carloads of stuntmen pulled up and as they got out it occurred to her then that, even though there were several actresses, she was the only stuntwoman. Maybe Quincy would have her double for all of them. The alternative was to have one of the men put on a wig and do it. Infuriating—but not uncommon. As she approached the group of them talking and joking with each other, her first thought was to ask.

Or would that make her look bratty? The first bit of doubt crept in.

Shit. Maybe I should just keep my mouth shut. So, she kept her words to greetings—and cringed when their sudden camaraderie came to a screeching halt.

Welcome to the boys' club.

Ken waved to her as he got out of another truck. Quincy got on the other side. It didn't surprise her that they were both here. The person who did surprise her was the make-up artist with her rolling suitcase full of concealers and mascara and eyeshadow making a beeline toward her. Sam would be wearing a helmet the whole time—one of the benefits was that she didn't have to sit in a chair for hours while someone turned her face into the spitting image of Lacey's. She looked at the other stunt guys and they shrugged.

"I don't think she's here for us," one of the stuntmen, Brent said. He was Caleb's double. The other men chuckled.

Hoss was doubling for Tristian. He shook his head. "Agreed."

The smiling artist approached Sam, her hand stretched out. "Hey, I'm Jules, and I just want to say it's amazing to be working with you today."

Sam smiled back. "Yeah, I think you have me confused with Lacey. She's not here yet. I'm just the stunt double." She waved Quincy over, who appeared to be studiously ignoring her as he talked to his assistant director, Cassidy.

"Quincy!" she shouted. "I need you for a sec."

Cassidy started over toward her.

"No, Cassidy, I want Quincy."

Cassidy stopped in her tracks and glanced back at Quincy. He looked up, his eyebrows raised under his baseball cap as if to say *who, me?* before jogging over.

"Hey, Sam! Looks like you've met Jules, the very best in the business—"

"I have, and I'm sure she is, but I don't need her." Sam turned to Jules as confusion spread across the woman's face. "Oh, sorry. Nothing personal."

Sam turned her attention back to Quincy. "Helmet." She lifted said object that she'd been cradling under one arm. "Makeup's just gonna run down my forehead and into my eyes, and nobody's going see my face anyway." She narrowed her eyes. "Right?"

"Sam," Quincy said, his voice all caramelly and warm. He put his arm around her shoulders, turned her around, and they walked away from the others. "We're family here. This is a non-union production, which means we've all gotta work outside our little prescribed roles, that's something I made clear right from the start, isn't it?"

"Yeah," she said hesitantly, not liking where this was going.

"So, I'm gonna need you to do some stand-in shots for Lacey while she's off getting her makeup done."

"I don't need makeup for that if all the camera's doing is taking a shot of me to figure out where she's going to stand." Something occurred to Sam. "Shouldn't she be here now? Won't the daylight be messed up if we're doing the stunts early and she's showing up later?" She gestured at the still-rosy early morning sky.

"We'll fix it in post. We're not gonna see the sky the way we're shooting, anyway."

"But the light—"

"Is my problem, and post's problem, okay, Samantha?" Some of that caramel was gone. "You worry about you, okay?" He patted her shoulder before he dropped his arm and they stopped walking.

"Here's where you need to stand. Let's get just a little foundation and lipstick on you so my camera guy can tell how much he'll need to zoom in to get Lacey's features, okay?" The sweetness in his voice was back, full-throttle. "I don't want to do anything to make you uncomfortable, but that would really help out Louis on camera one and I know, with this being your first time, that you're eager to make friends and not make any missteps. I'm here to help everyone, Sam. That's all I want." He patted her shoulder again. "You're doing great."

It's just make-up she told herself. She looked over at Louis the cameraman setting up his equipment, then at Jules who looked uncomfortable but was trying to hide it. Then at the rest of the stunt team, who appeared annoyed at the delay.

Don't be a brat.

"All right, yeah, whatever." She shrugged her shoulders. She didn't need anyone thinking she was a princess.

Quincy's face broke into a broad smile. "Yeah, that's what I'm talking about. Team spirit! Thanks, Sam." He waved Jules over and she looked immediately relieved.

"I do need to ask you something though," Sam said.

"Yeah, what's that, Sam?" She was already losing his attention as he looked away.

"Am I doubling for *all* the actresses?"

His attention snapped back. He looked momentarily stunned, then his warm smile was back in place. "No, no, you just focus on what you're doing for Lacey, okay?"

"Quincy—" She wanted to tell him he'd better not be using men to double for women, but he was already walking away and Jules was right in front of her unzipping her case.

In the meantime, Ken had assembled the rest of the stuntmen around a card table set with a small model of the road and several toy cars and motorcycles. Sam needed to be over there, now, going over what was expected for the day. She couldn't believe she was standing here waiting for her makeup. This was exactly what she didn't want.

"Jules." The woman had just loaded her brush and was halfway to Sam's face. "Do you mind if we scoot this on over to Ken and the rest? I really need to be there."

Jules looked over at the table. "Well, I wanted to do it right here because the light is different over there."

Sam tried to stay patient. "I'm not the lead, right? This is just for the stand-in. It shouldn't matter."

Sam saw her hesitate as she looked over at Quincy, who was already engaged with Cassidy again.

So this is my first stunt of the day. Jump now.

"Thanks for understanding," Sam said with a smile, then she started walking toward Ken. Jules followed right behind, sighing.

Great. I'm already looking like a spoiled brat.

But, she didn't have time to dwell on it. If she wasn't there for the meeting, Ken would have to explain everything twice, and that really looked primadonna.

"Hey," Sam said when she reached the table. The men looked up.

"Well, joining us after all, huh?" Hoss said. His voice was light but his eyes reassured her that, yes, she was being a pain. Sam had known she'd have to win over the stuntmen—male or female, that was just part of paying her dues—but now she definitely had an uphill battle. She hoped Hoss wouldn't be as big a jerk as Tristian. She knew the two were close and had worked on several movies together. It was written into Tristian's contract to use Hoss as his double.

"Just a little misunderstanding. But I'm here now." She looked at Ken, hoping he'd speak up, but he looked just as annoyed as the other men.

"As I was saying," Ken cleared his throat and pointed to a toy eighteen-wheeler. "This is where the gangs fight over the hijacked truck. We're doing the whole sequence in sections since we only have seven of you, not two dozen, so you'll be playing several different members. We'll do the fight scenes and car hits this morning, then the motorcycle chase as one gang tries to catch up with the truck."

He grinned and rubbed his hands together. "And *then*, we get to the real fun."

Ken moved a motorcycle up next to the truck. "By now the payload has been detached and is skidding along behind the cab, sending up sparks." He pointed at Mark. "You'll be driving the trailer in the hidden compartment, so we're gonna just practice with you first this morning."

Mark nodded.

"Meanwhile, Lacey's character Shawna is coming up on the passenger side of the cab where the door has swung open—"

Suddenly, Jules' brush was in Sam's face. swiping bronzer across her cheeks. Sam almost knocked her out of the way just on reflex.

"Sorry, I need to pay close attention to this part," Sam said.

The stuntmen looked at each other, none of them meeting her eyes.

"You paying attention, Sam?" Ken asked, and not too kindly.

"Yeah, the cab door's open, I'm standing, grabbing the handle, swinging in. That's what I read in the script."

"Okay, well, that was yesterday. We're doing this in segments now, like I said. First time's slow, because the camera angles have changed to capture your face—"

"Wait, what?" Now Jules was applying blush. Sam pulled back.

"Just through the visor, Sam," Ken said, annoyed.

"But, my helmet's visor is blacked out."

"Not anymore."

Anger flooded her chest. "I had an agreement."

Groans went up around her.

"We gonna do this or not, princess?" Hoss spat.

"Samantha," Ken said, using the same tone her dad did when he was scolding her. "This is a team effort. You aren't the director, are you? It's a two-second shot. Think of it as a plus for stuntwomen. Quincy wants realism. This way, the audience knows it's a woman and not a dude riding the motorcycle."

"Yeah, otherwise one of us could do it for you, you want out completely," Brent said.

What does he mean by completely? she thought. That didn't sound right. She saw Quincy look up and over at them, his brow furrowing.

Shit. Fire. Fuck.

"No, I don't want out. It's fine."

Ken smiled and nodded. "Good. So here's the change-up. We're doing the first shots going twenty miles an hour with Sam hanging on the truck."

"Wait. That should be Lacey doing that so they get her face, not mine."

Ken scowled. "You're doing it, not Lacey. You losing your nerve for this or what?"

"No. God, no. This is the easy part, barely a stunt. It's..." The rest of her objection died on her lips. *Don't be a princess.* "It's fine. Sorry."

Sam tried to concentrate on the new maneuvers but the rage boiled inside. Rage at Ken for treating her like this, rage at the other men around the table, rage at Quincy for what she considered weasel tactics. But mostly rage at herself for getting into this situation. Damn if she didn't want to call her mom and dad and ask for advice.

But she already knew what it would be—run don't walk away. *Now.*

And never get the chance to do that True Lies stunt. Probably even ruin my chances of doing any stunt in the future.

Her dad's words came back to her. *You'll need to really prove yourself to them.* Maybe she was overreacting. It was only one second of film time, and only her eyes, really. These guys had all done the same for their actors, right? She wasn't getting burned, not really. Maybe Lacey had decided she didn't want to do any of the stunt work. Sam would do the little stunts first, then the first real one—the jump from her bike into the cab—later.

Sam held still while Jules did her mascara. But the minute she was finished, Sam sent off a text to Eric.

Hey. Sorry about changing my mind, but I would like you here right now.

THIRTEEN

While Sam was on set that morning, Eric sweated in his hotel room as he put a call in to Watchdog's biggest computer guru, Elissa. He didn't like seeing the bikers again at Rafferty's the night before or the looks the locals gave them, along with a wide berth.

"What have you got for me on the Rosie Palms Gang?" he joked. Elissa was always up for a good laugh.

"Oh, I would *not* call them that within earshot," Elissa replied, uncharacteristically serious. "Why are you asking? Tell me you haven't seen them again."

Eric stood and walked to the window, hoping for a cool breeze. "I wish I could tell you that, but they were at Rafferty's again."

"Damn it."

He looked up and down the street as if a bunch of motorcycles would magically appear. "They were quiet though. Kept to themselves and the locals steered clear too."

"Yeah, I bet they did. Okay, listen up. These dudes are not to be fucked with. I can't find much, and a lot of it is hearsay, but if only half of it's true, then I'm concerned for you guys."

Eric stood up straighter. "Fill me in."

"You ever hear of a motorcycle gang called Devil's Deacons?" she asked, a trace of sarcasm in her voice.

"Of course I have." Everyone knew about the notorious gang, started all the way back in the Fifties. In the Seventies, they'd done concert security for a famous rock group that ended in several deaths.

"Yeah, the Red Hands are their support club in Arizona. They do the crap the Deacons won't touch. You know, the *really* nasty stuff."

Eric flinched. "Jesus. I can't imagine."

"Well, with me on board, you don't have to because I can tell you. They routinely run drugs, of course, and whatever the Deacons want them to do. But, oh my God, the torture. I read a report where they captured one of the Deacon's rivals, found some fire ants, then they took this guy's nutsack, sliced it op—"

"Okay, yeah, got it without the full visual, Elissa."

"Sharing is caring."

"Then I want you to never care about anything again."

That got her to laugh but she quickly grew serious. "I'm forwarding you all the info I have, which honestly isn't much. A few road names, some rumors, allegations. They're pretty good at flying under the radar."

Eric walked back to his computer and checked his email. "Got the files. Do you know if they have a clubhouse nearby? I want to know our chances of meeting up with them again."

"No idea where their clubhouse is. Or if they even have one."

He frowned. "They have to have one."

"Maybe not. They turn up all over the place, like nomads. Hopefully, they're just passing through town on their way to some demonic orgy."

"Maybe. Thanks, Elissa."

"Sure thing. And do me a favor? Tell Sam we're going rock climbing the minute she gets home. I miss my adventure buddy."

"Will do." He didn't want to ask where they were going.

Picturing Sam hanging by one hand on a sheer cliff face three hundred feet over the ocean did not sit well with him at the moment.

"Want me to shoot you over to Lach's office?" Elissa asked.

"Yeah, that—"

A text interrupted him. It was from Samantha.

"Belay that. I just got a text from her. Tell Lach I'll check in later."

Eric texted Samantha back asking what was wrong and got no answer. He pushed down the worry in his gut that told him things must have gone terribly wrong for her to change her mind. Most of all, he pushed away images of her injured body. He knew it was an irrational thought—if she were injured she wouldn't be texting him —but all the same, it made his stomach churn with acid to think she was in pain.

Eric closed his laptop and jogged downstairs to the van.

He tried calling her several times on the way to the set and left a message each time asking if she was all right. Sam finally texted back saying she just needed a 'second set of eyes' whatever that meant. Eric felt immediate relief knowing that she was safe.

Relief that was quickly replaced with more worry.

Eric squeezed the bridge of his nose as he drove up to the packed dirt parking lot near the ranch house, trying to chase away the last of a nightmare-borne headache. He'd been tempted to sleep down in the cool basement with the dogs the night before instead of in his sweltering room. He doubted he'd sleep any better down there with everything on his mind, but at least he wouldn't have sweated nearly to death. For once, he was thankful for the cold showers because he'd needed one desperately after walking Sam to her door—and then walking away.

When he did finally get to sleep, he had another nightmare that woke him up gasping. Luckily, Tim was still dead to the world as Eric jumped out of bed, still fighting back the images—men covered in blood, dogs howling in fear.

Help me, friend. Come with me now. The voice was so close on waking that Eric looked frantically around the room for the little boy who'd said those words so many years ago. But of course he was long gone.

Eric parked out of the way. Trailers lined the lot, some for the cast, others for set production, costumes and make-up, craft services, and one for Quincy. Cast and crew darted between the trailers, grabbing snacks and drinks at craft, then hurrying on to their next task.

The rest of his headache evaporated as he realized he was about to walk onto his first real day on a working set. No nightmare could compete against that lifelong dream.

Eric looked around for Samantha but didn't see her. He wondered if she was inside one of the trailers, or even the ranch house, which had been locked up tight the day before. He shot Sam a quick text letting her know he was there, then went off in search of her.

He didn't have to go far. The stunt crew had set up along the road on the other side of the ranch house. Two camera cars—a matte-black Porsche Cayenne and a rugged dune buggy fitted with crane arms ending in cameras—sat idling, ready to film some high-speed action.

But Eric's attention was quickly diverted to Samantha standing in the middle of the road as a Camaro came speeding down the dirt road straight at her. Even knowing it was a stunt, he picked up his pace until he was sprinting.

The car hit its mark and slowed, but to Eric's eyes, it wasn't nearly enough. Then bam! The bumper hit Sam's leg and she rolled onto the hood and into the windshield. She bounced off and disappeared behind the other side of the car, which kept moving as if nothing had happened.

When it passed, Eric saw her lying crumpled and motionless beside the road.

Her name lodged itself in Eric's throat. He sprinted faster.

Tristian came running across the road, screaming until he collapsed beside Sam.

"Shaaawwwnaaa!"

"And, cut!" Quincy shouted.

Sam sat up and pulled off her helmet. She beamed as Tristian stood and pulled her up to a round of applause. Eric slowed, heart still pounding, and joined in, clapping his hands as hard as he could.

I knew you could do it, Sam.

And she was only getting started.

So, why send me that first text asking me to be here? Samantha looked like she had everything under control. Maybe she just wanted Eric there to see what she could do. He rolled that idea around in his head, seeing how it felt.

Yup, it felt good—really good.

"All right," Quincy said. "I think we nailed it on that one. Let's set up for the semi chase, right after we get Jesse and Shawna's argument." He turned to Cassidy and started to give her orders to bring back a tray of sports drinks for everyone while Tristian and Lacey got into place, but she was already on it. Another woman trailed behind the actors and touched up Lacey's makeup as soon as she got into place.

Samantha spotted Eric. She gave him a smile and jogged over, looking like she was on top of the world.

"How's it going?" he asked her.

"Did you see?" she pointed over her shoulder with her thumb. "Just now?"

"Hell, yeah. You about gave me a heart attack." He quickly added, "It was incredibly realistic," before she started thinking he was going to tell her to quit doing the thing she so obviously loved.

"That was the third take." She rubbed her thigh. "Gonna leave a mark, but so worth it." If he thought the smile she gave Tristian beamed, the one she gave him outshone the sun. "Stick around and you'll see a real stunt though, with the semi later."

This was not the Samantha he was expecting. Her text had really worried him. Eric lowered his voice. "So, your text this morning. Is everything all right now?"

She nodded enthusiastically but kept her voice low too. "Yeah. I was just jittery and seeing things the wrong way. I think I was letting what my mom said about not trusting Quincy get to me, and I wanted your opinion. I thought for a minute that he wasn't going to actually use me, that I was more of a stand-in for Lacey than a stunt double. But this," she pointed again, "changed everything."

Relief eased Eric's heart. "Glad to hear it. And hey," he lightly tagged her arm, "you were phenomenal."

Red crept up her throat into her face. "Thank you," she said softly. "That...means a lot to me."

"What? I'm nobody. You should be more excited about Quincy's reaction. Looks like he loved it."

She shrugged a shoulder. "Don't underestimate who you are to me."

His heart stuttered. Before he could answer, she turned and motioned for him to follow.

"Come on. Let's watch Lacey in her very first scene." The impish smile on her face was adorable. "I'm so excited for her."

Eric couldn't help himself. He touched the small of Sam's back as they approached the rest of the crew. She reached behind her and squeezed his hand for a moment, long enough to make his chest swell.

Cassidy had returned with the drinks and now she and Quincy had their heads together over a tablet as they discussed the next shots.

"We'll need a close-up, then a tilt shot instead of going straight into the long shot, agreed?" Quincy looked up at Cassidy, who nodded, then went off to talk to the camera crew about the changes.

Lacey was getting the last of her make-up done when Samantha called out, "She looks great, Jules." The make-up artist looked a little surprised when she turned, then she smiled at Sam and thanked her.

Lacey gave Sam a little wave. Tristian stood beside her. There was something different about him and it only took Eric a moment to realize what it was. He looked at the man's shoes, and sure enough, the platform soles boosted him up a couple of inches.

Tristian looked bored and annoyed. "We ready yet?" he shouted to Cassidy. "Or are you going to jaw with Bart all day?"

"His name's Justin," Cassidy said as she jogged back to Quincy, her voice full of disdain.

"Cassidy," Quincy scolded in a good-natured way that got under Eric's skin all of a sudden.

The assistant director immediately apologized under her breath, then called for quiet on the set.

Eric's excitement grew. He wanted to see how the magic was made. Sam watched with equal intent beside him and he realized just how much they both loved this business. Even though she grew up in it, she acted as excited as he felt.

"Okay," Quincy said, "this scene is the heart and soul of the movie. This is where the audience knows at last how deeply Shawna loves Jesse. So, let's see what you got. And... Action!"

The cameras rolled as Tristian and Lacey—no, Jesse and Shawna—squared off.

"I want you so much, Jesse, you know that. But we can't be together, don't you get it?" Lacey grabbed Tristian's arm.

Tristian pulled Lacey to his body. "You can't be saying that to me, Shawna. Not after everything we've been through. You need me. I thought you might even love me."

Lacey's eyes filled with tears and her face became a study in emotional pain. She broke from Tristian's arms and walked three steps away before turning. "They'll kill you when they find out you're with the Feds. I can't..." She sobbed and Eric actually felt his heart lurch. "If I'm with you, they'll torture you, and *then* kill you."

"I don't care, Shawna. You're mine, understand me? *Mine.*" He started forward and Lacey threw her hands out in front of her to ward him off.

"Jesse, I'm leaving because I love you. Rage wants me and I'm promised to him."

"Don't talk to me about Rage. He's a fucking punk."

Tears streamed down her face. "I'm his property, Jesse. This," she gestured up and down her body, "this got sold to him before you and I ever met. But this," her hand went over her heart as she smiled through her tears, "this is yours. Always."

Her voice lowered and everyone on the set strained to hear her every word, riveted by her acting.

"So go. Get out of here and get safe. If you don't, if they kill you," she pounded her chest, "this will die inside me." She turned away.

"Shawna. Shawna, don't you dare run away," Tristian shouted. To Eric, he sounded like he was acting in a high school play. He'd seen the man act and act well before, and...this wasn't it.

Lacey picked up her pace. "Go! Get as far away from me as you can. Go!" And she took off running. Eric knew this scene led to the stunt Samantha just performed, where Shawna gets run down by Rage and kidnapped.

"Shawna? *Shawna!*" Tristian shouted after her before breaking into a halfhearted run. "Shawna, no!"

"And, cut!" Quincy said.

Lacey stopped running and turned, a bright smile making her face glow, the opposite of the heartbroken character she'd portrayed moments before. Both cast and crew clapped and shouted her name. And Eric thought she deserved every cheer.

I just witnessed the birth of a new Hollywood star. Sam looked up at him, her mouth smiling and agape, clearly amazed.

"Nope, nope, nope." Quincy waved his hands in the air in a 'cut' motion. "That was crap. Let's do it again."

"My thoughts exactly," Tristian said, glaring at Lacey, whose smile had dried up like one of the dusty riverbeds surrounding them. "I can't, with her. I just can't."

"What the fuck? She was great," Eric whispered to Samantha. "Can you tell me what exactly I'm missing?"

"The same thing I am. She was spectacular." Sam looked as confused as he felt. They both looked around at the rest of the crowd and saw their confusion mirrored back at them.

"Lacey," Quincy said. "You need to step it up, okay? Give Tristian something to work with. I know you can do this."

Lacey looked stunned. But she nodded and actually smiled at Quincy. Eric felt his heart go out to her in sympathy.

"Don't *smile* at him, Lacey," Sam growled under her breath. She glared at the director, who told Cassidy to shout for quiet.

They watched the same scene play out three more times. Quincy yelled cut and berated Lacey between each take. By the third time, it was obvious that she was exhausted and disheartened.

Tristian phoned in his performance each time.

"I can't," he repeated for the umpteenth time. "Not with her."

Quincy hung his head. "Lacey, sweetheart, why don't you take a break? Maybe you just need to warm up." He turned and found Samantha. "Sam? Can I have you step in for Lacey real quick?"

Samantha's brows knitted together. She glanced at Eric, then looked at Quincy.

"I'm...no. I'm not an actress."

Quincy looked shattered. "I never said you were, Sam, but I do need you as the stand-in, all right? We're losing the correct light here, so please. Or else we're all going to have to repeat this tomorrow and that's putting us behind schedule and budget."

The crew grumbled. Eric wanted to yell at them *No, it's not her fault.* It wasn't Lacey's either. Tristian was the problem, and for whatever reason, Quincy was backing him over Lacey and Samantha.

"You know what? I'm pushing. You don't have to do this," he told Sam, who was already stepping forward.

She craned her neck around and said, "It's okay. I'm just standing in." But she didn't look convinced by her own words.

"Sam?" Eric said. "You sure?"

She nodded, already committed.

Eric gritted his teeth. He hated to see her compromised like this, especially when there was nothing he could do that wouldn't make her look like a diva.

Sam beat her hand against her skinny jeans and a cloud of dirt went up. She was dressed identically to Lacey, except she was covered in dust.

"Can we get someone to take care of that?" Quincy looked around. Cassidy was already on it. She ran up to Sam and tried to brush the dirt off her sleeves while Sam patted her thighs.

Tristian leered. "I can help too."

Both women looked up, shocked into silence.

That did it. A blaze of red covered his vision and Eric rushed toward the actor. He stopped himself just shy of punching him.

"You will show respect, you fucking hack."

Tristian flinched before his cheeks flushed red.

Cassidy stopped what she was doing, looked quickly between the men, and stared down Eric.

"You, back off." She turned to Tristian. "And you owe both of us an apology. I won't tolerate disrespect like that on the set," she looked back at the director like she was daring him to disagree, "and neither will Quincy, understand?"

"That's right, Tristian, I won't."

Eric clenched his fists and got his breathing under control. If it weren't for Sam's pleading eyes, he would have taken Tristian's head off, top Hollywood actor or not.

Don't mess this up for her. She can eat a jackass like Tristian for breakfast. But his gut instinct to protect her roared in protest.

Tristian tried to stare Eric down but failed. Instead, he turned to Sam and Cassidy.

"Sorry that you can't take a joke," he mumbled.

Sam started to say something, but Quincy interrupted. "Come on, man. Can we please save the dramatics for the camera? Cassidy, Eric, get out of the way. Lacey, I thought I told you to take a quick break. Grab some water, cool off, okay?"

Lacey nodded, uncertainty in her eyes. Then she headed for craft.

Quincy watched her go, then turned to Sam. "Samantha, you know the scene. Maybe you and Tristian can try this. Be Shawna for a minute."

Again, Sam looked floored. "Are you serious? That's not what I'm here for."

"I know, but come on, be a team player. Just help me out here, okay?" Quincy poured on the honey.

Sam nodded. "All right. Fine."

Quincy's smile said he was proud of her. "All right. Tristian, take her in your arms."

Sam flinched when the asshole put his arms around her. Now, he looked genuine. This was Jesse holding Shawna, the woman he was ready to die for.

"Cassidy, can you get Justin to pull in for a closeup? Behind Tristian's head."

She looked surprised at him. "I thought we weren't—"

"I thought we weren't filming," Sam said at the same time. She looked at the cameraman who shrugged.

"So I can see it for the storyboards, Cass, all right?" Quincy sounded brittle.

Cassidy sighed and looked at Sam, who nodded reluctantly. "Justin? Close-up."

The cameraman complied.

"Okay. Good. Beautiful. Tristian, *now* you're on fire." Quincy looked around for confirmation. "Isn't he on fire?"

Heads nodded, some reluctantly.

"Now, Sam, please, just a line or two, okay?"

Sam startled and glanced at Quincy, then Eric. "Seriously?"

Quincy nodded. "Yeah, just to give him a lead-in."

Her expression said, *Okay, you asked for it.* Sam turned back to Tristian. "I want you so much, Jesse, you know that. But we can't be together, don't you get it?"

Eric tried not to crack up. If Tristian was bad, Samantha's delivery was ten times worse. Her delivery was flat, almost sarcastic. She didn't even look him in the eye but over his shoulder at the cameraman who was watching her on the screen and also trying not to laugh.

Then Tristian spoke.

"You can't be saying that to me, Shawna. Not after everything we've been through. You *need* me. I thought you might even *love* me." A tear slid down his cheek as he stared into Sam's eyes.

Sam's gaze snapped back to his in surprise. He was without a doubt Jesse, and his heart was breaking.

"One more time," Quincy said, his voice softer.

Tristian repeated the line. If anything, the second time was even more convincing. Sam actually looked moved enough to pass as Shawna.

Lacey walked up just then and watched the two of them. She looked like someone had just drowned her puppy.

"Yes! Cut!" Quincy punched the air. "That's what I'm talking about!"

"Cut?" Sam asked. "Are you sure this is just for the storyboards?"

Quincy sighed. "Do I need to explain—"

But he'd lost her attention as she looked over to where Ken was setting up for the semi-trailer stunt.

"What are you *doing*?" She pushed Tristian away and stormed across the road.

Right up to a skinny stuntman named Nick, who was putting on a long, dark woman's wig.

FOURTEEN

"What in the hell do you think you're doing?" Sam said as she ripped the wig off Nick's head. She would've ripped the tank top, moto jacket, and skinny jeans that matched hers off too if it wouldn't have gotten her arrested for assault.

"I'm getting ready for the stunt, little girl," Nick snarled back.

"Oh no, you're not. I'm doing this stunt, not you."

"Sam." Ken was suddenly there next to her, his hand hovering over her shoulder. At least he had the common sense not to touch her. "I've reconsidered this one and Quincy and I think it's too much for you."

The wig dropped out of Sam's hand. She barely registered Jules picking it up and running her fingers through its length before handing it off to another woman from costuming. How was it that people were suddenly popping up out of nowhere around her?

Tunnel vision from sheer rage. Sam took a deep breath to calm herself.

"Ken, please. I can handle it. We talked about this."

Ken rubbed his jaw. "I know we did, kid, I know. But I've been reconsidering. You already did some stunts this morning. Aren't you tired?"

"*Tired?* No, I'm outraged. I signed on as a stuntwoman and so far, I've been little more than a stand-in. As for getting hit by a car, I've been practicing that stunt with my dad since I was ten." *Just maybe not with a moving vehicle back then* she thought but didn't add. "So I'm not tired. I'm not even winded. And I'm not letting anyone else stand in for Lacey." She looked behind her, back at Quincy who seemed to be studiously ignoring the problem blowing up on his set. "Is this really *your* idea?"

"Boss, what do you want me to do?" Nick asked Ken.

"Fuck," Ken swore under his breath.

"Sam?" Now Eric had materialized along with Cassidy. *Jesus, is the Easter Bunny next?*

"It's too dangerous for you, Sam," Ken said in a voice that told her this was final. "I'm looking out for you, on behalf of your dad."

"That's not your place, Ken."

He looked at Eric. "Talk some sense into your girlfriend, would you?"

Girlfriend? Ken saw them dance *one* time. And to assume that Eric could tell her what to do? How dare he? Sam fumed.

"I'm doing this stunt or I'm walking."

"Jesus Christ," Nick said. "Drama queen." His eyes pleaded with Ken to make her shut up and go away.

Sam crossed her arms and looked at Cassidy. "And you can tell Quincy he can forget about using any of my footage." Her gaze shifted to Eric as she readied to tell him to stop being her babysitter.

But he was looking back at her with admiration.

"Yeah, I'll talk some sense into her," Eric told Ken, his eyes never leaving her face. "Sam, I think you absolutely can handle this stunt."

What?

"Furthermore, I think that you should follow through with

walking if you don't do this stunt." He turned to Cassidy. "Tell Quincy that."

Cassidy was looking at him like he'd lost his mind. "Okay, I don't mean to throw gasoline on this Dumpster fire of a situation, but aren't you the animal handler—no, wait, the *assistant* to the animal handler? What do you have to do with... Oh." She slapped her forehead as she looked between the two of them. "It's early for the on-set romances to be starting up, but whatever."

"We're not...nothing is...I mean. *No*," Sam sputtered.

Cassidy raised an eyebrow.

"I'm a family friend," Eric said smoothly. "I've known Sam for ages."

"He's taken me out for ice cream," she heard herself say stupidly. "Butter brickle."

Cassidy frowned. "What's a brickle?"

"See?" Sam gestured at Cassidy. "I'm not the only one."

Cassidy consulted her tablet. "Let's see if I can straighten this out. Ken, no one said anything to me about replacing Samantha with Nick." Her gaze flicked back up to him. "I still have her here in the notes doing the stunt. Quincy told me to come over here and handle things so I'm handling them. Nick, we need as many riders as we can get at one time on screen for the chase scene so that's what you're doing."

Then she looked at Sam. "You're on at the top of the hour, *Shawna*."

Sam grinned. "Thanks." Then she looked Eric in the eye. "And thank you."

———

Okay, so she wasn't making friends among the stuntmen today and that sucked. But, Sam was here to prove herself and all she could do was hope that at the end of the day she'd win them over with her skills.

As for Quincy? If the stunts didn't give her whiplash, he would. She couldn't puzzle him out. One minute he made her feel like the most important person in the world, but the next? Powerless.

And she wasn't the only one. Lacey was just as confused—no, more so. She and Sam caught up with each other before it was time for Sam to jump on her bike.

"Was I that terrible?" she asked Sam, sounding and looking devastated.

"No, you were amazing. Tristian was the one who sucked."

"Because of me." Lacey looked at her boots.

"Oh hell no. Because of him."

Lacey looked up. "But he came to life when he was with you."

"No, he just decided to stop phoning it in. *Acting.*" Sam tightened her jacket after she checked her elbow pads. "Lacey, I don't know what's going on for sure, but I don't like it." She looked Lacy over. "Did Ken check your bumpers?"

"No."

Seriously? "Then here, let me do it." Sam went over Lacey's elbow and knee pads, making little adjustments so that they were on correctly. Even though Lacey wouldn't be doing any hard stunts, she would be working with a moving vehicle.

"Thanks." She looked so crestfallen, it broke Sam's heart.

"Hey, you're doing an outstanding job. Don't let Quincy get to you."

"He's the director, Sam. Kinda hard not to let him."

"Quincy's just being moody on set. Wait until they review the dailies. Then they'll know what they have."

Lacey returned Sam's smile. "Thanks."

Sam checked her bike one more time. She made sure the frame was solid and undamaged before hopping on. Quincy sat in his chair watching her, acting as though he'd never spoken with Ken about the stunts.

"Action!"

Now it was Sam's chance to prove herself. One of the camera

cars—the dune buggy—kept up with her along the side of the road as she went zooming along on the stunt bike at sixty miles an hour to catch up with the semi. Her first move would be dodging the trailer after it detached. She knew that Mark was inside a hidden bottom compartment steering it, that he had screens showing him exactly where she was, but still, any number of things could go wrong. He could lose control, or she could skid at the wrong time. Even a bogey could come out of nowhere in the form of a scared deer doing the dumb and trying to cross the road amid their controlled chaos.

Don't think about what could go wrong. Think about what you're going to do right.

Heart pounding, Sam watched the semi hit its cue. Brent rode up on his bike dressed as Rage and 'unhooked' the trailer his character had rigged by messing with the king pin in an earlier scene. The trailer detached right where it should and the rigged landing gear sent up a shower of sparks that Sam rode through as three different cameras caught everything.

Now it was time to shift down. The actual stunt would be done at a slower speed—she couldn't imagine trying to attempt this at sixty miles an hour. The cab slowed and she watched for her next mark up the road to tell her when to make the jump. In the script, the driver was a fellow club member who had been shot and Shawna was going to jump in and gain control of the truck while trying to keep him from bleeding out. Lacey would do those interior shots—all Sam had to do was make the jump and get inside.

They neared the cue and the truck slowed. Sam matched the pace but was still worried when she realized they were going too fast. By her estimate, they'd blow right past it at ten miles over their designated safe speed.

Then as if the driver had suddenly done his math, the truck dropped speed faster than she'd expected. Sam adjusted quickly but they still hit the mark going five miles over.

I should skip it. My dad would kill me if he saw.

But the cameras were rolling and she needed more than ever to prove herself. The words came back to her. *Drama queen.*

The side door popped open and Sam reached for the door handle. She grabbed it just as she'd practiced. Her heart felt like a jackhammer—five miles' difference in speed didn't sound like a lot but she sure could feel it. Her legs left the bike and she let it go ahead of her while she dangled over the road, clinging to the open door. Sam swung around and into the cab, closing the door behind her.

"We came in too hot," she told the driver, a guy named Kel.

"Nope, change in direction. Quincy told me over the comm to come in at that speed. You didn't hear?"

What? She'd heard nothing over her comm. Sam took her helmet off and checked. It seemed to be working.

The truck slowed to a stop now that the scene was done. Sam caught her breath as adrenaline pumped through her body. She should have felt nothing but pride right now at completing her first big stunt, but instead, she felt confusion and a creeping sense of unease. Her dad had told her sometimes things change at the last minute, but in the middle of a stunt? And shouldn't it have been Ken making that call as the second unit director?

Between Quincy's antics earlier and this, she'd had enough.

As soon as the truck stopped, Sam was out the door. She marched up behind Quincy, ready to give him a piece of her mind. He turned away from Justin the camera guy and faced her with a huge smile.

"Let's hear it for our girl, huh?" he shouted and threw his arms over his head to clap. "First big stunt in the can and in one take! God *damn!*"

Applause filled the air around her. Sam spun and saw everyone from Quincy and Ken down to Jules applauding. Even Mark, Hoss, and Brent were putting their hands together for her. She'd done it. She'd won them over. Sam smiled and thanked everyone.

As Quincy started talking about the next scene, she tried to push her continuing unease way down to her toes. Sam still intended to talk to him about the abrupt change, but maybe not right at this moment.

Eric was grinning ear to ear. "You did it."

He had no idea that anything was amiss. To him, it was a perfectly planned and executed stunt.

What if he knew the truth? *He'd pull me out of here.*

The applause still rang in her ears.

Sam gave him her brightest smile. "Thanks for your support back there with Ken."

"I never doubted you."

Sam studied his face. Not a trace of bullshit. He meant it. Her stomach flipped over like she was still racing along on the bike. Like it had the night before. It was more than just the fact that he was incredibly sexy. Eric was kind. He was supportive.

He was real.

"Thank you," Sam said. "I owe you an apology."

He looked confused. "For what?"

"For being a complete pain about the whole babysitting thing. I'm sorry. You've been nothing but kind to me and I've been a jerk."

Eric chuckled. "Does this mean I don't need to avoid you on set anymore?"

"Not that you have," she teased. "But no. Please don't avoid me." Sam felt herself blush. "Especially if we happen to both find ourselves at Rafferty's again."

Now it was Eric's turn to feel the heat creeping up his throat. Sam liked seeing that, knowing she could turn him on with just a few words.

"We do have a dance to finish," Eric said, his voice rough.

FIFTEEN

Rafferty's was hopping every night thanks to the cast and crew of *Wheeler, Dealer*. Everyone had taken a shine to Mag's place throughout that first week, and started trickling in as soon as their jobs were done, which meant things really started picking up well after dark. The last scene often wrapped at ten pm or later—a sixteen-hour day for some. This was one of those days. Quincy was shooting a night scene but Eric wasn't needed so he decided to try and get Mags to talk a little more about the town.

And he hoped that Samantha would be in soon.

"The power's back on at the hotel," he said as Mags wiped down the bar in front of him.

She snorted. "Yeah, we'll see how long that lasts."

"Really? That bad around here?"

"That bad? You got eyes, don'cha? Whole town suffers regular blackouts. There's nothing for decent folks here anymore. People are talking about leaving, especially since the quarry gave out. No one wanted to rebuild anything and that includes the power grid."

"What about you? You thinking of leaving?"

Just then, a little boy darted out of the kitchen door behind the bar. Mags grabbed him with a laugh.

"You go on back in there, Cody," she ordered as she turned him around. The kid bolted back into the kitchen. "My grandson," Mags gave by way of explanation.

"Looks like a spitfire," Eric said. He forced a smile. The boy reminded him too much of another slightly older spitfire he'd met in Afghanistan, the same one who still haunted his dreams years later.

"He is. He and his mama are back in town, hoping to be extras on the movie." She shook her head. "Silly reason, but it's good to see them. They moved away a couple years ago when it looked like nothing was getting better."

"So, are *you* moving?" Eric asked again.

Mags sighed and looked at the jukebox as if the ghost of Glenn Frey would be leaning against it waiting for the rest of the band to turn up. Or maybe her husband, who she'd lost years back. She'd told Eric he'd been the love of her life.

Mags shook her head wistfully. "Naw. Jukeboxes are too hard to move."

In more ways than one Eric thought as he chuckled. "I hear you."

"The mayor was mighty pleased though when Quincy contacted him about using us for his movie," Mags continued. "Promised to upgrade the infrastructure, stabilize the power grid or some damn thing." She shook her head. "Nobody's seen it yet, though. Figured it'd be fixed by the time you all got here. People are grumbling. And not just about that."

Now we're getting somewhere.

"It'll be a while longer before we start shooting in town. Quincy's got a bunch of generators out at the ranch," Eric said. "We aren't hurting for power there."

"Yeah, the ranch." Mags' voice was anything but enthusiastic.

Eric started to ask about it when she looked up at the sound of the door opening.

"Hang on." She turned and went into the kitchen. Quincy stepped up to the bar next to Eric.

"Hey, how's it going?" The director clapped him on the back. "I've been enjoying your screenplay."

Eric was taken aback. "You're reading it?"

"I am. Helps me unwind."

"I hope it's not making you fall asleep."

Quincy laughed. "Nope, not at all. Still needs some work, but I'm already casting it up here." He tapped his ever-present baseball cap.

"I, uh, thank you." He picked up his beer and toasted Quincy. "I'm surprised to see you in here tonight."

"Yup, filming starts once the full moon rises over the ridge in about two hours. Long night ahead but I thought I'd stop and grab dinner. Craft is good, Rafferty's is better." He looked around the place. "I loved it here from day one. You know, when I was on my sabbatical. Mags won't let me shoot inside though or else I would."

Mags reappeared with a takeout bag.

"Right, Mags?" Quincy called.

Her brows knitted. "Right what?"

"You won't let me shoot in here."

"Nope." Straight-faced, she set the bag on the bar. "Here you go. That'll be ten ninety-nine." She picked up her bar rag and wiped at a non-existent stain on the edge.

Quincy gave Eric a smile and a look that said *Watch this*.

"Then just sell me the jukebox."

"No." She scrubbed harder, not looking at him.

Quincy kept on grinning. "How much for the jukebox, Mags?" he asked. "Come on, name your price."

Mags looked up, shook her head, and tossed the rag on the bar. "A million dollars."

"Done."

"I was joking."

"I wasn't." He pulled out a black credit card. "Ring it up. One million dollars plus ten ninety-nine for the burger and fries."

"I said I was joking."

He set the card on the bar and pushed it toward her with two fingers. "Ring it up, Mags."

She went from straight-faced to looking deeply upset. "You can't have my jukebox."

"I just bought it." He smiled even wider.

"I'm not running your card." She pushed it back at him.

"Come on, Quincy, I think you've taken the joke far enough," Eric said.

"It's not a problem, Eric," Mags said. "Because the jukebox is staying right where it is." She crossed her arms.

Quincy made a show of putting the card away. He laid a hundred-dollar bill on the bar, picked up his bag, and saluted Mags. The smile never left his face. As he stepped away from the bar, he leaned in conspiratorially and whispered to Eric, "We'll see."

Mags watched him all the way to the door. "Did he say what I thought he said?" she asked.

"Depends on what you think he said, but word to the wise: bolt that thing to the floor."

Mags nodded as she picked the rag back up. She sucked in her cheeks and turned away.

"Mags?" Eric asked, damn near ready to jump over the bar to make sure she was okay.

She turned back, tears in her eyes. "Ignore an old woman, T-B-H." The door opened again, sending in orange light from the setting sun. Mags shielded her eyes, then smiled.

"Here comes my rival," she said. "Your gal is here with her twin."

Eric tried not to turn around as he heard two women laughing and talking as they approached the bar. Then Samantha was standing beside him, her leather-and-vanilla scent filling his nose.

She looked his way and gave him a dazzling smile before she turned to Mags.

"How's it going, Mags?"

"Going just fine. What would you ladies like?"

"Two cheeseburger baskets, a beer for me, and a club soda for Lacey. She's still got a long night of filming ahead of her."

Mags set out two coasters in front of two bar stools. "We're gonna sit over there." Samantha pointed at their usual table but glanced at Eric again. "Ladies' night."

Eric smiled and nodded then took a sip of his beer. "You stunting tonight?" He already knew the answer.

Samantha shook her head. "No. At least not on set. Maybe on the dancefloor. If someone asks me." She winked as Mags brought them their baskets and drinks and went to the opposite end of the bar. Sam and Lacey went to their table and Eric went back to his beer and tried not to watch them.

Samantha Collins, you will be the death of me.

SIXTEEN

As soon as Sam and Lacey sat down at their table, Lacey grinned at her. "Sure you don't want to sit at the bar instead?"

"No way, this is ladies' night, remember?" Sam had convinced Lacey to skip the craft trailer and its cold sandwiches for dinner and come with her to Rafferty's for a hamburger. At least that was her excuse. Lacey looked like she could use a break away from the set and Rafferty's would be the perfect place for her friend to vent.

And our timing was perfect she thought. They'd gotten there as Quincy walked out carrying a takeout bag. He'd smiled and waved as they passed him in the parking lot and the two of them waved back, but Sam could feel the tenseness coming off Lacey.

"I just don't know what's going on with some of my scenes with Tristian," she confessed as they ate. "Quincy, either."

"Quincy's a perfectionist, just like every director. At least Tristian is actually acting now. Mostly," Sam said.

"Sure, after *you* fluff him." They laughed and rolled their eyes. "He's usually really on, but then sometimes, it's like he's..." Lacey trailed off as she shook her head.

"Phoning it in, I know. I've seen it."

"He seems to do it only when you're there. Not every time, but whenever it's a more intimate scene and you're around, he craps out on me but he's amazing with you."

Sam grimaced as the uneasiness she'd been fighting settled over her. "I know. They're keeping shots of Tristian's face for the film and mine for the storyboards."

At least that's what Quincy swears he's doing.

She kept her growing doubts to herself. Lacey didn't need to hear it and she didn't need to think it.

Lacey looked down at the table. "I don't think it's only for the storyboards."

"Lacey, Quincy's not going to replace you with me. I am not an actress, I will never be an actress. You've heard me deliver those lines. You think Tristian sounds like a robot? I'm worse."

Lacey waved her hand. "You aren't...terrible."

Samantha snorted and took a sip of her beer. "You are being generous and we both know it. Unless I'm jumping off a building or getting hit by a car, my acting sucks. And I like it that way. I just wish everyone else would buy a freekin' clue."

"Oh, God, then don't even *look* at social media right now." Lacey pulled her phone out.

"So you're going to show me what I shouldn't look at?" Samantha teased.

Lacey realized what she was doing and thumped her phone face down on the table. "Nope, you're right. I'm not." She popped a French fry into her mouth and washed it down with club soda.

"Except now I'm curious." Samantha propped her elbows on the table and laced her fingers together, then dropped her chin onto them. "Tell me. How bad is it?"

"Prue and Jaylee are convinced this is going to be *your* breakout role as Shawna."

"What?" Sam lifted her head and slammed her palms down on the tabletop. "Me?" She laughed in disbelief. "All they have to do is check IMDb online and see I'm listed as a stuntwoman, not as the lead. Lazy vultures is what they are."

"Are you sure? I'm worried that I'm actually getting replaced—they're saying I will be."

Sam tilted her head in sympathy. "Don't. You're not. That's just how Hollywood works though. It's mostly rumors and outright lies, anything to generate buzz about a project." Sam gestured for the phone. "Lemme see."

Lacey shoved the phone across the table. Sam picked it up. It was already queued to the loathsome gossiping duo. The banner across the bottom said they were interviewing a man who had the 'inside scoop' on *Wheeler, Dealer*.

"Ron Anderson. Oh my fucking God, I hate that man." Sam handed the phone back. "I don't even have to watch. He's a lying sack of shit."

"Well, he's an effective lying sack of shit. Everyone's talking about it." She seemed like she wanted to say more, but Sam didn't want to hear it. It wouldn't do either of them any good. It might even wind Lacey up even tighter and that's the last thing her friend needed right before shooting.

"Lacey, please, just ignore it."

She sighed. "I'll try."

"Chances are, once the previews come out they're going to spin it as you being the surprise breakout. You'll have extra hype. Trust me."

Lacey grinned. "I hope you're right."

Rafferty's filled up as they chatted about trivial things and finished their dinner until Lacey needed to leave. Samantha stood up and hugged her.

"I'm so glad we're friends, Sam. I mean it."

"Me too. Now go give them hell, okay? Quincy's not going to have a choice but to praise you. And you deserve every word. Ask anyone on set, not just me. They all think you're amazing."

"Thank you," Lacey said, looking a little more confident. She picked up her motorcycle helmet and tucked it under her arm. Then, her whole demeanor changed. Now Samantha was looking at Shawna—a woman not to be fucked with.

"You've got this, Shawna." Sam grinned.

"That's right, bitch, I do." 'Shawna' gave her a cocksure smile, then squared her shoulders. "Speaking of getting something, just remember I'll be out for a while tonight." She jutted her chin toward Eric, still sitting at the bar. He turned his head and smiled.

Sam held on to her heart, which wanted to hop on a stunt bike and jump the Grand Canyon to be near him every time he came within view, and now after their make-out sesh it was a hundred times worse. Rafferty's was already sweltering and Eric's presence sent the temperature even higher. Samantha couldn't help her smile. Just being in the same room with Eric made her worries seem small and easily conquerable, if they mattered at all. She could almost forget why he was really here.

Almost.

She hated the nagging voice in the back of her mind telling her that even if he was attracted to her, she was still a job to him. What would happen after the production wrapped and they went home? Would they see each other? Or would he tell her Jake was right? That she was just someone he'd needed to babysit, and now it was back to reality. Her smile faltered, even as she saw his as he looked straight at her.

"Not gonna happen."

"Never say never," Lacey said. "I'll see you later. Just make sure you put a sock on the doorknob."

Sam grinned and shook her head. "Go."

The minute Lacey left, Eric went straight to the jukebox and dropped in a handful of dimes one after the other. Scattered applause filled the room as people got up to dance.

Sam's heart raced with anticipation when he turned and crossed the floor to her table. They'd soon be up and dancing as they had a few times since their first night. But each time, someone had been with them. Lacey and Tim usually, but sometimes Ken and Quincy stopped by. Even Brent, Hoss, and Mark had warmed up since the first stunt and they'd all shared pitchers of beer together.

And at the end of the night, they all went their separate ways.

The night they kissed and Eric wanted to find a place where they could make love seemed like a distant memory—no, a fantasy she'd had. Something she wanted but never happened. He hadn't asked since then, and their dances were just that—dances.

Crazy to think tonight would be any different.

"Hey, handsome," Sam said as Eric sat down.

He refilled her beer mug before filling his. "Hey yourself. You looked lonely sitting here without your twin."

"Oh, so you decided to remedy that?"

"I did." He looked at her intently and she felt his stare all the way down to her bones. He was real. Even when they joked around, Eric was real and took her seriously.

I'm going to miss this feeling when we got back to California. A pit opened in her stomach. It was as if she'd jumped off a cliff and realized there was no air bag waiting for her at the bottom.

Stop kidding yourself. You're his job. That's all.

"What's going on in that head of yours?" he asked. "You look like you just swallowed one of the pool balls."

"Nothing," she said.

"Not true." He sipped his beer and continued to watch her.

She shrugged. "Fine. Lacey's still thinking that Quincy is going to replace her with me. Apparently, so does the rest of the world."

Eric shook his head. "Fuck the rest of the world. There's only here and now."

Sam started. She blinked rapidly. "That…"

"Surprises you that I feel that way?"

She considered his words. "Maybe not. I imagine there are some things you've had to let go of."

His expression darkened as he nodded again. For a moment, he was far away. Maybe she wasn't the only one wondering where this was going. Or maybe it was something else bothering him.

Eric finished his beer. Sam surprised both of them by standing and offering her hand. "Wanna dance?"

Eric immediately snapped back to the here and now. He stood up and took her hand. "Don't mind if we do." He led her to an empty corner at the back of the crowded dancefloor.

The next song came on. 'New Kid in Town.'

Their song.

You have to stop thinking that. It's only going to hurt more when you finally land and he looks the other way.

She leaned into him anyway. He brushed his hand down her hair. Just the thought of him holding someone else crushed her. She never wanted to go back. She wanted to stay forever in this dusty, hotter-than-hell roadhouse, sweat pouring down her back while Eric held her and they swayed to the music. She bit her lip to hold back the emotions that threatened to bring tears to her eyes.

He slid his hand up her back, and her skin tingled as she waited for him to touch that intimate place right on the nape of her neck that would completely disarm her.

Don't! she screamed inside even as her body readied itself to feel his fingers there, tracing little shapes on the nape of her neck, making her knees go weak, making her pull him just a little closer.

He tilted her chin up and gazed into her eyes, his own looking hazy and dead sexy.

"Do you watch me only because you have to?" she asked him. "Are we dancing because I'm still just part of the job, and this is a ruse?"

He blinked. "Does this feel fake to you? Like I'm acting?"

"You could be," Sam pushed, hating herself for pulling this stunt. "Like back at the ice cream parlor."

"Yes, that was a fake kiss," he whispered. "Necessary for the ruse."

"Unnecessary, because they were just customers." She looked

up at him through her lashes. "It's probably not true, but I like to think you just wanted to kiss me and used the first excuse you could for the opportunity."

Eric's gaze turned smoldering. "Did I?" His whisper was edged with a growl. "Did I want to press you against the wall, like this?" She felt her back go snug against the rough wood at the back of the dancefloor.

"Brush your hair back like this?" His fingers went to a stray lock clinging to her cheek and gently swept it back behind her ear, sending tingles down the side of her face.

"Come in close, like this?" He leaned down until their lips were millimeters apart and her eyes dropped to half-mast.

"I think you did," Sam breathed. "I think you want to kiss me right now."

He pressed his body against hers and she met every inch greedily. Then his lips brushed hers so softly she wasn't sure if she'd imagined it.

"Samantha." He breathed her name and her skin came to life. There was nothing she wanted more than to kiss him, right here right now. His other hand came up and cupped the side of her face.

Then he pressed his lips against hers and the world caught fire.

Her hands went to his hair and moved downward—down his broad shoulders, over his muscular back that tapered into his jeans, to the tight ass she'd been admiring since he'd first turned his back and she'd taken a good, long look.

He groaned and pressed against her. There was no mistaking his level of excitement as she ground against him shamelessly. They kissed harder, their tongues twining, lips pressing hard until she was sure hers would be bruised in the morning—

The morning. She didn't want to think about the next day when she'd probably regret all of this. When she'd feel like a fool as he went back to being her babysitter, probably pretending none of this mattered or even happened.

But for now, she was his, and she didn't want the night to end.

"They'll be filming for the next few hours," she said against his throat.

Eric nearly carried her through her hotel room door. Her hands fumbled with the lock and when she used the flimsy excuse that she wasn't used to actual keys, he outright laughed. Finally, the hateful knob turned and the door flew open as he swept her up and took her inside. He kicked the door closed behind them and it slammed way too loudly, which of course made them laugh all the harder.

"Shh, we really have to be quiet," Sam said, trying to stifle her laughs. "And we have to be quick."

"Two things I don't want to be are quiet and quick," Eric answered as he sat her down on the bed and stood over her. She laid back and he followed her down, kissing her throat until she stifled a moan.

"Let yourself go," he murmured.

"We can't be loud," she protested.

"Oh, yes we can. No way I can stop now." He was already taking off her shirt, unbuttoning it from top to bottom, and planting kisses on every newly exposed inch of her skin. She sat up so that he could pull off her shirt and jacket at the same time. Of course she was wearing a sports bra instead of something sexy and lacy but he didn't seem to care as he gazed hungrily at her.

"Not exactly date attire," she said.

He shook his head, amused. "Doesn't matter. You're gorgeous, Samantha. Stunning."

His eyes blazed. Then he reached behind his shoulder blades and did the one-hand shirt pull-off. Her eyes went straight to his impressive abs—and the small, puckered shrapnel scars scattered across his right side.

She wasn't expecting those and she tried not to stare, so she looked away quickly—which was almost worse. His lids fell and he looked to the side, so she quickly threw her arms around his shoulders and kissed him deeply. *Please*, she begged silently, *don't think I'm rejecting you.*

If his passionate kiss was any indication, he'd received her message loud and clear. She ran her hands down his back and that's where she found several larger scars. He'd been a SEAL and she could only wonder what had happened.

No wonder he'd reacted the way he did. She wondered if he'd ever been rejected for them.

But she didn't wonder long. His hands moved down to her belt and he quickly had her out of it. The button and zipper on her jeans posed no problem and she lifted her butt just high enough for him to push them down to her boots. He left her undies in place—again, stupid boy shorts she'd picked for comfort over sexiness. But again, he didn't seem to mind. Eric feathered his fingers over her mound, teasing her with light circles over the cotton until she dug her short nails into his back and bit back a moan.

"Sorry, sorry," she said, realizing she was clenching him tightly enough to add more scars.

He didn't bother answering, not with words. He bent down between her legs, pulled her underwear down, and his tongue swirled over her clit. The sensation was almost too much, but he held her down as she arched into him. God, had anything ever felt so good? She bit her lower lip to keep from calling his name, but she couldn't help the other sounds she made. And the evil bastard hummed against her clit in response.

Sam hooked her legs around his torso and squeezed. Eric ran his hands up hers to thumb her tightening nipples under her bra. She covered his hands, moving his fingers under the fabric until he'd pulled it aside.

"Too...much..." she panted.

He paused only long enough to say, "Let yourself go." Then his tongue went back to work—swirling, pressing, licking. He brought one hand down and thrust a finger inside her and that was it. Sam plunged over the edge as if she were performing one of her stunts.

"How loud was I?" she asked when she returned to earth.

Eric laughed—a wonderful sound as always. "Pretty loud."

Just then they heard a couple of people stumbling and laughing through the hall outside and they both froze. *Lacey couldn't be back already, and with someone, could she?* Thank God, the voices moved on down the hall.

"Okay, well, we aren't the only ones taking advantage of the late-night filming," Sam said. She scooted to the edge of the bed and sat up. "Now, it's your turn."

Eric grinned wickedly at her before pulling off her boots one by one. "Next time, we'll leave these on, but maybe without the bunched-up jeans."

Sam giggled as she kicked them off. "Could you take one of my socks and put it over the doorknob outside?"

"One of your..." He smirked. "Yeah, okay."

She laughed as he flew across the room and opened the door just wide enough to allow his hand through, and covered the doorknob with her sock. Then he turned and started stalking back across the room.

"You'd better be totally naked by the time I get back there," he said.

"Yes, sir." She quickly wiggled out of her sports bra and pulled her boy shorts all the way off. "Now, what about you?" She pointed at his jeans. "Bit of a barrier there."

"You want to take care of that?" He kicked off his boots, then stopped and stood in front of her.

"I do." Sam looked up into his face and gave him the naughtiest grin she could. He rewarded her with a hiss as he inhaled. The moonlight coming through the sheer curtains showed off his muscles and the sly grin he gave her. Sam undid his belt and pulled it slowly through the loops.

"Hurry, unless you want me to use that on you," Eric growled.

"Mmm," she answered, then tossed it aside. She unbuttoned his jeans, then slowly pulled the zipper down over his erection. He'd already dampened his boxer briefs with pre-cum and the sight of it turned her on, letting her know he wanted her.

"Tell me you brought protection," she said.

He nodded and pulled out his wallet before she tugged his jeans down. He pulled out three condoms and said, "I have more back in my room."

"All righty then, jackrabbit—"

Eric roared with laughter and Sam shushed him.

"I'll show you a jackrabbit." He tossed the condoms on the bed, stepped out of his jeans, and started to climb onto the bed when Sam stopped him.

"Stay standing right where you are." She ran a finger down his length over his boxer briefs and was satisfied to watch his cock bob and strain against the cloth all on its own as he groaned.

"Sam," he warned, his voice sounding strained.

"Just let me play," she said. Then she hooked her fingers into the waistband and pulled down. *And, oh. My. Goodness.* Of course she could tell how thick and long he was through the cloth, but then to actually see him?

Whoa.

And it was all hers.

But first.

"Take your socks off."

He blinked down at her. "Huh?"

"Your socks. They're still on. I am not sleeping with a dude while his socks are still on." She pointed at his feet. "Not unless we're in Alaska. I'll make an exception for Alaska."

By now he was laughing again, his cock bobbing, which made Sam crack up. She'd never—ever—had so much fun playing with a guy like this. Normally, she'd find herself with some guy who was starstruck, or she'd realize too late that he was pretty much there for the bragging rights. But with Eric, she was having honest-to-God fun.

Socks removed, Eric again tried to get on the bed.

"Nope. Stand at attention." She glanced at his curved erection, its head brushing his belly. "I mean, you know."

He was still shaking his head and holding back laughter when she took him in her mouth.

And that's when things turned serious. Eric's entire body shivered, his hands gripped her shoulders, and his eyes drifted closed.

"You don't have to..." he started.

"I want to. I happen to love doing this." She swirled her tongue around his tip to make her point and his breathing quickened. He kneaded her shoulders and she ran her hands over his gorgeous asscheeks until he clenched them.

"Jesus, Samantha," he said through gritted teeth.

Sam took as much of him as she could into her mouth and sucked hard until her cheeks went hollow. She brought one hand around to cup his balls, gently tugging at the skin before cupping them again. This close, she reveled in the cool, tangy smell of his skin.

"Sam," he hissed. "You need to stop. I can't hold back."

His body shuddered and she got ready for him to come. Instead, he pulled back and his cock slipped out of her mouth. He looked wild-eyed, desperate.

"Lie back," he ordered as he reached for one of the condoms. He tore the foil open and she grabbed his hands.

"Let me," she said.

He grabbed both her hands and looked deep into her eyes. "Can't."

She nodded and he dropped her hands. Sam scooted back onto the bed and watched him roll the condom down the length of his shaft. He lined himself up with her entrance, his gaze never leaving hers.

"You're sure you want this, baby?" he asked.

"God, yes," Sam answered. She reached down between them and guided him inside her.

And, oh, God, did it feel good to be stretched. He didn't hesitate or tease her, but went in as deeply as he could. She squeezed around him and he groaned.

"Oh, that feels so good, Samantha." He started to move inside her and she raised her hips. She pushed against him every time he buried himself until they had a perfect rhythm going. Sam was surprised when she felt herself start building to another orgasm.

"Your eyes are round, what is it?" Eric asked. "Am I hurting you?"

"No, oh, God, no. You're...I'm going to..." She closed her eyes and concentrated on the pleasure—and on Eric's chuckle.

"That's my girl. We're going to ride this one together." He started rubbing her clit in the small circles she loved. Sam gripped his shoulders as the next wave crashed over her. Eric threw his head back. Sweat beaded on his forehead as his body tensed and he pumped deep. He groaned out her name through clenched teeth before relaxing. Then he wrapped his arms around her and rolled with her to his back. She felt utterly boneless as she draped her body over his.

He stroked her hair as they both caught their breath.

I love you. The words came to her unbidden, but they were true. She loved him. He understood and respected her. And she loved the man he was. Real, honest. A lover of butter brickle ice cream.

She giggled.

"What?" He grinned.

"Brickle."

He looked at her like she'd lost her mind before he started laughing too.

"Awesome!" she said. "Every time I want to hear you laugh, all I have to do is say brickle in a bad British accent."

Which made him laugh harder.

I do love you, Eric Armstrong.

"Jesus, fuck, you're beautiful," he growled as he ran his fingers over her cheek.

She went stiff in his arms. This was what she was afraid of. She didn't want him to call her beautiful. She wanted him to be different from everyone else.

"Don't," she whispered.

"Don't what, Sam?" He propped himself up and studied her face. His expression had gone serious, like she was a problem he needed to solve. She looked away.

"Hey." He gently turned her face back to his. Now his eyes had gone soft. "Don't do this. Don't push me away, Sam. Not now. Not after this."

She was tempted to say something snarky, to do exactly what he didn't want and push him away. But instead, she told him the plain truth.

"It's all anyone ever says to me. How beautiful I am. It's all anyone cares about. My face. How I'd look on the screen in something skimpy."

"That's because they don't know you. I watched you fly through the air like an angel, but I'm not talking about something soft and white and sweet. You were on fire. You were vengeance and might. You're beautiful to me because you're strong and willful. The world doesn't see that part of you—yet. But they will when this movie comes out. And I hate that a little bit. I'll have to share the real you with the rest of the world."

Oh. Was that what was thinking back at Rafferty's, when his gaze went far away?

He shook his head. "I hate myself for saying that, because you need to be who you were meant to be, and all I can say is, get ready, world. You can't handle Sam Collins."

Sam shifted until she could look into his eyes. "You want to keep seeing me once we're back home?"

SEVENTEEN

Eric couldn't believe what he was hearing. Was Sam asking him if he wanted to keep seeing her after this—to make their relationship official—because that's what she wanted too? Or was it so that she could turn him down right now before things went any further?

He studied her gorgeous face and the serious look in her eyes, a look that had replaced the playfulness from only moments ago.

I'm no good for her. Of course she'll want this to end once we're back home. Why wouldn't she? I'm too serious. I'm broken inside and I bring her down.

"There is nothing I want more than to keep seeing you Sam, I just want to make that clear. But I understand why you'd want to leave me behind when we get back."

"Eric—"

"It's okay. I mean, I'm not exactly in my twenties."

She grimaced. "God, is *that* it? I'm sorry I told you Jake said you were too old for me. It's not true. I mean, you're only in your thirties, that's not exactly the age where you start getting in line at four-thirty for the dinner buffet."

Dammit, there she goes making me laugh again.

He shook his head. "I'm serious. I'm not a kid."

She stopped smiling and tensed. "I'm not a kid, either."

Shit. This is why this won't work. I keep fucking up.

"That came out wrong, and it's not what I meant." He pushed her hair back from her face. "You are in no way, shape, or form a kid. But you're young, Samantha. Young in here." He tapped her heart. "I'm not. I feel old some days. I've seen a lot of bad. Enough to turn me away from the world at times."

Sam's lips parted as if she'd just realized something.

"*That's* why you're writing a screenplay." She propped herself up on her elbow.

He frowned. "I don't follow."

"You've turned away from *this* world, so that's why you're creating a different one that you don't want to turn away from. A world you can love again, to replace this one that let you down so badly. Maybe you're writing it so that you can reconnect with this one."

"I..." He wanted to argue, say that she was wrong, that he wrote a screenplay only because he'd been a movie buff all his life.

"I love movies. I have since I was little. When there was nothing else to do on the ranch and Dad..." He shook his head.

"Dad what?" she asked quietly.

He shrugged. "Dad insisted there was no time for that shit. That ranch life didn't allow frivolities, as he put it. God, I hated that place. Still do. I haven't been back in years. Not since Mom died." Eric grinned. "Now, my mom, *she* loved movies. She could name every actor and actress going all the way back to...Jesus, the twenties, I think. Didn't matter what it was—eighties rom-com, classic black and white, action-adventure, horror—she knew them all. Loved them all. And she'd argue with Dad to let me watch them with her. Sundays were our day. Dad would get so pissed, and then he'd work me twice as hard the rest of the week. Called me lazy and soft. I didn't care. I lived for those Sundays when I could..." He stopped when he realized his eyes were wet.

"When you could what?"

"When I could escape into a world I didn't fucking hate so much. And I could do it with someone I loved, who loved me for... for who *I* was. Those movies saved us from being lonely. Saved me from turning out as mean and small-minded as my father." He looked at Sam's hand in his and wondered when he'd taken it and how long he'd been gripping it so hard. Her eyes were wet and he was afraid he'd hurt her." Eric eased up. "Sorry."

Sam shook her head. "No, that's not why I'm..." She wiped her eyes. "Your mom sounds like a wonderful person."

"She was awesome. You would have loved her. She would have loved you."

Sam smiled softly. "No wonder you wanted this job. This is still your escape. Even bigger than a screenplay because you can immerse yourself full-body into it." She brought his hand to her lips and kissed his fingers. "Eric. I'm sorry for ever giving you shit about being here. I was completely wrong and unfair and selfish."

"Samantha, you can shut that down right now. I told you that I wouldn't have taken this job if I knew it was to guard you. That was a lie. I could've still told Gina and Lach no and turned it down. Instead, I jumped twice as fast to take it, knowing I could keep you safe. That I could protect you. That I could spend actual time with you, in person."

He pulled her back down into his arms. She laid her head on his chest.

"You know I laughed out loud every single time you said something funny in a text while I was guarding Annalie. Your messages were the highlight of my day when we were out on the road. I hated that I felt like I had to keep them to myself. I wanted to show them off—not because the daughter of Bette and Grant Collins was texting me, but because I wanted to show the world that this smart, funny person existed. Murray caught me laughing a couple of times, but he was enough of a gentleman not to pry, but do you know how many times I wanted to show him one of your texts just so I could share my laughter with someone?"

He felt Samantha shake her head.

"It's true, Sam. You're amazing and I've known it since we met. I've loved you a long time now."

She took in a quick breath. He felt sudden wetness between his chest and her cheek.

"I love you, too, Eric."

"This isn't an escape for me, Sam. There's no damn movie set or screenplay that's going to reconnect me to this world. Because you already have."

Samantha's phone buzzed from somewhere inside her purse, waking them up. The room was dark and the air conditioning was off—another outage.

"Murph," she mumbled. Her face was tucked against Eric's pec.

It buzzed again.

"Better get that," he said halfheartedly as he nuzzled her hair. He didn't want to let her go yet. How long had they been asleep?

"Whoever it is, they're dead to me." Sam rolled over and picked her purse up off the floor. "Well, crap, it's Lacey. I like her too much so she's not dead to me." Sam read the text. "Yeah, she's really not dead to me because this is a heads-up that they're all heading back soon."

Buzz.

Sam read the text and laughed, then turned her phone to show Eric.

I'll keep walking if I see a sock. She'd followed her message with a winking emoji.

"Busted by your twin," Eric said as he started to get out of bed. "At least she's keeping us from getting busted by anyone else."

"Not that they'd see anything in the hall. When did the power go out again?" Sam turned on one of the battery-powered lamps Quincy had ordered for everyone. "More importantly, where do you think you're going?" Sam pulled him back into bed. Not that he fought her. "They'll be there another hour at least."

"Wishful thinking."

She looked him up and down. "But we still have a condom left. Time for round three."

Eric chuckled and wrapped his arms around her. "I think you miscounted. We used them all."

"Wait, what?" Sam grinned and counted on her fingers. "Let's see. First, you ate me out and sent me through the ceiling, but we didn't need a condom for that. Are you blushing? Okay, then there was our first time." She pulled his head down to hers and they kissed. "Which, I have no idea how, but you made me orgasm again. So, that was condom one."

"Right. Keep going." Damn, if he wasn't getting turned on all over again.

"And then after we talked, you turned me over on my stomach. Do you remember that?"

"I could never forget the sight of your lovely ass and the way you wiggled it at me."

Sam grinned. Her hand found its way to his cock which had already stood up to pay attention to her storytelling. She gripped his shaft and moved up and down slowly, adding a twist as she stroked. "You like my ass?"

"Oh, yeah, I do. And I really like what you're doing right now. But there was nothing like feeling how wet you were while you laid there and let me stroke your gorgeous pussy. Like this." He reached between her legs and was not surprised to find her just as wet and swollen now as she was before. "And then, it felt even better to run my tip over your lips. Up and down until you were begging me to fuck you. So I pushed in until I had that gorgeous ass right up against my belly. Now who's blushing?"

Sam giggled. "Okay, so that was...mmm...condom number two. What about...oh my God...number three?" She gasped as he slid a finger inside her while he rubbed her clit with his thumb.

Eric nuzzled into her neck and took over the storytelling. "I'm not done talking about the second one yet. I can't get over the way you squeezed around my cock like a velvet vise." He rubbed her faster as she closed her eyes and arched her back. "And then to feel you pulsing around me while you said my name—pure heaven, baby. I don't think I've ever come so hard in my life." He slipped her earlobe between his lips and bit down gently. Sam rewarded him by palming the tip of his cock and rubbing in circles. He groaned.

"So, the third one?" she gasped.

"Third one, let's see." He felt around the bed. "Yeah, it's right here."

"See? I *told* you!" She playfully slapped his upper arm and he laughed.

"Oh, for the third time? I was just looking into the future." He tried not to laugh again at the look she gave him. "Which is here, because we're going to use it right now."

"Give that to me." She snatched the packet out of his free hand and let go of him. He missed her touch immediately, but when she rolled the condom down his shaft, he had to hold himself back. Every touch she gave him was pure heaven. He eased her back, still pleasuring her until she was gasping and bucking against him.

"Eric, *please*," she begged.

"Please, what?" He couldn't help grinning at her.

"Inside me, now."

"Mmm, not yet."

Just before she came, he thrust inside her. She reacted immediately, clutching him. He watched her face, and at the last moment, she opened her eyes and gazed straight into his.

Nothing but fierce, proud beauty.

"I love you," he whispered into her neck after.

"I love you, too."

EIGHTEEN

Sam didn't want Eric to go to his room. She wanted to steal every spare moment she could with him, and they didn't have many left.

"I'm dying of thirst," she said. "I need a soda."

"I saw Edna restocking the cooler when we came in," Eric said.

"Me too. Care to join me?"

"Absolutely. I need to check on the dogs first. That okay?"

"Sounds great. Are they doing okay here?"

"They're better than we are right now. It's nice and cool down there." Eric kissed her, then pulled her up with him as he sat up. They quickly got dressed and opened the door. Voices rose from the front stairwell—everyone was back. Sam quickly snatched her sock off the doorknob and tossed it into the room. They stifled their laughter as they sprinted to the back stairs.

A faint light glowed from the front desk, a camping lantern that illuminated Edna's face as she read a book of Mary Oliver's poems. There was something so peaceful and calm about the scene that it made Eric take Sam's hand, and she let him.

Simple as that.

They continued down the last flight of stairs to the basement.

"You're right, it's so much cooler down here," Sam whispered.

All the dogs but one were asleep. Petey, a mix of lab and pit bull, sat at the front of his kennel as if he'd been waiting for them.

"Nothing to do but take him for a walk." Eric took down one of the leashes hanging on a peg on the wall. The dog wagged his stump of a tail. Eric let Petey out and clipped the leash to his collar. They headed back upstairs to the lobby.

Edna looked up briefly as she turned a page. "What can I do you for?" she asked as they approached her.

"Did the others leave anything?" Eric asked, pointing at the big red cooler beside the desk.

"A couple of Cokes, I think."

"Perfect," Sam said. "We'll take them."

Eric dug around in the ice-filled cooler, handed Sam a blessedly cold bottle of Coke, then insisted on paying for both. They clinked bottles—glass ones from Mexico, bless Edna's good taste—and Sam drank nearly half of hers in one go. She pointed at Edna's book and asked her, "I love Mary Oliver. What's your favorite line?"

Edna gave her a surprised smile. "I like the one where she asks you to tell her what you plan to do with your one wild, precious life."

Sam nodded. "I always liked that one too."

Edna leaned forward and asked in a conspirative voice, "You know what the right answer is, don't you?"

Sam tilted her head. "No."

Enda grinned. "Whatever you want."

Sam's grin turned into a big smile as she grabbed Eric's hand and squeezed it. "Then right now I want to go for a nice long walk in the moonlight."

Edna winked. "Good plan." She went back to reading, and Sam and Eric headed for the front doors.

About the only sound was Petey's nails clicking on the sidewalk. They walked quietly to a little park across the street to let him sniff around. The main street was dark and quiet, but that was every night, since half the storefronts were empty. Without streetlights blotting them out, the stars blanketed the sky above.

"Beautiful, aren't they?" Sam said.

Eric nodded. "Haven't seen this many stars in a long time."

"Since you left Montana?"

"You could see a lot of stars there, sure. But the last time I saw this many was Afghanistan."

"Oh, right." She watched Petey going tree to tree, sniffing. "You were a dog handler there?"

"I was, yeah." Eric squeezed the bridge of his nose.

"You don't want to talk about it."

"It's not that. It's other parts."

"You don't have to." She squeezed his hand, then took him in her arms. Eric held her tight and nuzzled the top of her head.

"You fell asleep with me tonight," he said.

"Yeah. Is that a problem?"

"It wasn't. Tonight."

Sam pulled back to look at him. "Is it a problem sometimes?"

His face went serious. "Sometimes." He focused his attention on the sky again. "I'm having a good night tonight. I haven't seen a sky full of stars or slept beside a woman in a long time."

"You have nightmares."

He looked back down and nodded.

"Bad enough that you don't let yourself fall asleep with a woman there."

Eric said nothing for a minute. "The first and only time I did, I scared her. Now, I don't."

"Do you still have them often?" She stroked his cheek.

Eric shook his head. "I hadn't for a long time."

Sam smiled. "Then it won't be a problem for us."

He pressed her hand against his cheek before clasping it in his and kissing her fingers. "I had one the first night here."

"Oh. What do you think caused it?" She looked back across the street. "Is it the town, the abandoned buildings?"

"No, it's not the town. I know exactly what it is." He let go of her hand and dropped his arms to his sides. She shivered without his heat against her.

"Hey." She grabbed his hand. "Then tell me. It might help."

A series of emotions crossed his face. A whole spectrum from doubt to a glimmer of hope. Finally, he took her in his arms again.

"It was a cold day in Kandahar. The middle of February. Perfect dogfighting season, according to the locals."

NINETEEN

"I'd been stationed in Kandahar for six months. This was my first deployment, and I was eager to prove myself. I had a talent for languages and quickly learned that what the locals spoke was a world apart from what I'd learned on base. Whenever me and the other guys went out, I was the designated translator."

Eric grinned at Sam. "And even knowing what I did, I still fucked up quite a bit. Some people were patient with my mistakes, but others weren't. I found that the best way to learn a language was to talk to the kids, who sometimes had more English than their parents. The trick to persuading them to give me a language lesson was of course befriending them. So I always carried candy."

"Ha. Kids are the same the world over," Sam said.

"Pretty much. Only, oftentimes these kids would also ask for cigarettes, but that's where I drew the line."

Sam nodded. "Obviously."

"The other way to a kid's heart was through sports. Unfortunately, one of the most popular sports in the area was dogfighting. The sport—if you can call it that, and I couldn't—had been banned under the Taliban. Men would go to a dog breeder's house, kill the dogs, and beat the breeder. Sometimes the breeder was killed too. When the Taliban was driven from the area, dogfighting became popular again. Some people still frowned on it since it was against the Koran. *Dogs cannot speak for themselves so we must be kind to them* was the argument that people who hated dogfighting gave for their reason."

"I never knew that," Sam said.

"Yup. But there were plenty who did like it. Poorer men enjoyed watching the fights as a cure to their boredom, or a way to drive up their adrenaline. Richer men, those with political positions and the ones high up in the militia placed huge bets on each battle. They even bred and sold dogs, sometimes getting as much as a hundred thousand dollars. Some of the bets went to twenty thousand. So dog fighting permeated every level of society. And in the winter? Dogfighting bouts became very common."

Eric drew in a deep breath. Could he continue? Sam looked at him expectantly. Yeah, he could. For her.

"I often mingled in the crowd undercover so I could overhear discussions and pick out the key players in the area. It was amazing what people talk about when they're at a sporting event, thinking that they were safe in a crowd."

He hesitated. "But that was the problem, wasn't it? People often thought they were safe in a crowd."

Sam kissed him. Then she led him to a nearby park bench and they sat. Petey trotted up to the two humans, took one look at them, then dropped his head onto Eric's lap for pets.

Dogs always know who needs them the most.

Eric scratched Petey's head absently.

"That day, I hung back on the edge of the crowd. I'd seen one of the local boys, Akbar, and wanted to keep an eye on him. Good kid, friendly, always quick with a lesson for some candy, but once I gained his trust, all he wanted to do was teach me enough so we could talk about dogfighting. He was smaller than the other boys, wiry, but very clever. He had his own dog. A scruffy mongrel he'd named Sting." Eric grinned. "Before you ask, yes, he named him after the singer."

Sam laughed lightly. "I like this kid."

Eric nodded. "I did, too. But the other boys called the dog Loser —the same name they called Akbar. Sting would never fight in the main ring. He had no chance against the locally-bred Kuchi dogs."

"Kuchi dogs?"

Eric nodded. "They guarded livestock, and they could get massive. Sting wasn't one of those. Poor Sting's fate was to whet the appetites of the champion-level dogs. But Akbar was ever-hopeful that Sting would fight.

"Wasn't he afraid Sting would die in the ring?"

"Oh, no, the dogs wouldn't fight to the death. They were way too valuable. Sting would have had a better life in the ring, ironically." Eric closed his eyes. "Except, he wouldn't have lived if..."

He felt Sam put her arm around him. He petted Petey.

"That day, when Akbar saw me, he raised his hand and waved, a huge grin crossing his face. 'Today is Sting's day,' he said. Every day was Sting's day, according to Akbar. The little boy never gave up hope. God, the kid was so thin that I knew he was giving every last scrap of food he had to his dog. And even the dog was thin. So I made sure to tell Akbar that chocolate was bad for dogs whenever I gave him an oversized candy bar. Which I did that day."

Eric remembered pulling the chocolate bar out of his backpack. It was still solid because of the cold. Akbar's brown eyes went round.

"He said, 'Thank you, my friend. I wish I could give this to Sting, but I won't. I promised you I wouldn't.'

"I told him, 'That's good Akbar. That one's for you.' I pulled out a Slim Jim and it quickly disappeared into Sting's mouth.

"'So who do you think will win today?' I asked him.

"'Well, if Sting gets his chance, of course he will win. But otherwise, I think Black Bear will.'

"Really? You think he has a chance against the Wolf?'

"'Of course he does. Sting helped train him.' He patted his dog affectionately, and I laughed at the two of them.

"'Well then,' I said, 'Black Bear will win.'"

Eric had run his hand over the boy's hair affectionately before walking away. While he was talking to Akbar, his ears were perked up for other more important, if not more interesting, conversations in the crowd. And he thought he heard one. Eric carefully made his way toward the two men who were speaking about betting and about other things. He was pretty sure it was troop movements.

"But I needed to get closer. To be sure."

Just then, the crowd roared as the next two dogs got ready to fight. Eric watched six men enter the ring. Two were green-jacketed referees. The other four held back two dogs, two men per dog, on thick ropes. The dogs barked and snarled at each other. Eric's targets immediately stopped talking and began cheering for the dogs. Black Bear was the clear favorite, judging by the crowd's cheers.

The men quickly but carefully turned loose their dogs and stepped back. The animals were immediately upon each other, barking, scratching, growling, biting, determining dominance.

"I could barely watch. It was bad enough that men fought each other, but to make loyal, faithful dogs face off against each other for entertainment and money? I couldn't stand it."

So while it was pointless to try and listen in on any conversations, Eric found his gaze drifting back toward Akbar. The boy loved Sting, and the dog loved him right back. Akbar laughed as the dog licked the last of the chocolate from around the boy's mouth.

"I took my eyes off him for one second, and when I looked back, he was staring straight at me with the strangest expression on his face. I watched as he let go of Sting's rope, and the dog went running off."

Can I do this? He looked at Sam in the starlight, quiet and patient. No judgment. No fear. Just love in her eyes.

"Akbar started yelling, 'Help me, friend!' He stared right at me, not at his dog running away, but at me to come and help him. He was desperate.

Friend, friend, come help me. Come help me catch him. Friend, friend, now, friend!

Akbar backed away slowly from the crowd, gesturing to Eric to follow him.

Eric started trotting toward Akbar, who smiled, turned, and began running after his dog. Eric picked up speed, following Akbar as closely as he could. The boy started down an alley. Eric turned to head around the building, hoping to block Sting from the other side.

And that's when the explosion tore through the crowd behind them.

Sam covered her mouth at Eric's words, then quickly dropped her hand and grabbed both of his.

"It threw me off my feet, sent me face down into the dirt. The ringing in my ears blocked out all other sounds at first, but when it faded all I could hear were men shouting and dogs screaming. When I looked up, there was no sign of Akbar, no sign of Sting. So I prayed that the two got away safely. And I thanked God for the little boy who saved my life."

"Eric. That's horrible."

"Ninety dead that day in the crowd. Even more wounded." Eric touched his side, the one covered in shrapnel scars. "It was a red-on-red attack."

"Red on red?"

"Local power struggle. For all I know, the two men I was listening to were the targets. They were among the dead. If I hadn't befriended Akbar, I would be too. I never saw him again, so I never got to ask, but I think he must have looked up in time to see the suicide bomber making his way through the crowd, or something tipped him off. And I'm the one he decided to save. Because I gave him a goddamned chocolate bar now and then."

"More than that. You gave him attention. You gave him kindness when everyone else called him a loser." Sam touched Eric's face. "You saved him a little bit every day you were there."

"It was just...so little, really."

"Not to him." Sam shifted on the bench until she was sitting right up against him. "No wonder you're having nightmares again. The dogfighting stuff is bringing it back."

"I'll be fine."

"I know you will." She kissed his cheek. "I'm not afraid of you. Of sleeping next to you."

That made him feel like a million bucks.

They finished their bottles of Coke and watched the stars.

Then something in the air changed. Maybe it was talking about Kandahar, but Eric felt on edge, as if someone might jump out at them from a dark doorway. The hair on the back of his neck stood up. He went on high alert, and Sam noticed immediately.

"What's wrong?" she asked as she surreptitiously looked back and forth.

"I'm just—"

"Protecting me. Got it."

"I was going to say feeling watched. But I don't see anyone. I think we should head back though."

They crossed the street, Petey still in the lead. "You're good, you know," he told Sam.

"Good?"

"You noticed the change in my demeanor immediately, and you looked around carefully," Eric said. "You're observant, and I saw you using your martial arts skills yesterday in that fight scene. You can handle yourself just fine, Sam."

She looked at him with surprise. "Thank you."

"It's true. But, it's still my job to make sure you're safe, and I will always take it seriously."

TWENTY

Sam and Eric climbed the dark stairs. At least the hotel had gotten the generator going so that a red light lit the steps enough that they didn't have to use their phones as flashlights. As soon as they got to the third floor, Sam spotted someone standing down the hall in front of her room. The shape was too big to be Lacey, but not bulky. Eric tensed behind her.

"Let me through first," he said in a low voice, pushing past her.

"Don't be silly, it's just Tristian." She recognized his build even in the dim light from the window at the end of the hall.

As they neared Tristian, he stood up taller once he realized Sam wasn't by herself.

"I saw you dash downstairs and didn't think you'd ever come back up. I need to talk to you," he shifted his gaze to Eric, "alone."

"I don't think so. I'm tired and I have a long day tomorrow."

"So do I," he whined. "So I wouldn't be here if it wasn't important. Now, send Dog Boy home so we can talk."

At that, Eric moved forward. Sam placed a hand on his chest to stop him.

"I've got this, Eric." She stood on her toes and planted a kiss firmly on his lips. "I'll see you tomorrow."

Eric smiled. "I know you do." He pulled her in close and kissed her again. "I'm still going to make sure you get into your room safely. And soon, I hope." The confident punch of a smile he gave Tristian made the man flinch. Then Eric headed down the hall to his room—where he leaned against the wall outside the door, arms crossed.

Good. Eric's presence would encourage Tristian to say what he had to say quickly, then leave. Truth was, she kind of liked what Eric was doing right now, which felt more like a safety net than anything overprotective.

"So, talk," she told Tristian. "But make it snappy."

He leaned against the doorframe. "Fine, I'll just get right to it. I'm convinced Quincy had you read for him and I'm wondering why you didn't spare us all the trouble and just take the lead for this movie."

Jesus. This is what he wanted to talk about?

"I didn't take it because I didn't read for Shawna's role. I wasn't even offered it."

"That's not what I'm hearing."

"Well, then stop reading the gossip sites because they're wrong." She pointed at herself. "Stunt. Woman."

"Well, that's just it, isn't it? You are a stuntwoman, and stuntwomen don't do stand-ins."

Sam rolled her eyes. "Quincy and I talked about that. I'm trying to help out here, just like everyone else. It's a non-union—"

"This goes way beyond the definition of non-union, Samantha. But I wouldn't expect a non-professional to understand that. I'm surprised your mother never taught you better."

"Wow. I think we're done talking now. And you can feel free to leave me alone from here on out." She reached for the doorknob and Tristian grabbed her wrist. He let go the second she glared at him.

"Wait, please. I'm sorry, that was totally out of line."

"You bet it was."

Footsteps behind her told her that Eric was heading their way. She looked over her shoulder. "Eric, it's cool. I've got this."

He shocked her when he put his hands up in a gesture of, *All right, if you say so.* He really did trust she had the situation under control.

Tristian gestured at the hotel room door, and presumably Lacey inside. "Face it. Quincy's filming you because Lacey sucks, Samantha."

"I beg to differ. Lacey is great on-screen. You're the one who's phoning it in."

He looked deeply offended. "I am *not.*"

"You are. Look, I thought you were great in *Only the Young Die Pretty*—"

"What about in *Balefire's Revenge*?" She watched insecurity creep over his features. "Quincy loved me in that and that's why I'm here."

"Oh, you mean *Invincible Gods Part Four*?" She said it just to watch him sneer. "Yeah, for a superhero movie, you were fine—"

"I did most of the stunts."

Sam knew for a fact he hadn't, but she brushed off his casual lie. "Right, but as far as acting goes, you were amazing in *Pretty*. I was expecting the same in this movie. I figured that's why you're here, to get back to your roots, too. Why aren't you doing your best now?"

That took Tristian aback. He stared at her as his jaw dropped and that look of insecurity flared. "I always bring my A-game."

"Well, I beg to differ. Honestly, I think you overextended yourself in *Invincible Gods* and hoped you could get your mojo back on this one. But, you haven't."

"I do whenever *we're* in a scene together."

"Those aren't scenes. I'm not acting, I'm standing in." She was tempted to add *I'm just your fluffer* but she wasn't that cruel. "I can't act. I'm terrible." Realization dawned on her. "The reason why you're better when it's me is that I *am* so bad. You're intimidated by Lacey because she's so good."

Tristian shook his head vehemently. "No. It's Lacey who's fucking things up. She's the one with zero talent, not me."

Sam was officially done with this bullshit. If he wasn't pulling punches then neither would she.

"Lacey's acting her heart out. She has to, since you're bringing the romantic chemistry of a dead eel to every scene."

His eyes blazed. "You really are a spoiled brat, you know that? I wanted to talk to you because I was going to tell you that I think you'd do a much better job, and that if you grew up, realized that Quincy's filming you because Lacey's dooming this movie, and then stepped into the role officially, we'd make an amazing team. I think we'd have Oscar potential with this. But forget it. I'd have worse chemistry with you."

"Oh, thank God, because I don't think I'd be able to stand your breath if we had to kiss."

His nostrils flared. "You little bitch."

She raised her hand to slap Tristian, but he grabbed her arm, then pulled her into a kiss. She felt his teeth cut her lip as he forced his slimy tongue into her mouth and—oh, gag—his breath was even worse than when he was talking.

Sam fell back on her martial arts training without even thinking about it and elbowed him in the gut, which thankfully broke the kiss.

"Jesus, your breath is rank! Lacey deserves combat pay for kissing you." She stuck her finger in his face. "Don't you ever, *ever* pull that shit again. I didn't want to kiss you, I want nothing to do with you, and if you ever try it again, I'll—"

The idiot reached for her. She didn't bother with a slap but decked him instead.

Tristian hit the floor.

Sam stood over him, calm and ready for his next move.

Then Eric was clapping as he walked toward them. When he got close, she could make out the huge, proud smile on his face in the red glow of the emergency lights. He offered Tristian a hand up.

Tristian looked at Eric's hand like it might sprout fangs and bite him. "Why you helping me up? So that you can hit me too?"

"No, man. I only fight real threats. Sam handled the situation just fine. All I'm trying to do is to get you up and out of here so my amazing woman can go to bed."

Tristian clambered up without help. He smoothed down his shirt while eying both of them as he walked backward toward his room. "You don't see it, but Quincy's burning you, Samantha. I hope he fucks up your career."

"He's not and he won't." She put every ounce of the confidence she didn't feel into her voice until Tristian disappeared into his room.

He's trying to burn you. First Lacey's suspicions, now Tristian's.

Big hands landed on her shoulders and massaged them. "You're tense. Are you all right?"

"Yeah. Thank you." She covered Eric's hands with hers.

"Don't let him get to you."

She shook her head. "He's not." It wasn't Tristian who bothered her, it was Quincy. She needed to talk to him. But first, she needed to have a hard conversation with someone else.

The next day, Samantha had the morning to herself. She stared at her cell phone for five minutes as her finger hovered over her mother's number.

At the last second, she hit her dad's number instead.

"Hey, sweetheart." Her dad's deep, warm timbre came over the phone, putting her instantly at ease. "How's my daredevil?"

"Am I catching you at a bad time?"

"No, not at all." She heard leather creaking and pictured him settling into his favorite library chair by the window. "So how's it going? You still in the Dark Ages at the hotel?"

Sam laughed. "I'm in my room right now because the power came back on again this morning and the air conditioner is working. Otherwise, I'd probably be calling you from Rafferty's."

"Rafferty's?"

"Oh my God, Dad, you would love it. It's this roadhouse straight out of the early seventies but the best part is the jukebox. It's practically a shrine to The Eagles." She paused as she thought of a certain track, and she shivered all over. "Seriously, it's like they found your collection of eight-tracks and went 'Yup, gotta stuff a jukebox full of this.'"

Grant laughed.

"The Eagles dominate but there's Boston, and Journey—"

"'Don't Stop Believin'?"

"Yeah, that, but even better. 'Still They Ride.' And of course Gerry Rafferty—"

"Baker Street?"

"You know it."

"You sound good, kid. Really good."

"I'm happy, Dad."

"Then I'm happy for you, sweetheart. So tell me how it's going on set."

"Oh, fine." *Time to do a little fishing.* "I'm sure Ken's given you a full report already."

Her dad cleared his throat. "He says you're doing a great job."

Uh-huh. "And that I'm a pain in the ass, right?"

Grant chuckled. "He phrased it as you aren't afraid to stand up for yourself and every stuntwoman who's ever lived."

She snorted. "Did he also tell you that they were getting ready to use a man to double as a woman?"

"He said that was Quincy's call and he didn't like it much." Her dad's tone had changed. "How's Quincy treating you?"

"Fine." Now that they'd come to it, she hesitated. "But he's not treating Lacey so well. Neither is Tristian."

Leather creaked and she pictured her dad sitting up straight. "What's happening?"

"It's...weird. And I'm trying to figure it out. It might just be my imagination though."

"Is your gut telling you it's your imagination?"

She let out a long breath. "Can I tell you what's happening and get your perspective first?"

"Of course, sweetheart."

Sam smoothed the comforter on the bed. "We're all pitching in together here, doing all sorts of jobs."

"Quincy's putting his own money into this. He'll save a buck on labor so he can add it to the stunt budget. Ken says it's big."

"And I get that. But I'm not just doing stunts but stand-ins for Lacey, especially with Tristian."

Her dad grunted. "*With* Tristian? Not Tristian's stand-in? Or I guess double if you're all pitching in."

"Nope, with Tristian. That's even odder now that I've said it out loud."

"Mmm. Agreed. What do you think is going on?"

"Well, Lacey is convinced that Quincy wants to replace her with me, that he's filming scenes ahead of when he finally convinces me to step in. I told her that's ridiculous. But last night, Tristian basically told me the same thing. Then...he tried to kiss me."

"What?" More creaking leather as her dad stood up.

"It's fine, I handled it."

"*You* handled it? Where was...I mean..."

"Dad, stop. Eric was right there the whole time. Let's not pretend I don't know he's my babysitter."

"Sam—" He sounded regretful.

"It's fine, Dad. I'm not mad about it anymore. He's not as overbearing as I was afraid he'd be. As a matter of fact, he knew I had the situation in hand so he stood by and let me play it out. If I'd been in any real danger, I know he would have jumped in, but it was just Tristian."

"So what happened?"

Shit. "I decked Tristian."

Silence. Then her dad erupted in laughter.

"I shouldn't be laughing, but Jesus Christ. Like father like daughter."

Now Sam stood up. "Wait, what?"

"I had occasion to hit the jackass once." Grant sounded almost embarrassed.

"I never knew that." Sam started pacing.

"Neither does your mother. And you won't hear any more about it because I should have kept my cool and it isn't important now anyway. But that man could piss off the Pope." She heard a faint chuckle. "He still have a glass jaw?"

"Like Waterford crystal."

He laughed again, which made Sam laugh too. Her dad's laugh was almost as satisfying to hear as Eric's. But Grant had an easy laugh and he did it often. Eric's laugh was more precious to Sam for its rarity.

"Sorry, sweetheart. Now, let's see. You're afraid that Lacey and Tristian are both right, and that Quincy is going to try and get you to step into Lacey's role."

"You hit it on the head, Dad." Sam worried her bottom lip as she waited for him to tell her to walk. She knew that's what her mom would say, along with a heaping helping of *I told you so.*

"Stuntpeople like us need to listen to our gut." She couldn't help but smile at the word *us.*

"What's yours telling you?"

Sam paced faster. "It's...I'm not sure. I know something isn't right, Dad. But I'm a terrible actress. I've said a few lines and he can't possibly want me to act."

Sam heard bike engines outside and looked out at the street below. Five motorcycles roared down the street.

"Are you on set?"

"No, I'm at the hotel. It's just some guys riding by."

"Random or a club?"

"I don't know. I think there's a club somewhere around here though. Not like the one you're in."

"Shhh. You're not supposed to know about that," he joked.

Sam smiled to herself. Her dad was a patched-in member of BACA—Bikers Against Child Abuse. They did God's work, making kids feel safe against their abusers.

"Are they a problem?" Grant asked, sounding concerned now. "This gang?"

She let the lace curtain drop and went back to pacing. "I don't think the town likes them much. But I haven't heard of anyone having a run-in or anything. Anyway, I don't think Quincy wants me to act. I mean, I'd have to sign a new contract and everything. It doesn't make sense."

"But your gut is still talking to you."

"Yes."

"Enough that you want to walk?"

The moment of truth. "The *True Lies* stunt, I really want to do it, and I'd never get the opportunity to do it in another movie. I can't even believe I'm doing it in this one. What if I said I still wanted to stay?"

She heard her dad sit down again. "Sam. You know how some actors are constantly in the news because they're on their fifth divorce or they're crashing cars...or kissing women they shouldn't?"

She snickered. "Yeah. Of course."

"As great as some of them are on the screen, a lot of them see their careers suffer because they're constantly getting in trouble in their real lives. Then there are actors like your mother, ones who become great, who become legends and have a long life to show for it too, who don't do all that crap. They live the most boring lives they can off the screen."

"Mom's hardly boring."

Grant laughed. "Point taken, but you know what I mean. The same holds true for any artist, no matter if it's a writer, or a painter, or what have you. It takes calm and discipline to show up every day and do your art, and your mom has discipline in spades. That goes for us stunt people too."

She smiled again at *us*. "So, what are you saying, Dad?"

"I'm saying that it takes a lot of discipline to live a boring life."

Sam laughed.

"You laugh, but when it comes to performing a stunt, a director might say we can do it. We can make that impossible jump. Or we even think to ourselves, fuck safety, the cameras are rolling. So to stay safe, we sometimes need people to tell us we've got feet of clay, Sam. That a situation is too dangerous. Both on and off the screen."

He wants me to walk. "Dad, I see where you're going with this."

"I don't think you do."

"Sure I do. You want me to walk," she said, resigned.

"No, Sam. What I'm saying is that it's up to you to decide what to do. If you want to do this stunt and you feel safe enough to do it, then stay."

That was not what she expected after his speech. "I do feel safe enough. I trust Ken to make sure it's safe."

"What about Eric?"

She couldn't stop her smile. "Yeah, Dad. I trust him too."

"Good. You need the right people around you who are going to keep you safe."

"You trust my judgment with him?"

"I do. But, I want you to trust your own judgment more than anything else. And your gut is still telling you something's not right. So, you need to do something about that."

"I need to talk to Quincy and ask him point-blank what he's doing."

"I'd say that's exactly what you need to do. Then, you can decide to stay or go."

Sam felt a tremendous weight lift off her shoulders. *God, if only Mom felt the same way.*

"But sweetheart?"

"Yeah, Dad?"

"Take Eric with you when you talk to Quincy."

"No worries, Dad. Because that's what my gut says too."

———

Quincy beat her to the punch minutes later with a text requesting a meeting concerning 'the previous night's events.' She answered his text, confirming that she'd meet him in his trailer on set.

Eric agreed to go, of course.

"And if at any point you don't like what he's saying and you want to walk, we walk," he said as they approached Quincy's trailer.

"What if I still want to stay?"

He gripped her hand and squeezed. "Then we stay. I know how much the *True Lies* stunt means to you. But I also trust you're not reckless enough to do it if you don't feel safe on set."

"What about off-set?"

There was that look—a predator scenting the wind for danger. "That's my job."

They climbed the steps to the trailer door and Sam knocked. She expected Cassidy to answer, but Quincy opened the door himself. He looked neutral, which for eternally-optimistic and cheerful Quincy Torrent, was downright glum.

"Hey, Sam, Eric. Come in." Quincy stepped back to let them pass. The air felt deliciously cool in the trailer.

Tristian sat at a round table. As soon as he saw Sam, he cradled his bruised jaw.

Quincy pulled out a chair for Sam. Eric sat between her and Tristian, and Quincy sat on her other side across from Eric.

Quincy clapped his hands. "Now, tell me what happened. Ladies first." He gestured at Sam.

"Tristian assaulted me."

"It was an accident. I slipped—"

Sam laughed. "You *slipped?*"

Quincy held his hands in a T shape. "Time out. You two are done fighting. Okay, Samantha, can you be more specific?"

Eric stared at Quincy. "She has to explain assault to you?" he asked calmly.

"No, man. Apologies, I'm just trying to get to the bottom of this."

Eric looked at Sam, a silent question in his eyes: *You ready to leave?*

She shook her head. Eric nodded back once. His hand found hers under the table and squeezed. His touch flooded her with calm. Eric had her back.

Sam continued. "Tristian tried to tell me that I needed to take over for Lacey, which is stupid, then he got belligerent about it until he forced a kiss on me."

Tristian stopped rubbing his jaw long enough to say, "That's not true."

Eric squeezed her hand again. "It fucking well is true and you know it. Eric witnessed it. I will put you down if you try anything like that again," Sam said.

Quincy narrowed his eyes at Tristian, who'd gone back to rubbing his jaw. "You never touch a woman like that if she doesn't want you to, am I right?"

Tristian said nothing.

He leaned forward against the table and narrowed his eyes. "Am. I. Right?"

Sam had never seen Quincy so pissed.

Tristian looked away. "You're right. You don't."

"Samantha is well within her rights to call the police on your sorry ass." Quincy took out his phone and slammed it onto the table. "Here you go. You can use mine right now."

Samantha could imagine the publicity that would cause. The public fights, the accusations. It would be a circus. And she could kiss the movie goodbye, and probably her career. This type of thing did not always go well for women. She had her mother as a perfect example.

"I...don't think I need to do that."

Quincy looked her in the eye. "I can't make you, Samantha, but are you sure?"

"I'm sure."

He turned his surprisingly baleful stare onto Tristian. "I want my set to be one big happy family. I thought you understood that. I didn't think I could make that any more clear. Then you go and you fuck it up, Tristian. I am never working with you again after this, do you understand?"

"Yeah."

"Apologize. Now."

"I'm sorry, Samantha."

"Thanks." She smiled the sweetest, fakest smile she could. "Now, stay away from me."

Quincy sighed deeply. "Nothing worse than a family feud. I love all of you and I want what's best for everyone."

"My jaw is wrecked," Tristian complained.

Quincy raised his eyebrows at the man. "Naw, you're fine, just a little bruising. We'll film the barfight scenes with you today. Sam saved the make-up gals the hassle of making you look beat-up." Quincy laughed at his own joke as he threw an arm around Tristian's shoulders and gave him a one-armed hug. "So, can we just do the bygones thing and get back to making this movie?"

Tristian nodded.

"Good." Quincy clapped his hands—discussion over.

Tristian got up and stormed out without another word.

Sam remained seated.

"We're *not* done," she said. "I have a question for you, Quincy. Something that you need to clear up for me."

His smile froze. "Anything."

"The whole reason Tristian confronted me is because he thinks you're using me to stand in for Lacey because I turned down her role, and that you're going to convince me to take it."

Quincy laughed. "That's ridiculous. We talked about this and you made it very clear what you wanted and didn't want and I'm respecting that. You're here for the stunts, full-stop." He stood up.

Sam remained seated. "So why are you filming me on those shots?"

"We went over that, Sam. I need them for the storyboards."

"Then why am I standing in with Tristian and not his double?"

Quincy paused.

"You're using me as a fluffer, aren't you?"

Quincy's eyes widened. He looked back and forth between Sam and Eric. "You know, I'd never put it that way, Sam. But...you do get a better performance out of him."

She crossed her arms. "It's not happening again."

Quincy waved his hands. "Nope. Never again. Promise." He turned, walked to the door, and opened it. "Now that we've cleared the air, can we get back to making this movie?"

"Almost," Sam said. "I want all that footage of us destroyed."

"Sure, sure. Absolutely."

"It won't be used in promotions or trailers, there won't be stills online. Nothing."

Quincy shook his head hard. "None of that, Samantha. The public will never see any of it, I promise." He drew an X over his heart with his finger. "Cross my heart and hope to die."

TWENTY-ONE

They left Quincy's trailer in the director's wake. Eric couldn't have been more proud of Sam.

"You were amazing," he said. "You didn't need me there at all."

"Yes, I did." She continued to march through the set, head held high. "You may not realize this, Eric Armstrong, but you make me feel stronger."

His chest tightened at her words. "Same here."

She stopped and looked him in the eye. "I do?"

"You do. I love you, Sam."

Her lips curled into the sexiest smile. "Good. Because I love you, too." She kissed him, not caring who saw them. "What's on your schedule for the rest of the day?"

"Exercising the dogs with Tim and then we have a meeting with a rep from the Humane Society ahead of tomorrow."

Sam turned serious. "The big dogfight scene. Are *you* ready?"

Eric nodded. "No nightmares for once. I've never told anyone the story I told you last night. I didn't think I ever could. Thank you."

"Anytime," she said softly.

His heart ached when he looked at Samantha. Surrounded by props and backdrops, they stood in a world of make-believe where anything was possible, even a relationship with her. But would it survive in the real world, or be left behind once the cameras stopped?

"You should get going. I'm holding you up," he told her.

She kissed him again, longer this time. "I'll see you at Rafferty's tonight." She whispered in his ear, "I need another dance."

Maybe it would survive after all. Eric would do everything in his power to make it happen. Sam was his.

Things were looking up. Eric and Tim's meeting with Jane Matthews, the representative from the American Humane Association, went well and ended earlier than Eric expected, so he sneaked over to Rafferty's to talk to Mags, hoping that with fewer crew members around, he could get her to talk more about the town. Eric couldn't shake the feeling that he and Sam had been watched the night before and it didn't sit well with him at all. No one had protested since the first night, but that didn't mean everyone was happy. Just...quiet.

He took a seat alone at the bar and Mags immediately pulled out a frosty mug.

"All by your lonesome again, T-B-H. So you've finally wised up and dumped Sam for me, huh?" Mags joked.

Eric laughed. "Both of you are too good for me." He toasted her and savored the ice-cold beer. It was perfect for another day under the hot desert sun.

"Grammy!" Cody ran through the kitchen door laughing. Mags scrambled after him but grabbed him just before he escaped past the bar.

"You little stinker," she laughed as she tickled him. "Go on back." She gave his butt a pat and he ran back into the kitchen. She looked at Eric. "It's a game now. Get away from Mama in the kitchen then try and get past Grammy."

Eric chuckled. "I see that."

"Good to have them in town. At the same time, I don't want them anywhere near this place." She smiled sadly and looked away, tears in her eyes. "Ignore an old woman, T-B-H. Mine's not the only sob story around here."

"Mags." He reached across the bar and patted her hand. "What's going on around here? I'm worried about you. Why are some people upset about the movie?"

She glared at the door, and Eric caught the sound of engines approaching. Motorcycle engines.

"It's them. Used to be, Red Hands would steer clear of us, but Quincy's drawing them right into Sagebrush and the mayor doesn't seem to care, the bastard. Idiot says this movie will put the town back on the map, that tourists will come and buy souvenir crap, and that's supposed to revitalize Sagebrush." She scoffed. "Meantime, the damn gang's ruining things in a town that can't afford to see much else go bad. You ask me, the mayor's tied in with them. Now Quincy wants my jukebox? Fuck him."

The front door opened and Mags looked past Eric. She went deadly serious.

In the mirror behind the bar, he watched half a dozen men walk in and sit down at a couple tables by the wall.

Fuck. The Red Hands decided to stop in.

"Excuse me," Mags said, and came out from behind the bar to take their order—something she didn't normally do. She didn't normally get quiet and pensive, either. Eric didn't blame Mags for being uneasy.

As she took their orders, Mags smiled at their jokes, but Eric could see how strained that smile really was. And when one of them smacked her bottom on her way back to the bar, the look of terror on her face betrayed the laugh she gave them. Eric started to stand, but she stopped him with one look.

"Don't you dare," she hissed as she passed him on her way back around the bar. He let her pour their drinks and put in their food order. In the meantime, he texted Samantha:

Do not come to Rafferty's right now.

Sam texted back:

Why? You twerking with Mags? She added a smiley winky face.

He grinned despite himself, then texted:

You already know who I want to dance with, smartass. But there's some trouble here so pass on the word if you can.

Chances were, filming had not wrapped up quite yet, but there was a lot of standing around and waiting on a set and if anyone had decided to sneak away for a beer, he wanted to prevent them from coming here.

What kind of trouble? Sam texted back, of course.

I'll tell you later he typed. Eric expected pushback but was surprised when Sam responded:

Ok. Passing along the word.

The warmth he felt in his chest was out of proportion to the simple words.

She trusted him.

So I need to honor that trust and make sure she stays safe.

Mags kept quiet and stayed at the other end of the bar until their food was ready. The fry cook took one look out the kitchen door and glanced at Mags. He disappeared back into the kitchen and then reemerged with baskets of burgers and fries on a tray and carried them to the table himself.

They were a thirsty bunch and drained their drinks quickly, shouting for more as they ate. Eric felt his phone buzz with a text, but he ignored it in order to keep an eye on Mags each time she carried a tray with pitchers of beer and shots of whiskey back to the tables. One of the bikers noticed him watching.

"Got a problem, fucktard?"

Eric just shook his head and turned back to the bar. He'd give anything to have Malcolm, Camden, or hell, even Jake at his back, and he definitely missed Blaze. Even the mere presence of a dog who looked like she could take your leg off often stopped fights before they started.

But the way to play this was to stay cool, stay disengaged, and watch them quietly in the mirror behind the bar.

"I said, you got a problem, *fucktard?*"

Well, shit.

"Fucktard's too stupid to know he's a fucktard," another voice said, and the men laughed.

Eric turned back around. Mags was already quickly walking back toward him, her face a mask of anger and fear.

"*Please, don't,*" she whispered.

He nodded but got ready for a fight anyway. His back prickled, telling him that at any moment one of them would be getting up, goaded on by his friends, and lumber up to him. He looked around for every available weapon. Of course, he had his piece in a holster under his shirt but he didn't want it to come to that. If he had to draw his gun, he'd already lost.

Called it. Psychic would be proud of me he thought ruefully as he watched the biggest biker stand and come toward him.

Eric turned around and slid off his bar stool. The guy was huge and hairy, with a red bandana tied around his head that didn't do a lot for restraining the long, greasy hair streaming out around it. The four patrons who were not with the gang got up from their tables and scooted out the door.

"Fucktard," the guy growled through a broken-toothed smile.

Eric grinned back and spread his arms like *Yup, right here, what do you want?* But his eyes were steel as he sized up the asshole. If he wanted a fight, he'd get one. The place had gone deadly quiet.

"Why were you looking at us?" Red Bandana demanded.

"I wasn't. I was looking at Mags, making sure she didn't need my help." Eric kept his voice calm as if they were only talking about the weather.

"Fucking gentleman, huh?"

"I guess."

"Mags can handle her own fucking self."

"Absolutely. But as you said, I'm a gentleman."

"I said you were a fucktard."

"Okay, I'm a gentleman fucktard. Now that we've established that, can I get back to my beer?"

"Fucktard," the guy repeated like a broken record.

"Thanks for the road name."

Bandana's hand landed hard on his shoulder.

Eric calculated his chances of surviving this encounter if the rest of the gang decided to join it. He couldn't count that low. Times like this he almost wished he was back in Afghanistan.

Friend! Come with me! Akbar's voice cried out in his head.

As if conjured straight out of his nightmares, Cody darted through the doorway again.

"Cody!" Mags shouted as she tried to grab the kid just before he got past the bar but she missed.

Eric turned, bent, and swung him up in his arms. Cody's protest turned to a laugh as Eric tickled him.

Red Bandana looked at them.

"Man, there's a kid here, okay? Whatever beef you got with me, he doesn't need to see it. We can settle up later, whatever. But not in front of the kid."

The biker gritted his teeth. Then he nodded once.

Eric handed Cody over to Mags. She pretended everything was fine for the little kid's sake, but her eyes told Eric otherwise. He gave her a chin-lift to go into the kitchen and she didn't hesitate.

Movement outside caught his eye. God help him if it was reinforcements.

The door flew open and a voice called out, "Fellas! Good to see you here!"

Quincy stood in the doorway, huge smile on his face, surveying the room like it was just another movie set.

Jesus Christ. Did the director have an actual death wish?

"Tigo!" he shouted at Red Bandana. "I see you've met one of our animal handlers. You talking shop?"

This is Tigo? Jesus. Now he had a face to match up with the road name from the files Elissa sent him.

Tigo straightened up and looked Eric up and down. "Fuck, Quincy. This one of yours?"

Quincy laughed like the man had just told the funniest joke. He sauntered into the room and up to Eric and Tigo.

"Yeah he's one of mine, aren't you, bud?" He clapped Eric on the upper arm. "Eric, I see you've met one of my advisers."

"Adviser?"

"Yeah. Tigo here has experience with dogs, too. And I can't make a movie about bikers without talking to bikers." He laughed like it was the most obvious thing in the world.

Eric looked back and forth between the men who were now shaking hands.

Tigo laughed at Eric. It wasn't a good-natured, hey-everything-is-cool laugh. It was more of an if-you-find-yourself-in-a-dark-alley-you're-dead laugh.

"My movie's about an outlaw gang, but these guys are legit, aren't you?" Quincy said. "Hell, they were my inspiration just as much as Sagebrush. Their expertise lends the realism I'm looking for."

"Quincy!" One of the other men waved him over. "Shut your mouth and come have a drink. You too, Tigo." Wood scraped against wood as he kicked a chair out.

Quincy's smile wavered the tiniest bit. "Sure, yeah, Nitro. Everything's on me, guys."

Nitro. Their leader. Fuck.

"Better fucking be!" Nitro said. His laughter roared throughout Rafferty's.

"Later, Fucktard." Tigo walked to Nitro's table.

Quincy turned back to Eric. "Sam told me where you were.

They need you back on set for break down. Go on now, your beer's on me."

Jesus Christ. Quincy actually thought he had this all under control. This wasn't a movie set. This was real life. Did he even know the difference between fact and fiction anymore? Or did he just think he was above it all?

Eric was betting on the latter.

"Everything cool, Eric?" Quincy asked.

"Copacetic, boss. Except it looks like you're fucked."

Quincy gave Eric a perplexed smile. "I'm fucked? *I'm* fucked?" He scoffed and looked around as if he were performing for an audience and his next line was going to be *Can you believe this guy?*

"You think you've got those guys on a leash? You don't. I know who they are, what they can do, and I'm your best defense against them and you're gonna need it."

Quincy looked uneasy again as if Eric had gotten through to him. But it lasted only a moment.

"No, it's cool, man. They're fine. I got this."

Eric poked his finger into Quincy's chest. "You have no idea what you're doing right now. You think the world is your set? It's not." He pointed at the bikers. "They're *real*, Quincy, and they're not here to fuck around. Whatever deal you have going with them is gonna get you killed. That's your choice. But you're also fucking with your cast, your crew, and the whole damn town."

"Naw, I'm good, man, I'm good. And tell Mags it's all good." He walked over to the tables and sat down as Nitro yelled for Mags to bring another round.

Eric turned to check on Mags, who was standing in the kitchen doorway. Cody was nowhere in sight, thank God.

She came out and he asked, "You need me to stick around?"

Mags shook her head. "My daughter took Cody back to my place. Best if you go too. Quincy's got 'em under control."

"Mags."

"*Go*, T-B-H. I'm serious."

He laid down a big tip on the bar, then walked out. He need to call Watchdog, ASAP and let them know he'd figured out where the Red Hands' clubhouse was. The only place it could be.

And that Quincy was a stupid, delusional motherfucker who was in way over his head along with the whole town.

After what happened tonight, so was Eric.

He didn't miss the jukebox's choice of songs as he left. Eric grinned ruefully as 'Desperado' played behind him.

TWENTY-TWO

Samantha ducked a blow from Brent and dropped to a crouch. She swung her right leg out in a coffee grinder and swept his legs out from under him, sending him sprawling.

"Awesome," Ken said, watching them. "That's gonna look great on film."

Sam sprang up and helped Brent to his feet. "Thanks, Ken."

"You've come a long way, Sam," Brent added.

"Only because you're teaching me cool stuff right and left. Thanks for showing me how to do that one." They high-fived.

Sam felt her phone buzz in her costume jacket pocket. "One sec." She pulled out her phone and read the text from Eric.

Do not come to Rafferty's right now.

Still riding the high of a good practice session, Sam texted back:

Why? You twerking with Mags?

You already know who I want to dance with, smartass. But there's some trouble here so pass on the word if you can.

All her good humor evaporated. Eric was being serious. A barfight maybe? But when he told her to tell the rest of the crew, she wondered if maybe the townies had decided once and for all that they didn't belong there and had gathered at Mag's place to cause trouble.

"Hey, Ken, Brent? I just got a text from Eric. He says to avoid Rafferty's for the moment. Not sure what's going on, but I'm passing on the word."

Ken frowned. "Yeah, okay."

"You think we've worn out our welcome?"

Brent nodded. "I've seen it happen before."

"We got the big dogfight scene tomorrow though with the locals as extras," Ken said.

She typed an alert into the app they all used for communicating and got an error message.

"Shit. This thing is so buggy." She tried again and got the same thing.

"Yeah, half the crew doesn't even use it now," Brent said.

"Have you seen Quincy or Cassidy?" Sam asked. "Maybe they can make an announcement."

"I know where Cassidy is, so I'll go tell her. Last I saw Quincy, he was over by the ranch house. Let's find them, then meet back up here for more practice."

"Sounds good. I'll go find him. Thanks, guys." Sam jogged off in the direction of the ranch house. She told everyone she passed to avoid Rafferty's for now and to spread the word. A good thing too, since things were winding down for the day.

When she got to the house, she looked around but didn't see Quincy. *Maybe he's inside.* She'd seen him go in a couple of times after shooting. Sam climbed the steps to the porch and tried the door. She opened it and went inside.

Quincy must have changed his mind about doing all the interior shots on a soundstage she thought as she looked around. She'd been in a clubhouse before and this had all the hallmarks of one. It looked like the lovechild between a dive bar and a motorcycle garage. A beat-up leather couch lined one wall beside a wet bar made of plywood painted black. Bike parts were strewn across the floor. Cigarette burns covered a low table in front of the couch The dingy yellow walls showed lighter-colored squares that told Sam some art had been removed from the walls, probably the original art replaced by posters of motorcycles and half-naked women.

But the stench of stale cigarette smoke, motor oil, beer, and cheap air freshener hanging in the air defied the idea that this was a temporary set, though Quincy was known for going to extremes with his realism. He'd pumped the smell of blood and smoke onto a soundstage during a disaster scene in *Invincible Gods*, to the point that the actors were practically hurling—so the gossip went.

Gossip confirmed, I guess.

Sam heard noises coming from somewhere deeper in the house. It sounded like someone was watching TV. As she made her way down a dim hall, the sound resolved into a crowd shouting and dogs barking. The sound quit abruptly like someone had turned off the TV and Sam stopped in her tracks. Her heart was beating as if she were breaking into someone's home. It almost felt that way.

Ridiculous. This place was abandoned for years.

A new sound took the place of the crowd noises. A woman's voice.

Wait, is that me?

Then she heard Quincy talking to himself. "That shot. Yeah, that one. Perfect. Yes! Got her face straight on in that one."

Why was Quincy looking at the dailies or editing footage in here, when the production trailer was only a few yards away?

Only one reason came to her—privacy. And why would he need that?

Got her face straight on in that one.

Because he was burning Sam after all.

And then she heard something that made her blood run cold. Dogs—barking and snarling like they were ready for a fight while a crowd cheered. The sounds were muffled, obviously from the footage, not live. She'd watched Eric and Tim wrangle the dogs through several shots on set already, but Sam never heard the dogs snarling like that, and never with a crowd. That was supposed to happen tomorrow. This was different footage.

Quincy chuckled. "Yeah, look at that big killer. Need to get more of him."

Her blood froze even as her mind tried to deny what she was hearing as impossible.

This was footage from a real dogfight.

A toilet flushed in a room right in front of her and she jumped. The door opened and a big guy she didn't recognize stepped out, took one look at her, and shouted, "Hey, what the fuck?"

"Quincy, I was looking for Quincy."

The director appeared behind the giant dressed in jeans and a black Ghost Rider t-shirt.

"Sam? Hey, what, uh, are you doing here?" He clapped his hands.

Sam eyed the giant who had now crossed his arms like he was a bouncer, Quincy was a nightclub, and Sam wasn't invited. All notions of confronting Quincy died.

"App's not working, so I wanted to let you know Eric says we all need to avoid Rafferty's now. Not sure why."

Quincy exchanged a look with the hulk. "Yeah, okay. Probably something I should look into. Hey, do me a favor and spread the word."

"Already on it," Sam said.

"Great. Okay, everybody outta here." Quincy clapped again and pushed past the giant, who stared down Sam.

She didn't need a verbal warning. Sam turned around and followed Quincy out, the giant right on her heels. He slammed the door behind them and locked it. Quincy broke into a run as he headed for the parking lot. Sam descended the steps and then turned around.

The dude stood in front of the door like a sentry.

She turned again and started walking back to the practice area. One thought went through her head—how to sneak back into the ranch house and check out that footage. Something was very, very wrong here.

She pulled out her phone and texted Eric:

Meet me on set ASAP.

She'd tell him what she saw and suspected—that not only was Quincy Torrent a lying son of a bitch, but that he'd gone for a little too much realism.

Then with Eric's help, she'd make her plans to ruin him.

TWENTY-THREE

Eric got into his truck and checked his phone. *Shit.* The text he'd missed was from Sam telling him to come to the set ASAP. He started the engine and put in a call to Lach as he sped back to the ranch. He told his boss about the confrontation with Tigo and the Red Hands.

"Already on it," Lach said. "Once Elissa completed her report, Gina's friends took an interest."

Fuck. Gina's 'friends' tended to be FBI and CIA—and those were just the ones who admitted to being in the alphabets. God knew who else she worked with.

"Why are they interested?"

"Well, it's rumored that in addition to drug running and basically carrying out Deacons' orders, the Red Hands have been getting into human trafficking."

"Fuck."

"But, the Feds haven't been able to find enough credible evidence. Anyway, we started looking for a place to rent some miles out of town," Lach said. "Quincy found himself a location remote enough that Gina didn't have a bead on anything fast and close we could use, but we got a place now. Walker, Nash, and Gina are on their way now. She's insisting that she be there, just to poke around."

Lach sounded a tad annoyed at that. Eric could hear the pen clicking in the man's teeth.

"What's wrong with Gina being here?"

"Not a fucking thing," Lach grumbled. "Except I need her...*we* need her here."

Eric smirked, then was glad he wasn't on a video call for Lach to see it.

"So you're sending me the FNG?" Walker Dean had started at Watchdog while Eric was on the road with Malcolm guarding Annalie.

"Yeah. He may be new to us but I think you'll find he knows his way around a situation. The Red Hands have got clubhouses scattered across Arizona, but this one wasn't on anyone's radar. You sure the ranch is one of them?"

Eric shifted in his seat. "Not one hundred percent, but I'd place a bet in Vegas."

"Jesus, I can't believe Torrent's involved with them."

"More than involved. The way things went down tonight, I'd be willing to bet that he's paying them to use it. It would make sense out of him keeping it locked up. Might be things in there they don't want us to see."

Plastic clicked on the other end and Eric imagined Lachlan shifting the cut-down pen from one side of his mouth to the other. "I'll have Elissa check out Torrent's bank transactions. Anyone ever go in there?"

"If you're asking if it's an active hornet's nest, not that I've seen."

"If that's what's happening and they don't have their club, no wonder they're hanging out at Rafferty's. They're like a bee swarm without a hive—and today they tried to sting. And that puts *everyone* working on the movie in the middle. I can't believe Torrent is that big of an idiot."

Eric turned off the highway onto the road leading to the ranch. "More like that big of an ego. He's treating them like they're exotic pets he's got on a short leash."

"I've known exotic animals to turn around and bite their owners if the leash is short enough."

"Yeah, and if it's too long, they can bite everyone around them. We're shooting the dogfight tomorrow. Lots of extras from town are gonna be on set."

Lach grunted in agreement. "You won't be alone there. Gina already has a plan."

"Of course she does. Thanks, Lach. I appreciate the backup."

Lachlan grunted again. "So. How hard will it be to pull Samantha out of the shit?"

Eric blew out a breath. "She's Sam. She fought hard to be here. I watched her do her first big stunt and she's been nothing but amazing ever since. And every time the *True Lies* stunt gets mentioned, she comes alive."

"So in other words, you're gonna have to dynamite her outta there."

"That's what I'm telling you."

"Bette wears a groove in my office floor every time she's in here. The woman makes pacing by wheelchair into an art form."

"Tell her I'm on my way to the set now to pick up Sam. If you'll shoot me the address to the safehouse, I'll take her straight there."

Lach snorted. "Yeah, the safehouse. You're gonna love it. Gina's absolutely thrilled. Take Samantha there and let Gina and them sort the rest. Samantha's still your number one priority."

"Yes, she is." *Shit.* Did his voice give too much away?

Lachlan paused. "Am I going to have to give you the Whitney Houston speech?"

Oh, shit. "No, sir. Bodyguards don't date the principals. Got it."

"Yeeaahh." Click-click went Lach's pen across his teeth. "Just keep your head in the game."

"I am. There's too much at stake otherwise."

"Well, Gina and them should get there tonight and you'll have your backup tomorrow."

Eric shook his head as if Lach could see it. "Quincy is out with the gang right now and this might be my only chance to sneak back onto the set and poke around the ranch house after I drop off Sam."

"No way."

"Lach, this is my only chance—"

Lach's irritation seeped over the call and filled the truck. "Eric. Do you know what your problem is here?"

"I—"

"Lemme finish. Actually, you know what *my* biggest problem is right now? Besides hiring a bunch of jackasses like you who fall in love with their principals? And don't you dare try to deny it."

Fuck.

"No, Lach, I didn't know you had any problems."

"You're all smartasses, too. Every goddamned one of you. But what makes you stand out from this particular crowd, Eric, is that you stand out from this particular crowd."

"I'm not following."

"Your problem, Eric, is that you think you're supposed to go this alone. You've got to learn to trust your team and know that we have your back no matter what." Sounds of clicking plastic filled the line as Lach paused.

"Let me put it to you this way. You think you're supposed to do all the stunts all by yourself, out on your lonesome, without any sort of safety net. Well, my friend, Watchdog *is* your safety net. And that's what my problem is in this case. I sent you in there alone when I shoulda given you backup right off the bat like I did with Annalie's detail. I set you up to go off and be the lone hero. All I can say is I trusted someone outside of Watchdog to help you when

I shouldn't have, and now here we are. Never should have assumed Ken Adams would put Sam first, let alone you. So, grab Sam, then stay put until your team gets there, understood?"

"Yeah, Boss. Got it."

He got it, but he sure didn't like it.

TWENTY-FOUR

Sam wasn't an actress, but she was good enough to convince Ken and Brent that everything was fine. They ran through a few more fight moves before Eric texted her saying he was in the parking lot. She breathed a sigh of relief that he was safe from whatever trouble he'd found. Ken called it a day a few minutes later and she jogged to Eric's truck.

As soon as she got into the truck, Eric pulled her in close for a kiss. Just being in his arms calmed and centered her. Whatever Quincy was up to, she could handle it.

"So, before I get into my little adventure, what happened at Rafferty's? Is Mags okay?"

Eric immediately tensed. "What adventure? Are you okay? Shit." He let her go and started the engine. "We're getting out of here."

"Whoa, calm down. Yeah, I'm fine. Just had some weirdness with Quincy. So, is Mags okay?"

"Yeah, she's fine. Speaking of Quincy." Eric pulled out and onto the road heading back toward the highway. "You're not going to like this."

"Neither are you."

Eric glanced at her. "What happened on the set?"

"Long story short, I'm pretty sure he lied and he's burning me. I went into the ranch house to—"

"Wait, wait, wait!" Eric shouted. "You went *into* the ranch house?"

"Yeah. And you should see it."

She was ready for Eric to be upset, but he surprised her with a laugh. "Yeah, I bet I should, but I don't have to. Teamwork."

"Teamwork?"

"Yeah. I'll explain once everyone is here." When he got to the end of the road, he turned in the opposite direction from Sagebrush.

"Where we going?"

"I'm taking you to a safehouse." He held up his hand before she could protest. "Just until we can figure out what's going on."

"And if that's the duration?"

Eric pulled over to the side of the road. "I'm going to do everything in my power to make sure the filming goes on and you get to do your stunt. But, Sam, you are the most important thing in the world to me. I've watched you work, and I know you're going to have a million chances to do amazing things. But you're not going to have a goddamned future if I leave you unprotected and something happens to you." He grabbed her hand and squeezed it. "And I can't see a future for myself without you in it."

The intensity of his gaze should have scared her. Instead, she'd never felt safer, even as her heart pounded.

She held his gaze as she told him the truth. "Neither can I."

The safehouse turned out not to be a house at all, but three 'glamping' yurts on some scenic acreage behind a locked gate about twenty minutes from the set.

Sam actually laughed when she saw them. "You're kidding me. When I heard safehouse, I was expecting something, I don't know, with actual walls."

"Yeah, Lach warned me the pickings were slim, but..."

"Ooh, I see a hot tub though." She grinned at Eric. "How long do we have before they get in?"

"Don't tempt me." Eric pulled up to the closest yurt and parked. He got out, walked around the truck, and opened the door for her.

Sam took Eric's hand and hopped out. He closed the door and she paused, studying him. Sam hated the worry in his eyes and knowing that she was the one causing it. He smoothed down her hair then twined the end of a long lock in his fingers and pulled gently. She shivered and stepped closer. She ran her fingers along his arm up to his neck and slid them behind his head to play with the hair at his nape. Now *he* shivered.

"Careful," he said, his voice rough. He put his arms around her until she was pressed up against him and couldn't miss how much he would have preferred it if they'd had the whole night to themselves.

Sam's boots made her taller to match Lacey's height, so she didn't have to go too far up on her toes for her lips to meet his. He tilted his head and kissed her greedily. Her nipples pebbled against his chest as he pressed her against the truck. Eric slid his hand down her body until he was cupping her asscheeks. He lifted her and she wrapped her legs around his waist. All thoughts of the ranch house disappeared in the smell of his skin, the feel of his tight body, and the taste of his lips. She opened to him and he explored her mouth. He groaned and that only drove her wilder.

"You're tempting me," he growled.

"Into the hot tub? I think it would be a great idea."

"And then what do we do when the rest of them drive up?"

"Sprint to the nearest yurt, of course." She kept her expression bright-eyed as if what she was saying was the most rational thing in the world.

Which cracked Eric up, as she'd intended. She joined his laughter.

"I love you, Sam," he whispered, making her heart melt.

"I love you, too." She ran her hand down the side of his face. "When we've gotten past this, I want to show you how much."

She'd intended to make him feel more at ease, but instead, he tensed up again and looked around.

"I have to make sure we're secure here." He set her back down gently. He wasn't playing now. He was dead serious.

She nodded. "I am safe, thanks to you." She touched his cheek. "What do you need me to do right now?"

"Follow me. I'll make sure everything is copacetic with the first yurt. Then, I need you to stay in there out of sight." Something in his tone told her he thought she'd fight him on it.

"You got it."

And yup, he gave her that almost disbelieving look.

"Eric. I trust you. And I'm not going to make things difficult for you. I get that the set is potentially dangerous and it's your job to make it safe."

He shook his head again, a slight smile on his lips.

"What?"

"You. I'm still getting used to you not wanting to fight me at every turn."

"Well, I'm already used to you being in my corner, so put on your racing brickles and catch up with me."

He laughed hard, then brushed his lips against her forehead. "I am crazy in love with you."

They went inside the yurt.

"Wow, this reminds me of that old show, *I Dream of Jeannie*," Sam said. "This could be the inside of her genie bottle."

"No doubt."

She watched as Eric went around the room looking behind the

billowy curtains lining the round walls. Then he searched under the round bed in the middle of the room.

"Looking for monsters?"

"Yup. The human kind. Or any trace that they might be listening." He pulled out some sort of contraption and turned it on. "No bugs though. We're good."

"This'll be fun." Sam fingered the mosquito netting tenting the bed. The place was honestly cute. She wished they were renting it under better circumstances.

"I need to check out the other two. Stay here."

"Yup. Got it." Sam sat on the edge of the bed and started to pull her boots off. "What?" she asked Eric as he paused to watch her.

"Just thinking this would be fun under better circumstances."

Sam beamed. "Great minds."

Eric left and she was tempted to strip down completely and surprise him, when she heard a car engine getting closer. *Damn. No time to play.* The sound snapped her back to reality like a gut punch when she hadn't braced for it. She wasn't stupid—once she told them what she saw in the ranch house, she'd have to fight to stay on set, and that was the best-case scenario. What if everything shut down?

But worst of all, Eric could get in trouble for being in a relationship with her.

She almost left the yurt then remembered that Eric would want her to stay put in case whoever this was, wasn't a friendly. But as soon as she heard the dog barking, she smiled and poked her head out the door.

Gina, Nash, and Walker were already out of the SUV and letting two dogs out—Fleur and Blaze. Blaze ran straight for Eric the moment she laid eyes on him.

"Hey, girl!" He went to his knees and hugged the dog, who decided she needed to try to lick his face off as quickly as she could. "I missed you, too."

"Hey." Sam stepped out and waved at Gina. "You can inform my mom that I'm alive and well."

"Excellent," Gina said, walking toward Sam, Fleur at her side. They hugged. "She'll kill me if I tell you this, but she's been restraining herself from calling you every minute since you left."

Sam rolled her eyes, then immediately felt bad about it. "I guess she was right."

Gina shrugged. "About some things, maybe. But not about everything." She turned and headed for the second yurt before Sam could ask her to elaborate.

"We secure?" she asked Eric.

"Secure."

"Good. Let's convene in here and brief." She climbed the steps without waiting for the others. Gina was usually pretty abrupt in Sam's experience, but she seemed even more so now. Something weighed on her, and Gina was doing a surprisingly crap job of hiding it.

Nash walked up to Sam and gave her a one-armed hug. "Elissa's like to kill me since you left. She's dragged me up and down every last cliff along the California coast. She misses her climbing buddy."

Sam laughed. "Just a few more weeks, and I'll take her back off your hands, Nash." Or at least Sam hoped it would still be a few weeks and not a few days.

After they'd made themselves comfortable in the yurt—another dead ringer for a plush genie bottle—Eric went first and described his encounter with the Red Hands at Rafferty's. Sam's heart sank with every word he spoke.

"I wanted to go back and recon the place tonight, but I don't think we have to." He gestured at Sam. "Sam's already been inside. Wanna tell us what you saw?"

Sam took a deep breath. "After hearing your story, I'm one hundred percent convinced that place is one of their clubhouses. I didn't get to see much, just the front room, which is part bar, part motorcycle repair shop. There were paler spots on the wall where I imagine they had their insignia and photos hanging, but took them down and hid them."

She tried not to look at Eric's face while she talked about hearing Quincy as he looked over the footage, because any worry she saw there would derail her. "Before I could confront him, this guy that I'd never seen on set before stopped me in the hall. I'm pretty sure he's a Red Hand."

She didn't have to look at Eric to know he was upset. The swift intake of breath told her everything she needed to know about where his mind was.

Gina opened her bag and took out a tablet. "Think you could ID him?" She tapped a few times on the screen and handed the tablet to Sam.

"Sure." Sam looked over the mug shots and zoomed-in photos that looked taken from a distance. After a moment, she found a familiar mugshot. "That's him. This guy." She tapped on the photo which opened to another page and handed it back to Gina.

"TJ Bailey," Gina said. "Just this year we have drunk and disorderly, second-degree assault on a peace officer, possession with intent to distribute methamphetamine, but the list goes on."

"And you were in there with him." Eric's voice was flat.

"Yeah, I think he was there to guard Quincy."

"So there are hornets in the nest after all." Eric looked at Nash, Gina, and Walker. "This just changed the game."

Sam sensed where they were going. "Don't pull me." She looked from one face to the next. "I'm not in any particular danger."

Walker shook his head. "Like hell you aren't. You confronted one of them."

"I wouldn't call that a confrontation at all. I played both dumb and nice and I left immediately. No confrontation."

Gina frowned. "Tell us again what you heard on the video."

"I'm pretty sure I heard my own voice. And Quincy definitely sounded excited to get my face. Okay, whoever's face he was watching, but it's got to be mine."

"You said you heard dogs." Again, Eric was playing his cards close to the vest.

"Yeah. They sounded all riled up. And they sounded real. I mean, like they were actually getting ready to fight, not like the dogs on set."

Eric looked at the others. "Son of a bitch."

Gina nodded.

"What?" Sam asked.

"Second location. Probably another clubhouse close by would be my guess. And Quincy filmed an actual fight there."

Sam felt nauseous. "Why?" She looked at Eric, who looked stricken. "He can't use the footage. And I just don't want to believe he'd do something like that."

"No one wants to believe it, Sam, Eric said, softening his voice. "But it sounds like he did. And, he's looking at footage of you and we don't know why. I know you want to respect him. I want to think the best of him, too. But we can't."

She bit her lip and looked at the floor. "No. You're right. I can't assume anything about him." She looked up in time to catch Gina's expression. She was looking at Eric like she was impressed. It only lasted a moment but it was there.

"But you can't pull me," Sam insisted. "If you do, it'll tip him off, and whoever he might be working with. Because I refuse to believe he's just doing this because he can."

Gina stood up and walked to the door and back. "I hate to say this is a good call because I want to keep you out of harm's way. But you're right." She looked at the men. "This will tip them off if Sam just disappears. Eric, I'll back your call."

"Against my mom," Sam said. "She's wanted me out since day one."

Gina nodded. "But this just got bigger."

"Sam stays in," Eric said. "She can handle herself."

Sam felt her heart fill to near bursting.

Gina studied Eric. "You're going to need backup for sure." Then she smiled as she looked between Sam and Eric. "When we get home and you explain yourselves to Bette." She paced again. "In the meantime, we still need to get in there and have a look around. I'm hoping we'll have a chance to do that tomorrow."

"I want back in, too," Sam said. "If he has footage of me he's turning into some sort of promo or..." She didn't even want to think of all the alternatives. "I want to destroy it myself."

TWENTY-FIVE

The dogs snarled and barked and bit each other. The crowd yelled and goaded them on. A white-hot blast sent Eric reeling.

He sat straight up in bed, wrestling with the last of his dream. He immediately looked around, hoping not to find Samantha out of bed and looking at him like he was a monster.

Or worse...looking at him through a blackened eye.

But she was there beside him, unhurt, and trying to calm him.

"Eric, hey, you're in Arizona. You're safe." Sam stroked his arm. "It's Sam. Come back to me."

"I'm all right." He ran his hands over his face. "And I'm so fucking sorry." *I shouldn't be sleeping next to her. She should be in with Gina, and at the very least, I should be on the floor.* They hadn't even tried to deny their relationship the night before and insult everyone's intelligence, so when it was time for bed, they took one of the yurts while Nash and Walker took another, and Gina and Fleur had one to themselves.

Blaze was at the side of the bed, too well-behaved to jump up but looking worried as hell as she stood there with her nose pointed up at Eric.

"No need to apologize, ever. I know." She wrapped her arms around him and he reflexively pulled her closer. "Jake used to do this sometimes."

"Do what? Act like he was..." He left the word *crazy* out.

"Like he was remembering, hard. It's all right."

"It's not all right. I'm not..." But shame wouldn't let him finish, even if she understood.

"It's tomorrow. You're worried. I get it. The nightmares will go away again once this is over."

"I don't know if they will, Sam."

She looked into his face and then kissed him. "If they do or they don't it doesn't change *us*, Eric. Nothing will."

"You say that now."

"Dammit! I do say that now, and I'll say that tomorrow, and the day after, and the day after that."

God, she was beautiful when she was determined. And he'd never seen her more determined than she was right now.

He grinned as his heart eased. "All right."

"All right?"

"Yeah. I believe you. And I believe *in* you."

Early the next morning, Eric helped Tim unload the dogs for their big day on the set. Jane from the American Humane Society was already there, steam rising from her travel mug as she inspected the set ahead of the shoot. She stopped and smiled when she saw them —or rather, the smile was for the dogs. To say Jane was a dog-person was putting it mildly.

While she looked over the excited pups—who rewarded her efforts with big sloppy kisses—Eric studied the gathering crowd of extras. Quincy had hired townies almost exclusively and paid double what they normally would have made, so the rumor went. Most would have shown up for free just for the novelty, but Quincy insisted on 'paying real money for real work' as he'd put it. Eric gritted his teeth as he listened to some of them praising his generosity.

If only they knew what kind of person they were really dealing with.

He hadn't mentioned his suspicions to Tim about the footage Sam overheard the night before. He wanted to be sure it wasn't just his imagination or prejudice coloring his observations. And there was no need to get the man upset.

The extras had already been through costuming and makeup, so he was surrounded by people in jeans, biker jackets, sunglasses, and bandannas. Friends he'd made hanging out at Rafferty's now looked like tough strangers. And then he saw Mags and a woman who looked like her but younger in their get-up and smiled.

"Wasn't expecting to see you here," he told her.

"I got my arm twisted," Mags replied.

"By your daughter?" He turned to the other woman who smiled and introduced herself as Mae.

"No, by this little tyrant." Mags turned in time to catch Cody running at her. He was in costume, too.

Eric suppressed a shudder. Quincy was going for a little too much realism for him.

Especially if what I think is true.

Just then, he spotted Nash and Walker in full costume, posing as townies. He couldn't believe how relieved he felt knowing he had his own 'pack' there at his back. He didn't see Gina, but knew she had to be somewhere. He carefully made his way over to his brothers.

"Hey," he said. "Where's Spooky?"

Nash chuckled. "Really?"

"She's good," Walker said.

"Right here, Shep," someone said behind him. He didn't turn right away, but when he did, he was face to face with a woman he'd never seen before. Even when he looked right into her dark brown eyes, he had no recollection.

Until he realized Gina was wearing contacts. Which of course made him think of the lyrics to the Eagles' song 'Lyin' Eyes.' In this case, she'd disguised her golden eyes quite well.

"Spooky."

She grinned, grabbed his hand, then punched him in the arm, hard. "Fucker!" she cackled loudly in a very un-Gina-like voice then moved on until she'd disappeared into the crowd. Eric surreptitiously put the tiny comm she'd slipped him into his ear.

"Damn, she's amazing," Walker muttered under his breath. Eric heard his voice doubled in his earpiece.

"This is just a Tuesday for her," Eric said.

Walker shook his head. "I can't believe the bikers are here."

"Of course they are," Eric said. "*Realism* is important to Quincy. He called them his consultants. And I suspect they're here to keep an eye on their property. Make sure no one snoops."

"But to have them in the crowd like this," Walker said. "It's reckless."

"Agreed."

"So while you're doing your thing, we'll be spread out in the crowd," Nash said, "keeping an eye out and ready to stop any real fights. If the town's as angry as you say it is..." He didn't need to finish the thought.

They all knew the day would probably end ugly.

Eric nodded. Looking around again, the crowd was definitely clustered into two groups—townies and Red Hands. Even without their patch vests and in costume like the rest, they were easy to pick out. They mixed with the others like oil and water.

Or fire and gasoline if we aren't careful.

No sign of Tigo or Nitro, which bothered Eric. He wondered if they were in the ranch house.

"Time for Operation Hearts and Minds," Gina said over their comms.

"Whoo-wee, so this is a movie set," Nash drawled, loud enough for anyone to hear him. "So excitin'!" He laid his Southern accent on extra-thick. People had a tendency to dismiss him as a dumb hillbilly whenever he let his South show—much to their mistake and sometimes demise. Nash was one of the smartest people Eric knew, especially when it came to tech.

Nash headed off one way, while Walker headed the other, spreading out among the crowd. Time for Eric to get back to Tim.

On his way back to Tim and Jane, Eric spotted Sam. She was wearing a bleached-blond wig and sunglasses—another extra in the crowd. She was talking to Lacey but when she saw him, she lowered her sunglasses, held his gaze for a moment, and winked, sending his heart pounding.

Focus, jackass.

Quincy was standing at the edge of the crowd next to a platform that rose above everyone. He was talking to several cameramen. Eric watched him carefully for any signs that he was upset about the night before, or that he suspected Sam and Eric were up to something. Sam had texted earlier that Quincy hadn't approached her about being in the house, but then again, it was a particularly busy morning.

"Has he spoken to you yet, Tim?" Eric asked, jutting his chin in Quincy's direction.

"No, he hasn't. He's been talking to the cameramen all morning. I have zero direction so far."

Jane looked between Eric and Tim. "He didn't talk to you yesterday either?" She made a note on the tablet she carried everywhere. "I thought a director's job was to direct. And I thought that included the actors, even if they have four feet." Her voice dripped with sarcasm.

"Yeah, that's how it's supposed to work," Tim said, obviously annoyed.

They waited a few minutes more and finally, Quincy broke away from the cameramen and headed toward them.

His smile grew the moment he saw Jane. "There she is! There's the lady of the hour."

Jane looked anything but impressed. She didn't bother taking the hand he stretched out toward her to shake, but started right in. "Tim and Eric are doing a fantastic job of taking care of these dogs, but I still have some concerns today."

"Sure, sure, of course you do. Their safety is my priority," Quincy said, ignoring the dogs winding around and between the four of them.

"Then why haven't you given them any direction? This is a very complicated scene, and even though these dogs get along beautifully, there's always the chance that one of them is going to get overexcited and nip and bite." She gestured all around them, indicating all of the people. "If someone even moves the wrong way, a dog could take it as a sign of aggression and lash out."

"But you just said these dogs behave beautifully. I'm not concerned. I have complete faith in Tim and Eric here." Quincy beamed at them like he was a proud parent. Eric swallowed down his irritation. Looking at Tim, he thought the man was doing the same thing.

Quincy clapped his hands together, ending the thread.

"So I'm here now and I'm here to direct." He pointed at a flat area where the dogfight would be staged. There were two concentric circles painted in the dirt. The inner circle was the edge of the dogfight and the larger outer circle marked off the edge where the crowd would stand. "As you can see, there's three feet between where the dogs end and the people begin. Don't you think that'll be enough?"

Jane inspected the circles. "Make it *four* feet. At least." She studied Quincy. "You know what? Make it five."

Quincy looked around until he spotted Cassidy. She appeared to be in a serious conversation with one of the extras—who Eric realized was the mayor. "Cass! I need the circle enlarged by two feet."

Cassidy looked at him funny. "I don't understand."

Quincy huffed. Close up, Eric noticed the dark circles under Quincy's eyes, which were bloodshot. He rubbed at them.

Jane spoke up. "I want at least five feet between the dogs and the rest of the crowd, please."

Cassidy actually looked relieved. She shot a quick look at Quincy then called over the best boy with his seemingly unlimited supply of tape to explain what they needed.

"All right, you got your extra space." Quincy rocked on his heels, his smile tight and forced. "Which means I need to go back and tell my camera guys that all the direction I just gave them is now complete crap. This sets us back a good hour, but hey, anything in the name of safety, right?"

Jane stared him down. "That's exactly right. We'll be waiting in the dogs' air-conditioned trailer while you sort that out, then maybe you can direct the actors."

"The actors? I already spoke to Lacey and—"

"The *dogs*," Jane said. "And their handlers."

Quincy smiled again. "Of course. The dogs." He looked at Eric and Tim like *can you believe this shit?*

Eric just smiled back. So did Tim, who stepped closer to Jane.

"Yeah, okay." He clapped his hands again. "I'm needed elsewhere." He turned on his heel and strode back to the camera operators.

Jane breathed out hard through her nose. "I don't like that man." She dropped down to pet the nearest dog, who happened to be Pretzel, a pit bull lab mix. "You don't either, do you, baby? No, you don't," she crooned.

Quincy took his time getting back to them. No surprise there. In the meantime, Eric kept tabs on the crowd, which now growing restless under the increasing heat as the sun rose higher.

Leather and denim was not the most comfortable material to wear when the temperature rose into the nineties with no sign of slowing down, and the crowd was getting into an ugly, itchy mood. Worse, rumors were already spreading that it was 'some primadonna's fault' and that translated unfairly to Lacey. She and Sam had retreated to her trailer for the moment, which relieved Eric. At least he didn't have to keep an eye on them, and Lacey didn't have to listen to the bullshit. But it also gave people more ammunition.

Gina, Nash, and Walker all reported in regularly and what they said troubled Eric even more than grumbling about an air-conditioned trailer.

Quincy had directed the townies to be dressed as one gang and the Red Hands as the other.

"We're ready to break anything up," Gina said. "But we are ridiculously outnumbered. Continuing Hearts and Minds."

"Copy."

Hearts and Minds was a soft tactic they used for crowd control. Basically, they were walking harbingers of goodwill, trying to keep people positive and calm. Eric watched as Walker handed out water bottles to a group of people looking like they were about to combust. Nash did what Nash did best and cracked a joke that had a group of pissed-off bikers laughing their asses off. Hearts and Minds was tricky and kept you thinking on your toes, but it was totally effective, and his teammates were experts at it.

Finally, Quincy decided he'd talk to Tim and Eric. With Jane looking on, he outlined the scene. The rival gangs were pitting their dogs against each other in a fight that would pay off in cash and territory. One gang would accuse the other of cheating by coating their dog in hot sauce to irritate the other dog's mouth. After hurling insults back and forth, they would fight each other—including the dogs.

"We're going to do some establishing shots, show the dogs snarling and barking at each other. He held up his hand before Jane could protest. "You know we're using the dogs one at a time so they aren't aggressive toward each other."

Jane glared.

"And we have the motion capture suits so we can CGI the fuck outta them after. Make it look like a real fight, and no doggies get hurt. Are we good?" He smiled back.

Jane nodded once.

Quincy gave Tim and Eric some additional direction. Two camera operators would be walking around the ring with them, one filming each man, and they needed to learn how to stay out of the opposite camera's range. A couple of practice rounds later, they were ready. A cheer went up among both townies and Red Hands when Quincy climbed up on the platform with another camera operator to oversee the shot. Finally, they were getting to it.

Pretzel and another of Tim's dogs, Rawhide, a German Shepherd had been suited up with round sensors all over their bodies that would track their movements. Tim, dressed as one of the bikers, went around the inner ring first with Pretzel as the crowd cheered and booed according to their side. He gave the command for Pretzel to bark and snarl and act aggressive. Cameras whirled around them on cranes and dollies, capturing the action.

Then it was Eric's turn. He and Rawhide took a turn around the ring. After spending time with the dog, Eric could read his body language, and Rawhide was more than happy to be there, knowing that his favorite treat waited for him at the end. Eric gave him the command to 'attack' and Rawhide let loose with barking and snarls that would have stopped a bear in its tracks. The crowd played their part—shouting, stomping their feet, waving their fists. But one voice made itself distinct from the others.

Cody's.

The kid had a ringside spot where he cheered louder than the adults.

"Friend!" Eric heard him shout. He pointed at Eric.

The world tilted.

Keep it together.

Eric was on the opposite side of the ring from where Tim had stopped, so when the shooting was done and the shots put together in post, it would look like the two dogs were ready to attack each other. CGI would cover them, turning them into animals that looked scarred, injured, and ferocious. But this position gave Eric a perfect view of Cody, who cheered and waved at him, shouting *friend* the entire time.

Prickly sweat trickled down the back of Eric's neck. He felt chills despite the heat. It had been a cold day in Kandahar, the dead of winter, and the ground was frozen when the boy he'd befriended looked up in fear...

Eric scanned the crowd again, and there she was. His Sam. His reality in a world of make-believe. She was looking right at him. Her lips parted, and she spoke one all-important word that took away all the fear and uncertainty.

Brickle.

Eric turned away from the cameras in case they caught his smile and laugh. Goddam, but he loved his goof. The only woman in the world who could bring him joy and laughter in the middle of a shitstorm.

They'd filmed different takes for an hour when Quincy shouted, "Cut!" for the last time.

He conferred with Cassidy who shouted, "Moving on," meaning it was time for the next setup.

Jane nodded at the director in approval. Tim and Eric had done their jobs. The dogs were safe, no one was bitten, and it was time to let the furry actors take a break in their trailer. The crowd had done its part too, cheering and shouting, though some of the Red Hands shouted for the dogs to actually fight.

Tim and Eric led the dogs back to their trailer while the crew set up for the next scenes. As soon as he got inside Nash's voice came over the comm.

"Hearts and Minds aborted. Hostiles. Need you, Shep."

"I need to get back out there," Eric told Tim. "The crowd."

"Yeah, I hear you," Tim said. "I'll take care of things and sign off with Jane."

Eric headed back out and just in time—it looked like the crowd was ready to fight without any direction whatsoever. The two sides were shouting at each other and it wasn't over the dogfight.

"I told you scum to stay away from my shop!" one man yelled.

"Fuck you, I wouldn't buy your shit anyway," one of the Red Hands shouted back.

Eric broke into a run and when he got to the crowd, a hand landed on his shoulder.

He turned to see Tigo's fist flying at his face.

Eric arched backward and felt the breeze left by Tigo's meaty hand just missing his nose. He threw his upper body forward and his head connected with Tigo's, sending the man stumbling backward. Another hand landed on him but Eric was ready. He spun and hit Nitro with a powerful hook that snapped the man's head to the left.

Around him, Red Hands were attacking pissed-off townies. Eric searched for Sam, Mags, and Cody. Knowing Sam, she was probably having the time of her life. But God help his fury if anything—*anything*—happened to Cody.

Tigo stood up and honest-to-God charged Eric like a mad bull. Eric sidestepped but decided to help his old friend along by grabbing the back of his vest and waistband and increasing his speed so that he barreled right into Nitro, who'd barely recovered from Eric's punch. The two went down in a heap and Eric didn't give them another thought as he went wading into the crowd looking for Cody.

He spotted Mags first. She was holding Cody, pressing his head to her neck and using her body as a shield as she tried to get out of the crowd with her grandson. Eric led with his shoulder through the crowd, careful not to hurt anyone needlessly, but landing a few thumps where they needed to be landed. He reached Mags and wrapped his arm around her while turning and shielding them as they passed through the crowd to safety.

"Is Mae okay?" he asked Mags.

"Yeah. She stepped out to the ladies' room just before it started."

"Take Cody to the dog trailer," he told her. "Tell Tim I sent you."

She nodded and ran toward the trailer.

"Eyes on Little Sister?" Eric asked his team, knowing Samantha would absolutely cringe at her code name.

"With me," Gina responded. "Double, too." That meant Lacey. "Packages secured."

That was a relief. Sam was safe.

Eric looked up at Quincy on his platform like Caesar lording over a fight in the Colosseum. The guy looked like he was getting off on the violence and chaos he'd engineered. Eric started back through the crowd straight to the platform when he caught Quincy's eye. At least the man had the decency to flinch.

"People!" he shouted. "Enough! Cut!" He clapped his hands over his head.

Nothing happened.

He tried again. "Cut! Enough! Stop!"

Quincy finally looked afraid. He scanned the crowd until he found someone he wanted. "Nitro!"

Eric turned in time to see Nitro. He put his fingers in his mouth and a high-pitched whistle cut through the shouting.

The fighting slowed, mostly because the Red Hands stopped their aggression on Nitro's command.

"Scene's over!" Quincy yelled, much to the confusion of the townspeople. Eric heard several people ask *This was acting?*

The two groups separated as the crew passed through the crowd, physically separating them where necessary.

"What the hell?" Eric said over the comm.

"Just what I was going to say," Walker answered.

"Grade-A manipulator," Gina added.

Eric watched Quincy climb down from the platform and approach Nitro. They spoke quickly, then Nitro whistled again. The Red Hands all turned and headed for the parking lot.

"All right, I think we're gonna wrap early for the day," Quincy shouted. "Thanks, everyone. Make sure we have your names and then watch for yourselves in the credits."

Eric practically rolled his eyes. *That won't happen. And does he really think he can bribe these people that easily?*

Judging by the grumblings, nope.

But Quincy had gotten what he wanted, so Eric figured he didn't care. He quickly got back up on the platform and watched as his crew worked crowd control.

Eric turned to find Gina, and hopefully Sam and Lacey.

"Spooky, location."

"Double's HQ."

Lacey's trailer. Good. Eric headed that way, passing Nash and Walker, who were checking on people. He grabbed Nash.

"Go check on Tim. There's a woman and her grandson, Mags, and Cody there. Make sure they're okay. I'll catch up with you."

"Roger." Nash jogged off toward the dogs' trailer.

Eric stepped into blissfully cool air when he opened the trailer door. Gina and Sam were standing on either side of Lacey, who was sitting on a couch. Gina looked cooler than the air—her typical self. Both Blaze and Fleur were curled up at her feet. Sam looked pissed, and Lacey was completely distraught.

"How we doing?" he asked Gina.

"Authorities are on their way," she told him. "I won't be surprised if this shuts it all down."

Eric shook his head. "We're lucky no one was seriously hurt. What a stupid, stupid waste, and for what? One man's ego."

Lacey looked even more upset. Sam hugged her. "I think I need to get Lacey back to the hotel." Her voice sounded strange, almost wooden.

"You okay?" Eric asked. "I mean, under the circumstances."

She looked away as she nodded.

Of course she's not okay, dumbass. She's just kissed the big stunt goodbye.

"I'll take you," Eric said.

"No, I'm sure you need to stay here," Sam said. "It's okay. I've got her." Her eyes implored Eric to understand. He nodded.

"I just want to get out of here," Lacey said. She smiled weakly at Eric, then at Gina. "Thanks for your help. You got us to safety."

Gina waved her off. "Shouldn't have been necessary."

Sam and Lacey headed for the trailer door. Eric held it open for them. Sam and Lacey aimed for the parking lot and disappeared into the milling crowd.

TWENTY-SIX

"You think they bought it?" Lacey asked Sam as they changed course. They moved through the crowd toward the ranch house.

"Yeah, no thanks to my beyond non-existent acting skills," Sam said. "Thank you so much. I owe you big time."

"Sweetie, I feel sick just thinking about that footage of you. What if Quincy's making some creepy little movie out of it? You need to get it before the cops get here."

"Yeah, I'm just afraid they'll padlock the door, then confiscate everything and God knows if I'll ever get my hands on it after that. If someone leaks it—"

"Say no more."

"It's killing me to lie to them, to Eric, but this way they have plausible deniability. I'm the only one responsible for tampering with evidence." *If I get caught.*

They'd circled around to the back of the ranch house and stood under the window Sam guessed belonged to the room where Quincy had his editing equipment set up. "Can you get in?"

Sam grinned. "I was made for this." She hugged Lacey. "You'd better head back to the hotel."

"You sure you don't want me to stay? Keep a lookout?"

"No, I'll be fine. The Red Hands all took off."

"I think I'd be more afraid of Gina finding you."

Sam grimaced. "Exactly. So get outta here, but be careful."

Lacey gave her one last smile before she sneaked away toward the parking lot.

Sam turned her attention to the window while she pulled on a pair of supple leather gloves. Yup, the window was old and the wood frame was showing dry rot. It took almost no effort for Sam to break in. She crossed the dim, dusty room and walked around a table with a keyboard and several monitors. Quincy's editing console. Sam pulled out the metal folding chair and sat down. She clicked the mouse and the screens lit up. The middle screen showed a desktop and she immediately began rooting through files that were named by date.

"Fuck." Her first impulse was to grab them all and trash them. Yeah, she was probably breaking the law and tampering with evidence, but she could justify trashing clips of her face because they were her. *Her* images, and she'd be damned if she let anyone have control over them.

But then there were the dogfighting files—if that's what she actually heard. Those she couldn't trash in good conscience. Her heart hurt thinking of those poor animals locked up and hurting somewhere. They needed to be found and saved.

And she'd never be able to look Eric in the eye again. The stricken look on his face when she talked about what she'd heard. No. She'd have to preview the files one by one and leave the dogfighting ones as evidence.

Her fingers flew as she opened the first video file. Sure enough, there was a closeup of her face as she told Jesse how much she loved him.

"Motherfucker," she swore under her breath. She dragged the file to the trash icon and then opened the next one. It was a variation on the first file and quickly joined it in the trash. Then

Sam had an idea. She looked at the file sizes and opened the biggest one. She nearly fell back when the room filled with the sound of barking dogs. Sam scrambled to find the volume control but the images on the screen tore her attention away.

Two dogs were squared off across from each other, snarling, growling, and straining as hard as they could on their leashes. Two burley men per dog held them back. The dogs were covered in the circles that would capture their movements so that an editor could hide the truth later. Neither dog looked like it was sporting any current injuries, but Sam could see old scars running through their fur. Drool hung in ropes from their maws. It flew with every bark and spotted the reddish earth, turning it the color of old blood. She had no doubt that this footage would find its way into the movie and no one would ever know two dogs had suffered for real.

"Let loose the dogs!" one of the men shouted. Sam hit pause and caught her breath while her heart hammered in her chest and she fought the urge to puke. She closed the video and dragged it away from the others on the laptop. Again, she was tempted to just drag the rest to the trash and then delete all of them. Surely, that video was evidence enough?

But what if it isn't? Or, what if there are other files that would make even better evidence?

Sam looked for the second largest file and opened it.

Sam-as-Shawna looked at her from the screen. The back of Tristian's head was slightly off to the side.

"I want you," she said in the worst, most unsexy voice imaginable to Tristian.

Then the scene cut to a new one.

"What. The actual. Fuck?"

It was a shot of a man with Tristian's shaggy movie hairstyle. She knew his road name and had seen him for the first time earlier that day when he'd stopped the fight.

Nitro. The leader of the Red Hands.

"I want you too, Samantha. I always have," Nitro said on-screen.

The scene changed again to the back of Tristian's head and Sam's face as she 'reacted' to the words.

Sam covered her mouth in shock. So this was what Quincy was up to. He didn't just pay the Red Hands for use of their clubhouse. He was making a private movie of Sam and Nitro together.

She heard the floorboards creaking and footsteps crossing the room behind her only a moment before a hand went around her head covering her mouth and a needle went into her arm.

Son of bitch snuck up behind me when the dogs were barking on-screen. Sam struggled against her captor, but already her head was going fuzzy and her limbs heavy. Nitro's hair brushed against her cheek, flooding her with revulsion.

"It's Jesse. I didn't want to scare you away, you pretty thing," he said in her ear. He watched the screen as the scene played out. "I love this scene. I couldn't let the cops get my movie, could I? Looks like you had the same idea."

Sam bucked and tried to break free. But her eyelids were so heavy. Sam felt herself slipping into unconsciousness as Nitro's voice followed her down into a nightmare.

"But I don't need the footage. I have you now, after all this time," he whispered. "The real thing. My own little star."

Where am I?

God, her head hurt. Sam tried to move but that only made her want to puke. Gentle hands eased her up into a sitting position as she gagged. They turned her head so that she could throw up into a bucket. The metal edge felt cool against the bottom of her chin. Judging by the smell, this wasn't the first time she'd done it.

"Eric?" she rasped, spitting the last of the bad taste from her mouth.

"No, baby, it's your Jesse. I've got you, honey. You'll feel better soon."

Sam moaned and struggled as her nightmare turned into a worse reality. How could she ever mistake this son of a bitch for her beloved?

She wrenched her eyes open. He was holding her—oh sweet Jesus—on a bed with a dingy comforter. At least she was still dressed in her costume from the set, though the bleach-blond wig was gone. So, he hadn't seen her naked or taken advantage of her that way. *Thank God.*

How long had she been out? And where was she?

He's taken me somewhere else she thought dimly. *Oh, God, how will Eric find me now? I've got to get out of here.*

"Hey now, no struggling," Nitro chided as if he were talking to a misbehaving child. He reached across her and set the bucket on a nightstand. His keys jingled on his belt.

They were propped up on a pile of pillows against the headboard of a narrow bed. Sam blinked and tried to get her eyes to focus, to figure out where she was. A bare bulb overhead lit what looked like a bedroom with one window. There was a single nightstand on the side closest to her. Her wig lay discarded on a wooden chair across the room. There were movie posters on the walls featuring a young woman.

No, not a young woman. Blown-up photos of Sam as a teenager.

Sam gagged again. Nitro stroked her hair and rocked her.

"I couldn't believe it when Zachary told me Quincy Torrent was wanting to shoot a movie around Sagebrush," Nitro said.

Zachary? Her head swam. The name was familiar. *Zachary Fischer. The mayor.*

"He was against it," Nitro went on. "Said it would bring the wrong kind of attention to the town and might risk our little operation. But I saw a different opportunity. A once-in-a-lifetime chance." He kissed her temple and she shuddered. "To see you here, in the flesh. My little star."

Sam shook her head. Every fiber of her wild soul wanted to fight, but she clung to the rational voice in her head telling her to stay calm and think her way out of this.

Wait for your opportunity the voice said. *Like you're waiting for the right time to jump from the bike to the truck. Timing is everything and you need to buy time for Eric and the others to find you.*

They will *find you. And they'll save you.*

Nitro nuzzled her. "So when *the* Quincy Torrent marched up to my door and knocked, I invited him right on in. He and Zachary took a seat and I explained what it would cost for him to do business in the town. It was gonna cost *you*, baby."

"Me?" she mumbled, pretending not to understand what she knew all too well. Quincy had done worse than burning her. He'd sold her out.

Nitro chuckled as if she were just the cutest little thing. "Well, not *you* exactly. A movie of you. Of us. Just for me and no one else. And no deepfake crap. You."

Quincy's words came swimming up from her memories. *The public will never see any of it, I promise. Cross my heart and hope to die.* The bastard had told the truth. Sam chuckled bitterly.

Nitro smiled. "Yeah, you like that, huh? Just you and me in our own little movie. Now that you're here though, we can make a real one. No Tristian fucking St. Paul pretending to be me." He held up a hank of her sweat-soaked hair. "And we'll wash this crappy color out of your hair because you're so pretty as a blonde." He pointed to one of the giant photos. "Like in that one."

"Not my real color," she mumbled.

"Yeah, honey, I know you had to dye your hair for the part, but we'll fix it."

"No." She pointed a shaky finger at the photo. "That's not my real color. I dyed it different colors all the time. To hide in plain sight. I had to hide," adrenaline flooded her system, bringing her out of her haze, "from sons of bitches like you."

"Samantha." Nitro's voice stayed soft and chiding even but he tightened his arm around her. "I never met you before now, but I *know* you. If you just get to know me, you'll understand how much I need you. How much I loved you all these years and knew you were mine just by looking at your beautiful face, little star."

The rational voice in her head pleaded with Sam. *Calm, stay calm, and let them find you. Play along with him. Play dead if you have to.*

Rage flooded her. Her one precious wild soul howled.

"You son of a bitch. You aren't a big man, you're a coward. You watched me from the shadows. You watched me in town. You watched me at the park. You watched me leave my house. You watched me with my mom, with my dad, with my friends. You watched me online as I grew up. You watched that damn ticking clock. You watched me *all my fucking life* and I had no recourse. You tried to rob me of my childhood. You think you have me now, but you don't. You never will. All you have are pictures and you will never have *me*."

Sam elbowed Nitro in the solar plexus as hard as she could. His eyes opened wide as he lost his breath and his hold on her. She rolled and lunged for the metal bucket. He tried to grab her as she swung back around and slammed the bucket into the side of his head, stunning him.

Sam rolled off the bed and staggered to her feet. The world did not want to hold still for her. She stumbled across the room to the wooden chair and picked it up. It came crashing down onto Nitro's head while he was still trying to breathe. She hit him again.

Footsteps in the hall outside told her she only had seconds. Sam turned Nitro onto his side and unhooked the carabiner holding his keys on his belt. Someone pounded on the door.

"You okay? God fucking dammit it, Nitro, this was a stupid idea."

She pulled up the window shade, looked out into the night, and hoped she was on the first floor. No such luck. But she was only a story up and she thought she could make out a strip of long grass directly below her.

Sam opened the window, scooted onto the sill, then turned and lowered herself down, trying to shorten the distance she needed to fall as much as she could. Arms stretched, she relaxed her body to soften the impact before letting go. Sam bent her knees and did a mid-air turn as she fell. She landed on the balls of her feet and immediately tucked her body to roll forward away from the house.

Not bad, except I want to puke again. She heard dogs barking from somewhere behind her along with the sound of their bodies hitting a chain link fence over and over, like they were trying to escape. She remembered the video and felt even sicker about not being able to help them immediately, but she swore that if—

No. When.

When she got out of this, she'd make sure they were rescued.

Sam got to her feet and looked around until she saw a row of bikes. She ran towards them, wondering which one was Nitro's. She squeezed the key fob on his ring of keys and the indicator lights on the Kawasaki at the end flashed.

Awesome.

A door slammed open behind her and she picked up speed. She remembered some joke about a man pulled over for drunk driving telling the officer he had to drive because he sure as hell couldn't walk. Sam wondered what the hell Nitro had drugged her with and hoped she could ride better than she could run.

She mounted Nitro's bike, turned the key, and decided to find out.

Sam turned the bike and sped down the dirt road away from the house. It didn't take long before she heard another bike racing behind her. Sam put on speed and felt the bike want to tango under her. It was built for speed, but the handling left much to be desired. She had no idea where she was or where she was going except away from Nitro. The sky wasn't entirely dark. The just-past-full moon was hiding behind a ridge, judging by the light. If she could just stay ahead of this guy behind her long enough, maybe she could see a larger road or even a small one that might let her lose him among the hills and canyons.

The moon broke over the ridge, letting her get a better look at the terrain. She came to the top of a hill and saw several paths below. Down she went into a shallow valley where trails tangled. Yup, she needed to lose this guy behind her quick. He was good, matching her tricks and turns down smaller roads. If she'd been on a different bike, she could have gone off-road into the canyon and lost him completely. Now that she was on a motorcycle she was in her glory. No need to be afraid. She'd escaped. One more stunt— without a safety net.

No, that wasn't true. She knew in her heart that Eric was on his way.

Up ahead, she saw what might have been an actual road and started toward it. At least there, she might be able to figure out where she was, or maybe stumble onto a gas station, a house, something. God, her head was killing her. She may have escaped, but she couldn't keep this up for long.

The bike started to ride rough. *Fuck.* Something was definitely wrong with it.

She lost acceleration, and with it, the bike became harder to control, but at least she was on an actual road now. She heard the rider behind her gaining fast. Distracted by her bike, she just missed a turnoff that would have taken her among some boulders.

Then up ahead she saw two more bikes coming at her fast. They knew the trails along here better than she ever would.

They must have taken a trail that let them out ahead of me. I'm getting herded.

Only way out is back through.

Sam slowed just enough to do a wide turn that almost laid the bike down. She sped back the way she'd come, her stomach lurching as she realized *just* how close the guy was. She flew past him, hoping the Kawasaki would hold together long enough for her to hide.

Except now she had three bikes on her tail. And no idea if any more waited for her up ahead.

Come on, where can I turn off? She knew the next turn was close...or at least she thought so. It was still dark, and things looked different coming back the opposite way. The good old boy who'd been chasing her had apparently waited for his two buddies so they could ride together in a big wall of coming-to-fuck-you-up, which had given her a little time, but now they were gaining.

Gaining fast.

She *just* missed the turn-off. They were going to catch her, no doubt about it.

Another engine roared over the sound of the motorcycles behind her. She risked a look over her shoulder.

And saw Eric's truck speed across the road from the turn. It stopped, blocking the bikes. With any luck, they'd laid them down.

Sam whooped.

She heard the truck coming closer and looked in her mirror. Eric was providing her with cover. When she turned back, she saw another headlight coming straight at her. She turned off just in time onto a dirt trail leading up a brush-covered hill, with plans to abandon the bike somewhere along there and hide until Eric followed her up, then jump out and signal him.

Eric blocked the road momentarily, just long enough to keep the other biker away and for her to disappear around a bend.

Then she heard the worst sound in the world behind her.

Gunshots.

Sam needed to focus on what she was doing and trust that Eric would be all right.

He's a retired SEAL. There's no one tougher. He'll be fine.

Please, God, let him be fine.

She rode up the hill until she didn't hear anyone behind her.

She killed the engine and rolled the bike into some sagebrush. The moon was high, lighting the landscape. She was exhausted and starting to feel her adrenaline crash. Her heavy head was threatening to abandon her neck and go rolling down the hill.

Everything was quiet.

Oh, God, what if they shot Eric? She couldn't hide in the brush knowing he might be injured. She needed to get to him, now. Sam started down the hill, hoping she was wrong. Hoping that Eric was fine and that would meet her on foot halfway down.

He'll always be there when I need him.

Eric Armstrong was the real deal. He didn't pretend to be someone he wasn't. He was kind and funny, quick to help anyone on set. He was a good man, down to his bones.

And he believed in her.

Sam believed in him, too.

She'd almost reached the road at the bottom of the hill. Her head was pounding and she staggered, then dropped to her knees. Only a little farther to the road and Eric. She could make it. She was tough. He believed in her and he'd come to rescue her.

A shadow fell over Sam, blocking out the moonlight. She turned and looked up at Nitro.

"You were wrong. I do have you, little star. I have you right here and now. You were so fun to chase but now you're gonna come with me. We're gonna die together if that's what we have to do."

He pulled out a gun and aimed it at her. Her one precious life was about to end.

Shots rang out and Nitro staggered backward. His gun went off and the bullet hit the dirt a few feet away from Sam, close enough to make her cry out in fear. But Nitro was down and she didn't think he'd be getting back up again.

"Sam!" Eric sounded terrified. "Are you hurt?"

Then she was in his arms.

"I'm all right. You saved me."

He swept her up off her feet in a giant bear hug. She wrapped her legs around his waist and they stared into each other's eyes. The smile he gave her made her weak in the knees. Not just because he was drop-dead gorgeous, but because it was genuine, and just for her.

"Well, that was fun," Sam said.

"I was fucking terrified," Eric said at the same time.

They both laughed, lightly at first, until Sam's turned into something approaching a sob.

"Shh, baby, I've got you now. It's over. You're safe."

She leaned forward until their foreheads touched and closed her eyes.

"Maybe next time, we can just go out for ice cream instead," she said, feeling herself slipping back down into unconsciousness.

TWENTY-SEVEN

The next time Sam opened her eyes, she was in a hospital room.

She felt someone holding her hand. Her first thought was that it was Eric, but the hand was much too soft to be his. She opened her eyes to find her mother sitting in her wheelchair next to Sam's bed, clutching her hand and smiling at her through her tears.

"Well, kiddo. You certainly gave us a good scare."

"Sorry, Mom. I know that's only supposed to happen up on the screen."

"Damn right it's only supposed to happen up on the screen."

Sam looked around. She and her mom were the only two people in the room. "Where is..." She stopped herself before she said Eric.

"I sent everyone out the minute you started to stir. I wanted a word in private with you first."

Sam braced for it. A tirade from Bette the actress, the one who always got her way. And as much as she hated to admit it, her mom was right in this case. Quincy had betrayed her, had betrayed an entire town just to see his own creative vision come true. She should have known better. And even not knowing better, she should have at least listened to Bette, who did.

"Mom, I know sorry doesn't even cover it," she said. Bette held up her other hand to stop her.

"That's enough out of you, young lady. You're going to let me talk and you're going to listen this time."

Sam closed her mouth and nodded, resigned.

"I know what I'm talking about when it comes to this business, wouldn't you agree?"

Sam nodded.

"What I obviously don't know is how to respect my own daughter's life choices."

Wait. That stopped Sam cold.

"What did you just say?"

"Darling, I have been blind and deaf to who you are, and for that, I apologize. I applied a double standard to you as opposed to your brothers and let them do their own thing. When Grant Junior went off to become a lawyer, I let him go with my blessing. When Jake went off to join the military, I didn't send in a covert squad of GI Joes to wipe his butt." Bette smirked. "Oh, but if I could have, I would have done that."

Sam laughed softly.

"But I didn't, that's the thing," Bette continued. "And I didn't treat you the same as I did your brothers. Instead, I sent in Eric to babysit you on your first real job."

Sam looked Bette in the eye. "Is it because you think I'm somehow weaker? That I can't handle myself?"

Bette shook her head. "No, that's not at all why. It's because I thought your life up to that point had been a rollercoaster ride compared to what you wanted to do, which to me was careening down a mountain in a real car with no brakes. I wanted you to become an actor like me because that's what I understand. I get that world, and I thought I could guide you safely through it. But, that's not *your* dream. Being a stunt woman is the dream in your heart. Your father tried to tell me and I didn't listen to him, either. I was afraid. And both my fear and my stubbornness have put us all at odds, and it hurts. I hate it when we fight, I really do. And that's *my* fault." Tears filled her mother's eyes.

"Mom," she started, but Bette shook her head.

"I never should have discouraged you from doing what you do best and kept you from the dreams you had. Instead, I tried to protect you in all the wrong ways. I tried to throw a net over you when I should have been putting a net *under* you."

Sam grinned at that.

"By trying to keep you close, I pushed you out. And I can't blame you. You weren't ever going to find what you needed at home. I overreacted and I practically pushed you at Quincy in my own way." She looked down at her lap. "I was wrong and I'm deeply regretful and I'm sorry."

Tears blurred Sam's vision. She couldn't remember the last time her mother had actually admitted to being wrong. And she was completely serious. This was not Bette the actress. This was Bette the mom.

Sam gave her mom's hand a squeeze. "I should have listened to you too though, Mom. I should have had the faith to know that my chance was coming eventually. That Quincy was a bad idea, and not the only option I had."

Bette shook her head. "You couldn't have known everything. None of us did. Quincy made a deal with the devil—no, two devils —when he came to Sagebrush."

"There's no way that Quincy is going to be allowed to continue with the movie, am I right?"

Bette smiled sadly. "You're right, sweetheart. Quincy is out. He's in so much trouble right now for so many reasons, reckless endangerment for starters." Her smile took on a vicious edge. "And there are definitely civil suits in his future."

Sam sat up. "Was anyone hurt badly?"

"No, everyone is fine, thank goodness. It could have gone so much worse. No, for one thing, Quincy's in deep shit with the Humane Society. Jane decided the dogs were in way too much danger, even if they were in their trailer. The other producers learned what happened and of course, they stepped in and halted production."

"So no movie now, huh?"

"Oh no, there will be a movie. The producers knew who they were dealing with, so they hedged their bets. This production was insured up to the gills so there has to be a movie. They had a meeting early this morning and decided to see what footage had been shot and what they could scrape together with that and release it straight to streaming, *if* they could get anyone to even pick it up."

"God, that's worse than no movie at all. Poor Lacey. Poor everyone." Sam studied her mom, whose turned-down mouth said one thing while her twinkling eyes said something else. "What?"

"Well, I happened to Zoom in and crash that meeting."

Sam's hopes rose. "And?"

"When they said minimal viable product, I said I don't think so. I've always wanted to produce a movie, so what could be better for my first project than a movie with my daughter in it?" Bette looked into Sam's eyes. "But I'll only go forward with this if it's all right with you."

Sam smiled so big, her face hurt. "Yeah, Mom. That's fine with me. If—" She put her finger in the air—"I still get to do the *True Lies* stunt."

Bette laughed. "Yes, of course you get to do the *True Lies* stunt, God help me. And your father will be working with Ken. He's very excited to be back on a set."

Sam's eyes pricked with tears again. "Thanks, Mom." She scooted as close to the edge of the bed as she could and hugged her mom.

"All right, this meeting is adjourned," Bette said. "I don't think I can keep everyone out a minute longer anyway."

Sam looked at the closed door. "So, uh, who all is out there?"

"Well, your father and Grant Junior, of course. Jake and Rachel are here, too."

"Really?"

Bette nodded. "That dear girl postponed one of her concert dates and they rushed to Arizona the minute they'd heard what happened."

"How *is* Jake?" Sam asked tentatively.

For the first time, her mother seemed truly troubled.

Sam covered her mouth. "He and Rachael aren't having issues, are they?" Besides her parents, Sam couldn't think of any married couple more in love than Jake and Rachael, and that was saying a lot. Happy couples surrounded her.

"No. I mean, not the way you might think. They love each other very much, and they'll see each other through all ups and downs." Bette blinked rapidly. For all her acting skills, she couldn't hide true pain from her daughter.

Sam had a sad, sick feeling in the pit of her stomach. Rachael had said that once she got her career established, she wanted to start a family. She was certainly established now.

"Did they—?"

Bette shook her head. "It's not my place to share, sweetheart. Just give your brother some time and patience, and Rachael all your love."

Sam only nodded and swallowed the lump in her throat.

Bette brightened. "But they are going to be so happy to see you awake right now."

"So...anyone else out there?" Sam asked, her tone mock-casual.

Bette grinned. "There's a whole pack of Watchdogs, if that's what you're asking."

"A whole pack?" Sam said with a grin.

A rapid, impatient knock on the door interrupted them.

Bette rolled her eyes. "Well, one in particular is scratching at the door to see you."

"Mom—"

"Sweetheart, I think he's wonderful. So does your father." Bette leaned forward. "But the most important thing, the only thing that matters, is that *you* think he's wonderful."

"I do. Eric *is* wonderful."

"Then by all means," Bette rolled her chair to the door, "I'll leave you two alone."

TWENTY-EIGHT

Eric waited outside the hospital room while Bette spoke to Sam. As much as he knew the women needed to talk, he wanted to be in there with Sam right now, to hold her in his arms and reassure himself that she was all right. Blaze paced beside him up and down the hospital corridor. She'd been by his side all through the night as he watched Sam sleep, unable to close his own eyes out of the irrational fear that she'd vanish, nothing but a wishful dream. In the morning, Sam's parents came in with her oldest brother, a prosecutor married to his job, who looked like the spitting image of his father. After introductions, Bette told him Gina, Walker, and Nash were waiting outside.

Along with Jake and Rachael, who'd just flown in.

When Sam stirred and Bette ordered Grant and Eric out of the room, the others were in the small waiting room at the end of the hall. Jake stood up the minute the men walked in.

"Cool your engines, son," Grant said. "Mom's talking to her."

Jake growled and sat back down. Rachael kissed him.

"Might as well get comfortable," she said, smiling. "I certainly learned that lesson."

Jake smiled, about the first smile Eric had seen on the man's face in months. He took his wife's hand in his and kissed it.

Eric left the room to pace the hall. He wanted to be the very next person Sam saw. When he got to the end of the hallway he turned to see Jake standing alone by Sam's door, watching him.

"I'm going in there next," Eric said without preamble when he reached Jake.

Jake nodded, to Eric's shock.

"And if she'll have me, I plan to continue my relationship with her, whether you like it or not."

"Didn't think you'd do otherwise." Jake smirked. "If you told me any different, I'd have to punch you."

"Man, what the fuck?" Eric growled, too angry and exhausted to care. "You ride my ass for months about even looking at Sam and now you're saying this shit?"

"Dude, I was wrong—no, I was a complete asshole. And I'm still being an asshole and I'm sorry." He held out his hand for Eric to shake.

Eric nodded and shook Jake's hand. "Yeah, fine. But can you tell me why? What's your problem with me? That I'm too old? That's what Sam said. It's bullshit, you know."

Jake clenched his eyes shut. "Fuck. No, that's not what I think." He opened them again and all Eric saw was pain. "I'm..." He pressed his lips together until they turned into a pale line. "Rachael and I might not be able to have kids."

"Oh, shit, man. I'm sorry."

Jake took a deep breath. "The medical issue is mine. And, I've been taking it out on you by being an overbearing asshole when it came to protecting my sister from hurt. It's all twisted up in here." He jabbed his forehead. "But, Rachael found out what a dick I was being and set me straight. She sent me out here, too. I'm sorry, man."

"Me, too," Eric said. "I hope you two can find an answer."

Jake nodded. "Thanks." He looked at the closed door and shook his head. "Jesus, Mom, share, will ya? There's a man in love out here." He made a fist and pounded on the door.

Eric laughed. "Oh, sure. Say you're sorry then get me in trouble with Bette."

"Dude, welcome to the family. You poor sucker."

The hospital door opened and Bette came out. "She's all yours," she told Eric. Then her gaze shifted to Jake and she frowned. "*You* are a rude monkey."

Eric didn't bother listening to the rest. He needed to get to Sam *now*.

The worry in his heart melted into pure joy when their eyes met. Eric crossed the room in what felt like two steps and she was in his arms. He smelled her sexy vanilla-and-leather scent and kissed her within an inch of her life.

"You saved me," she whispered as she stroked his face. "I knew you would, but how did you find me? I don't even know where I was."

"It was all in the dogfighting files that you left on the computer," Eric said. "Gina saw Lacey alone in the parking lot—"

Sam smiled and shook her head. "I knew she would. Tell me Lacey lived to tell the tale."

"She did. She put up a valiant effort that lasted all of five minutes. That's honestly longer than some people trained to withstand torture hold out against her." He was pretty sure he was only half-joking. "But, she finally told Gina what you guys did."

"I'm sorry. It was stupid, and I wasn't thinking." She shivered in his arms, and he hated feeling it. "But the thought of my face getting leaked when I had no idea what he'd done, and just thinking about what he *could* do with the footage—"

"Hey." Eric kissed her lips before she could say another word. "You were upset. And, you had every right to be. He used you."

"I promise I'll bring you along on my next adventure."

"You'd better." He stroked her cheek. "So, by the time we got into the ranch house, you were already gone. We found the empty syringe on the floor along with your phone. We had no idea who had taken you, but of course we suspected it was one of the bikers. We didn't know why either, until we looked at the computer screen and opened a file off to the side."

"The footage of the dogfight. I separated it out and planned to trash the rest."

"Good thing you did. That was the first one we looked at. We thought maybe they kidnapped you because of what you'd seen. We sent a screenshot of the house behind them and a couple of the surrounding hills to Elissa and she identified the location online. I could only hope that was where they took you. While she was doing that, we checked the trash and found another big file."

Sam smiled grimly. "You saw the movie that Quincy had spliced together of me and Nitro. I had it open when he sneaked up behind me. He must have thrown it away since he had me in real life."

"His name is Jesse Colin Wilson. He's a sick fuck. *Was* a sick fuck."

"Thank God he's gone," Sam said quietly. "What about the others?"

"Feds have rounded up most of the bikers, and the dogs are at a shelter. Jane's overseeing that personally." Eric paused and tried not to think about what could have happened to Sam if they'd chosen the wrong location to look for her first. "I'm glad you didn't go downstairs in the ranch house. The basement was full of cages."

"For those poor dogs?" Her voice held onto a shred of hope. But the look in her eyes told Eric that she suspected the truth.

"No. For people."

"Oh my God." Tears sprung into her eyes and Eric held her tightly.

"No one was there. The good news is, Gina and her friends found them." Eric couldn't bring himself to tell her it was two women and three children. "They're safe now. They're getting help."

Sam bit her lip as a sob tried to escape.

"I'm so sorry, baby. I didn't mean to upset you like this."

"No, it's okay," she said. "I'm so glad those bastards are in custody. And I'm glad that Sagebrush is going to be okay now too." Her eyes widened. "Zachary Fisher, the mayor! You've got to—"

"We know, baby. He was in the middle of it, working with the gang and getting his share of profits for turning a blind eye to whatever they smuggled right through town. He's in custody right along with them. I'm sure they'll have a lot to talk about in their cells."

Sam tucked her face into Eric's neck. He felt his skin grow wet as she cried. He held her and rocked her, reassuring her that she was safe.

Eventually, her tears dried. She pulled back and looked at him.

"I'm done crying," she said. "Everyone is safe now and I have things to celebrate."

"If you're talking about the movie going forward, I know all about it. Congratulations, babe. This is wonderful."

"It's wonderful for everybody. I cannot wait."

"Me neither. I'll be there to watch you fly."

TWENTY-NINE

Okay, breathe Sam told herself. *This is the moment that you have been waiting for, the one that you have worked toward your entire life, from the moment you sat down next to Dad on the couch and watched his stunts for the first time.*

Sam looked out over the early morning desert landscape stretching out in all directions. Ahead of her lay one mile of perfectly flat road. And after that was a sheer drop off a cliff.

Sam's job today was to fly straight off that cliff.

She'd looked over the stunt bike countless times. It was brand new, never used in a stunt before, but one could never be too careful when it came to things like this. The old joke, of course, was safety third, but in this case, safety definitely came first.

Her dad had looked the bike over, too, before he purchased it. No way was he going to let his little girl ride an inferior bike into the best stunt ever.

Drones hummed and flew past Sam as their operators sent them through a test run. She heard footsteps on the gravel behind her and turned, hoping it was Eric. She saw her dad instead.

"You ready, daredevil?" he asked, squeezing her shoulder. She knew what he really meant. The scene was uncomfortably close to what she'd just been through.

She leaned her head against his shoulder for a moment. "I am very ready. And so is this guy. "She patted the suited-up dummy already sitting on the bike. "But are you ready to watch me do this?"

She couldn't mistake the nervousness in his eyes even as he nodded and said, "Yes, I am."

"And Mom is...?" Her voice trailed off.

"Not going to be watching you perform this stunt until it's safely up on a screen. She never could watch me do mine in real life either."

Sam clucked her tongue. "She is the bravest woman I know, except when it comes to this."

"Well, cut her a little slack. You are her only daughter, after all."

"Yeah, I guess I can do that, considering she's footing the bill." Sam looked around at the crew running back and forth, getting everything ready. The excitement in the air was damn near intoxicating. The set had been running like a well-oiled machine the past couple of weeks since Cassidy was promoted to director. Bette had had a gut feeling about her, and when she approached Cassidy about the position, the woman jumped at the chance to go from an admin role to directing.

So many faces on set, but she didn't see the one she wanted there the most.

Eric's.

"Dad, have you seen Eric?"

"Oh, yeah, he's around here, don't worry. He wouldn't miss this for the world."

Sam smiled. No, he wouldn't miss it. He promised.

Sam talked to Ken one last time, and then she was ready.

"All right, people," Cassidy said. "Just a reminder. In this scene, Shawna has been kidnapped by Rage and is on the back of his bike.

He's running from the feds and Jesse who's been working for them. As revenge, Rage has taken Shawna. Knowing he's out of options and will probably be facing the electric chair, he's decided he's taking Shawna down with him." Cassidy smiled at Sam, who gave her a thumbs up. "And...action!"

Sam was off.

Yup, this was a tricky one. The bike was rigged so that she could control it while maintaining the illusion that the dummy was Rage taking Shawna on a death ride straight off the cliff. Her first mark was the sign ahead that read BRIDGE OUT and the second was the balsa wood blockade two hundred yards past it that she would crash through right before the big escape.

Her heart pounded as she sped along the center of the road. They had to time it just right or she was going over too. The drone's cameras would capture several angles as the bike dropped off the cliff into a hidden net far below the camera's range. If Sam's timing was off, she wouldn't be killed outright, but she certainly could suffer a lot of injuries.

But that was the risk. One she was thrilled to take.

And there it was behind her—the sound of helicopter rotors. In her mind's eye, she could see the whole thing as if she were one of the drones flying high above it all. The Fed's helicopter speeding to catch up with the doomed bikers. The rope ladder lowered from the door with Hoss dressed as Jesse clinging to it and desperately shouting Shawna's name.

Sam turned her head and 'spotted' them at the first mark by the sign. She had half a mile left in front of her and that was *nothing*. She got ready as the helicopter's rotors grew louder and Hoss was right above and behind her.

Second mark—she crashed the bike through the balsa wood barrier. No turning back now. She was committed. The cliff's edge loomed ahead of her, nothing but blue sky beyond as everything started to turn dreamlike in her head. She swore time both slowed down and sped up. Hoss was right above her and she reached up, then pretended to miss his hand. Once again they pretended to almost touch when the bike swerved—Rage's attempt to doom Shawna to die with him.

The tiniest doubt whispered in her ear: *Hoss will miss and you'll go over the edge and break every bone in your body. How's that for your one precious life?*

But Sam easily pushed it away. She'd survived Nitro. She could survive anything.

And Eric would be on the other side of the leap, waiting for her when she landed.

Right there in front of her was the cliff's edge where the road ran out. She lifted her arms one last time and relaxed her legs, preparing to slip right off the bike.

The front tire left the road and went over the chasm.

Hoss. Come on, Hoss.

Time stood still.

She felt the bike falling away under her and she hung suspended in the air, supported by nothing. There was no difference between flying and falling. The moment when anything can happen.

Hoss grabbed her arms tightly.

The bike was gone, on its way with Rage to oblivion at the bottom of the canyon. The helicopter flew straight on into the blue sky, headed for the opposite side of the canyon. Sam looked around thinking how beautiful the world was. How perfect. How alive.

When the helicopter made it to the other side, she saw someone waiting for them to land.

Once they were safely down and the drones had captured all the footage they needed, Eric came forward with the biggest, proudest smile on his face. She jogged to him for a hug, but instead, he dropped to one knee in front of her.

Her jaw dropped open and she covered her mouth.

"Sam Collins. The woman who makes me laugh, who shows

me constantly how good life can be. The love of my life. Will you..."

"Yes, yes! I will!"

His smile turned mischievous as he reached into his jacket and pulled out—

A pint container that read *Butter Brickle.*

Sam burst into laughter.

"Will you eat ice cream with me?" Eric asked.

"Yes, dammit, I will eat ice cream with you for the rest of my precious fucking *life.*"

"Good. You first." He handed her the pint.

She laughed again when she felt its slight weight. She shook it and was pretty sure what she felt rattling around inside was a ring-sized box.

Sam opened the container. She was right.

It was not full of ice cream, butter brickle or otherwise.

THIRTY

Kyla Lewis

Kyla Lewis hated, *hated*, meeting with Ron Anderson but she had no choice. *The man is slimier than the goo in an okra pod* she thought as she stirred her bowl of gumbo at Tony P's and looked out at the marina. It was much easier than looking at the man seated across from her. For one thing, Anderson was constantly smiling like he knew something you didn't and that whatever it was had sharp teeth and was standing right behind you ready to pounce.

But the man somehow always managed to be in the right place at the right time with his camera aimed in the direction of the next trainwreck moment before it happened, which made him the darling of the talk shows and an invaluable source of intel.

"So, are we ready to discuss a price?" he asked as he cracked open a king crab leg, sending a spray of juice in her direction that fortunately landed short of her blouse.

She turned her head slowly back to him. "Not until you give me something I can actually use, Ron. Last time—"

"Last time was not my fault. You didn't move fast enough on it."

Kyla smiled and smacked her lips as she shook her head. "What you gave me was day-old bread you were trying to pass off as fresh. That's not going to happen again." She brought the spoon to her lips and blew on it, hating the way he watched her mouth. She wasn't the type to flirt to get her way.

"This is fresh, Kyla. This is so fresh you wouldn't believe it. It's the break you need. You know the one I'm talking about."

"Heard that one before." She tore off a piece of buttered bread and popped it in her mouth while he cracked open another leg. The sound was getting to her. It was too much like—

No, don't think about it.

He put the end of the leg up to his mouth and sucked out the meat. Kyla noticed the unused fork and knife she'd lined up earlier were askew. She nudged them back in place, making sure their ends lined up perfectly. If she wasn't careful, she'd lose herself in the task.

"Look," Anderson said through a mouthful of crab meat, "I'll knock a little off the price to make up for last time, even though that was on you."

She looked at the spot between his eyes to avoid looking directly into them. She didn't want him to realize she was curious. Ron never wanted to knock any money off his transactions. Most of the time, he didn't have to. Even stale, his intel was still good and true. Ron Anderson may have been a lot of unpleasant things, but he was not a fabricator. Where others spread rumors, he uncovered the truth.

The one and only trait that Kyla could appreciate about the man because she had it in common with him. As an old-school reporter, Kyla was dedicated to the truth.

"Give me a hint at least, then we'll talk price." She tried not to count the lines on his forehead. She remembered from the last time she counted that there were four.

Dammit, now he was smiling like the thing with sharp teeth

right behind her had just opened its mouth. He knew she wanted the intel, wanted it badly.

Ron set the crab leg down on his plate and sat back in his chair. "All right. Get up and go to the bathroom. Look at every person along the way."

She frowned. "Why?"

"Just do it and when you come back, I'll give you your hint."

She sighed and took her napkin off her lap. She folded it into a neat rectangle and laid it on the table so its edge lined up with the knife and fork.

Asshole probably just wants a good look at my ass. The bathrooms were behind her so she turned and walked toward them. She surreptitiously studied the faces as she walked past each table. There weren't many, as this was mid-afternoon between lunch and dinner, when the place would fill up.

An older couple who she knew as regulars here but didn't know their names. A sunburnt family in matching Disneyland tees. Another couple sitting across from each other, her back to Kyla and his face in perfect view.

And dear God, what a face. Solid jawline with a day's worth of stubble. Full lips like a statue of a Greek god. Dark brows that matched his hair. But even as he kept his eyes down and focused on his plate, he couldn't hide their blue color. He filled his shirt out nicely, too.

Kyla looked away quickly. He was sitting with a woman, so he was taken.

Why would I even think that? It's not like I'm going to walk up and ask him out.

Kyla went into the ladies' room and waited a few minutes before returning to the table. She'd hoped to get a look at the woman's face, but they'd paid their bill and left. Anderson watched her walk all the way back.

She sat down. "Okay, you had your fun."

"The man and woman."

"What about them?"

"You didn't recognize them?"

"No. What show are they on?" He had to be an actor. No one that good-looking lived in L.A. without at least being in a commercial.

Ron chuckled. "No show. The man you saw was named Walker Dean. He's with Watchdog."

Kyla straightened up. She'd heard the rumors. "Okay, so...what?"

Ron lowered his voice. "They did a little job in Hawaii a while back during a triathlon. No one's supposed to know about it, but I do. And I can put you in touch with someone who knows a whole lot more."

Hawaii. She'd heard the rumors.

Kyla didn't bother to act disinterested or dumb. Ron knew already, and she wouldn't insult the man by trying to hide her excitement.

"Fine. Name your price. But I still want that discount."

Kyla and Walker's story continues in Watchdog Security Book 8: More Than Rumors. https://amzn.to/3D9yKsG

ACKNOWLEDGMENTS

As always, thank you, Lovely, for giving me a chance.

Trinity Wilde, I don't know how I'd get through a day without you! Caitlyn O'Leary, you are always amazing. Riley Edwards... Tiki, my Tiki! Ophelia Bell, Godiva Glenn, Carrie, and Emily, who, along with Trinity are in my amazing online writers' group that keeps me going, whether we're swapping recipes, book ideas, or joking about the general absurdity of it all (Best Job In The World!) Bella Stone, where have you been all my life?! Thanks for the sprints, the chocolate, the Tatos, and of course, who can forget the gobshite? Gary Jonas, thank you for the unending encouragement, the brainstorming, and for lifting me up just ahead of the cliff on this one. Becca Jameson, who always makes me laugh. Sara Judson Brown, Soul Sister extraordinaire! Rayne Lewis for all the Chica Checks—love you, girl!

Love and gratitude to you all!

OLIVIA'S LOVELIES

Never miss a release from Olivia Michaels by signing up for the Olivia Michaels Romance Newsletter. Be the first to read advance excerpts, see cover previews, and enter giveaways at https://oliviamichaelsromance.com/

Follow on Amazon at https://amzn.to/3sECMCk

Follow Olivia on BookBub at https://www.bookbub.com/authors/olivia-michaels

Follow on Instagram at https://www.instagram.com/explore/tags/oliviamichaelsauthor/

Want more? Come be one of Olivia's Lovelies on Facebook. I can always use another ARC reader or two...
https://www.facebook.com/groups/639545290309740/

https://www.facebook.com/oliviamichaelsauthor

ALSO BY OLIVIA MICHAELS

Romantic Suspense

Watchdog Security Series (Ongoing)

More Than Love

More Than Family

More Than Puppy Love

More Than Paradise

More Than Thrills

More Than Words Can Say

More Than Beauty

Watchdog Protectors Series (Ongoing)

Protecting Harper

Protecting Brianna

ABOUT THE AUTHOR

Olivia Michaels is a lifelong reader, dog lover, gardener, and a certified beachaholic. When she's not throwing a Frisbee for her fur-baby, harvesting tomatoes, or writing, you can find her playing in the surf, kayaking, or kicking back on the sand and cracking open a romantic beach read.

Made in the USA
Las Vegas, NV
26 October 2022

58210812R00168